Anonymous

Catholic Almanac of Ontario for 1895

with clergy list - approved by the archbishops and bishops of Ontario

Anonymous

Catholic Almanac of Ontario for 1895
with clergy list - approved by the archbishops and bishops of Ontario

ISBN/EAN: 9783337336066

Printed in Europe, USA, Canada, Australia, Japan

Cover: Foto ©Andreas Hilbeck / pixelio.de

More available books at **www.hansebooks.com**

ILLUSTRATED

Catholic Almanac of Ontario for 1895,

WITH

CLERGY LIST.

APPROVED BY THE

ARCHBISHOPS AND BISHOPS OF ONTARIO.

The Catholic Calendar is, in fact, but the Almanac of the " New heavens and the new earth," which the Lord of Mercy hath created for Himself and us. It faithfully represents to the Christian soul the annual course of the " Sun of Righteousness" passing through his cycle of love, to warm and to cheer, to nourish and give growth, to " the planting of His right hand" in the vineyard of His Church.— *Wiseman.*

PUBLISHED BY

THE SISTERS ADORERS OF THE PRECIOUS BLOOD.

TORONTO:
CATHOLIC REGISTER PRINT.
1895.

CONVENT OF THE PRECIOUS BLOOD.

INTRODUCTION.

By HIS GRACE MOST REV. JOHN WALSH, D.D.,

ARCHBISHOP OF TORONTO.

THIS ALMANAC is intended for the instruction and edification of our faithful people, and will, it is to be hoped, be a welcome visitor in every Catholic home in the land. It contains much information on a variety of subjects that have a special interest for the Catholics of Ontario, whilst the reflections written for each month will be found attractive and instructive reading for Catholic families. It is therefore a useful, though unpretentious publication, and deserves generous encouragement and widespread patronage. Cheap publications of this sort are a great want in the homes of our people. Frequently a few costly books will be seen that are seldom or never opened, and are kept for show rather than for use, whilst cheap Catholic publications that would be within easy reach of our people, and that would be at once interesting and instructive, especially to the young, are rarely to be found. This Almanac is gotten up to help in its own way in supplying this want, and we therefore bespeak for it the active interest, sympathy and encouragement of the clergy and the generous support and patronage of the laity. A good book is a blessing to a family; it is a silent but effective friend and benefactor; it teaches and admonishes, it counsels and consoles, it points out the narrow way of duty that should be followed and the broad road of sin that should be shunned ; it nourishes the mind with good and holy thoughts, and stimulates to meritorious deeds and to good, virtuous lives. It sows the seed of truth and virtue in the soil of the soul, which eventually grows and ripens into a rich harvest of Christian virtues and good works.

A bad book, on the other hand, is one of the most powerful weapons wielded by Satan in the ruin and loss of souls. There is no more effective means of propagating destructive falsehood and of spreading the blight and poison of evil than a book that is bad, because of the falsehood it inculcates, the attacks it contains against the Church of Christ, the lessons of immoral thoughts and actions it quietly suggests or openly teaches.   A bad book is an evil, silent and impersonal, but effective and destructive.   "Great as the Sea" is the destruction it causes in individuals, in families and in society generally.   The antidote to the poison of bad books is the propagation of good Catholic publications.   The Apostolate of the Press, carried on in the publication and propagation of good Catholic newspapers and books, is a work of the last importance and of the utmost necessity for Catholic interests in this country.   As we are circumstanced in this country very much as the Catholics in England, the following words of Cardinal Manning will be to the point here : "The whole literature of this country (England)," says his Eminence, "is written by those who sometimes unconsciously, sometimes consciously, assume an attitude of hostility to our faith.   I say sometimes unconsciously, because being born in that state they often do so without being aware that they have received an heirloom of false principles and of false histories respecting the Holy Catholic Church.   Without knowing it they are perpetually incorporating them with what they write, so that the greater part of the literature of this country, which is in the hands of us all, contains a systematic contradiction of all that we believe.   The newspapers which fill the whole country day by day are animated by a spirit which is against us ; and they are filled by details and narratives and correspondence, and with fables, fictions, fabrications and absurdities—anything that can pander to the morbid appetite, to the craving for scandals against Catholic institutions, Catholic priests and Catholic nuns."

This is but too faithful a picture of the condition of things in Western Canada.   For years the atmosphere of the country has been foul and reeking with the stench of the moral filth vomited forth by immoral women and fallen, apostate priests against the Holy Catholic Church and her faithful priests and consecrated virgins, and greedily swallowed by infatuated multitudes.   It is, however, a comfort to know that a lie, though sometimes long lived, can in the long run be killed by the sword of truth.   It is for us Catholics to make use of the agency of the Press to refute falsehoods, to correct misrepresentations and to spread abroad the light of Catholic truth.   No matter how great may be the odds against us, no matter how discouraging the prospect, we should toil at this labor of love in faith and hope.   We should not cease to plant and water in the confidence that God will give the increase.   The Catholic Church is revealed truth, embodied, unchangeable and imperishable.   Let us defend and proclaim it ever, and its divine Founder will ensure its triumphs.

ASTRONOMICAL CALCULATIONS FOR 1895.

Calculated expressly for this Almanac

Chronological Cycles.

Dominical Letter	F	Solar Cycle	28
Epact	4	Roman Indiction	8
Lunar Cycle, or Golden Number	15	Julian Period	6608

The Year 5655-6 of the Jewish Era commences at sunset on October 3.
The Year 1313 of the Mohammedan Era, or the Era of the Hegira, begins 24th of June, 1895.
The 59th year of Queen Victoria's reign begins June 20, 1895.
The 119th year of the Independence of the United States begins July 4, 1895.
The first day of January, 1895, is the 2,413,105th day since the commencement of the Julian Period.

Eclipses in 1895.   (Eastern Standard Time.)

There will be five eclipses, three of the Sun and two of the Moon.
I Total Eclipse of the Moon March 10. Visible in North America. Magnitude of Eclipse, 1.627. Moon's diameter = 1.

	D. H. M			H. M.
Moon enters Penumbra	10 7 57 P.M.	Moon leaves Shadow	11 0 25 A.M.
Moon enters Shadow	10 8 51 P.M.	Moon leaves Penumbra	11 1 21 A.M.
Middle of Eclipse	10 10 39 P.M.		

II. A Partial Eclipse of the Sun March 25. Ends at sunrise in the Maritime Provinces.
III A Partial Eclipse of the Sun August 20. Invisible in North America.
IV. A Total Eclipse of the Moon September 3. Visible in North America. Magnitude of Eclipse, 1.557. Moon's diameter = 1.

	D. H. M.			D. H. M.
Moon enters Penumbra	3 9 48 P.M	Moon leaves Shadow	4 2 54 A.M.
Moon enters Shadow	3 11 0 P.M.	Moon leaves Penumbra	4 4 8 A.M.
Middle of Eclipse	4 0 57 A.M		

V. A Partial Eclipse of the Sun September 18. Invisible in North America

Morning and Evening Stars.

Venus is an Evening Star to September 18, then Morning Star. Mars is an Evening Star to October 11, then Morning Star. Jupiter is an Evening Star to July 10, then Morning Star. Saturn is a Morning Star to April 24, an Evening Star to November 2, afterwards a Morning Star. Mercury is a Morning Star about March 24, July 22 and November 10, and an Evening Star about February 9, June 4 and October 1.

Venus brightest Aug. 14 and October 26. Mars not being in opposition during 1895 the satellites will not be visible. The Satellites of Jupiter are not visible from June 12 until August 8, Jupiter being too near the Sun.

The Seasons   (Standard Time)

Sun enters Aries—Spring begins	March 20th, 4 p.m.
Sun enters Cancer—Summer begins	June 21st, noon.
Sun enters Libra—Autumn begins	Sept. 23rd, 2 a.m.
Sun enters Capricorn—Winter begins	Dec. 21st, 9 p.m.

Holydays of Obligation in Ontario.

All Sundays in the year ; Circumcision of Our Lord, January 1 ; Ascension of Our Lord, May 23 ; All Saints' Day, November 1 ; Immaculate Conception, December 8; Nativity of Our Lord, Christmas Day, December 25.

On days of obligation every Catholic who has reached the years of understanding is obliged, unless hindered by sickness or other sufficient cause, to hear Mass and rest from servile work.

Fasting Days of Obligation.

All the week days of Lent ; Wednesdays and Fridays of Advent ; the Ember Days, four times a year, being the Wednesdays, Fridays and Saturdays next after (1) the first Sunday in Lent, (2) after Whitsunday, (3) after the 14th of September, (4) after the third Sunday in Advent ; the Vigils of Pentecost (June 1), of the Solemnity of the Assumption (August 17), of All Saints (October 31), of the Immaculate Conception (December 7), of Christmas (December 24). If a feast fall on Monday the vigil is kept on the Saturday preceding. Sunday is never a fast day.

Abstinence Days.

All Fridays in the year, excepting Christmas Day when it falls upon a Friday ; Wednesdays and Fridays in Lent and Advent ; Saturday in Holy Week ; the Ember days ; the Vigils of Pentecost, of the Solemnity of the Assumption, of All Saints, and of Christmas.

On a day of abstinence flesh meat is not allowed.

Solemnizing of Marriages is not allowed, except by special dispensation, from the first Sunday in Advent until after Epiphany, and from the beginning of Lent until the Sunday after Easter.

RATES OF POSTAGE.

LETTERS addressed to any place in Canada or the United States, 3 cents per ounce or fraction of an ounce. Local or drop letters for local delivery 1 cent per ounce. Where delivery by letter carrier has been established, 2 cents per ounce. Letters addressed to any country in the Universal Postal Union, which embraces Europe (including Great Britain and Ireland), the larger part of Asia, certain portions of Africa, and a number of countries in South America, are 5 cents per ⅓ ounce.

POST CARDS.—Post cards for delivery in Canada or United States are 1 cent each ; for delivery in Postal Union countries, 2 cents each.

NEWSPAPERS.—Newspapers and periodicals printed and published in Canada, mailed by the publishers in the Post Office at the place where they are published, and addressed to regular subscribers in Canada and the United States, or to newsdealers in Canada, are transmitted by mail to their respective addresses free of postage. British newspapers and periodicals brought by mail to Canadian booksellers or news agents, may be reposted by them to regular subscribers in Canada free of postage If brought otherwise than by mail they may be reposted at the rate of 1 cent per pound, and United States or other foreign newspapers or periodicals however imported may also be reposted to subscribers in Canada at the same rate payable by postage stamps. Newspapers and periodical publications printed and published in Canada, issued less frequently than once a month, addressed to regular subscribers and news agents, are liable to a rate of 1 cent per pound, or fraction thereof. On all newspapers and periodicals posted in Canada, other than those addressed from the office of publication, to regular subscribers or news agents in the Dominion, the rate will be 1 cent per four ounces. Single numbers of newspapers and periodicals weighing not more than one ounce each may be posted if prepaid by postage stamp ½ cent each.

MISCELLANEOUS MATTER.—On all book packets, pamphlets, circulars, prices current and other matter wholly in print, and on packages of seeds, cuttings, bulbs, roots, etc , the rate is 1 cent for each four ounces or fraction thereof

On maps, prints, drawings, engravings, lithographs, photographs, circulars produced by a multiplying process easy to recognize, but not type written, nor in such a form as to resemble type writing; exhibitor's entry tickets for Dominion or Provincial Exhibitions, botanical and entomological specimens, when properly put up, so as to prevent injury to the contents of the mails; sheet music, whether printed or written, including music books whether stitched or bound ; book or newspaper manuscript, whether type written or hand-written, printer's proof sheets, whether corrected or not ; such partly printed and partly written documents as deeds of land, mortgages made under seal (including chattel mortgages), insurance policies, renewal receipts when attached to the policies, insurance receipts sent in bulk from head offices to agents, militia and school returns, customs manifests, voters lists when written or partly in writing, school or college examination papers, municipal assessment rolls, Provincial Government returns on official blanks, and all partly printed and partly written Provincial Government documents, statute labor returns, municipal returns in general, blank broks, printed forms entirely blank and printed stationery, the rate of postage is 1 cent for each two ounces.

PATTERNS AND SAMPLES.—On patterns or samples of merchandise or of goods for sale, not exceeding 24 ounces, the rate to any place within the Dominion is 1 cent per four ounces.

CLOSED PARCELS.—Closed parcels not exceeding five pounds in weight may be posted at any Post Office in Canada for conveyance to any other Post Office in the Dominion at the following rates : For each parcel weighing not more than four ounces, 6 cents ; for each additional four ounces or fraction thereof, 6 cents.

For Great Britain and Ireland the rate is 20 cents for one pound and 16 cents for each additional pound. The limit of weight is eleven pounds

MERCHANDIZE.—On merchandize of all descriptions not entitled to pass at a lower rate, and not excluded from the mails by the general prohibitory regulation with respect to objectionable matter, the rate is 1 cent per ounce or fraction thereof.

Registration,

All classes of matter sent by inland post may be registered, and the fee therefor is 5 cents.

Free Letters.

All letters and other mailable matter addressed to, or sent by, the Governor General of Canada, or to or by his Secretary or other Officer at Ottawa.

All letters and other mailab'e matter posted from the Public Departments at Ottawa and franked as being of an official character ; all correspondence addressed to the Ministers in charge of the said Departments or to their Private Secretaries, or to the Deputy Heads or Secretaries of the same, or to any branch or division of a Department, or to the officer at the head thereof in his official capacity and under his official title.

All letters and other mailable matter addressed to or sent by the Speaker or Chief Clerk of the Senate or of the House of Commons, or to or by the Librarian of Parliament, as well as all mail matter directed to the Senate, to the House of Commons or to the Library of Parliament at Ottawa.

Letters and other mailable matter addressed to or by any Member of the Senate or of the House of Commons while at Ottawa during any session of Parliament, or during the ten days next before the meeting of Parliament.

Letters and other mailable matter addressed to or sent by the Chief Post Office Inspector, or to or by the Post Office Inspectors on Post Office business.

All letters containing a remittance on account of the Public Revenue sent by any Postmaster in Canada to a Bank or Bank agency ; and all remittances or acknowledgments sent by a Bank or Bank agency on account of Public Revenue to any Postmaster in Canada.

Month of the Holy Infancy.

THIS month is like a mile-stone on the road of life. It tells us how far we have travelled on that road, but it cannot say how far it will extend into the hidden future ere it reaches the grave that lies open and ready for each of us. Time is the road to eternity, and each day is as a march on that road :

"To these walks on the journey to eternity," says St. Bonaventure, "our spirit is invited and encouraged to God, who offers Himself as our companion on the way, for He is the way by which we should go. As Isaias says, 'This is the way, walk in it.' For thus the spirit heareth. Come, my beloved, begin with thirsty longing for eternal things, which answers to the first stage of right intention. Let us enter on the plain by devout meditation of eternal things, which constitutes the second journey. Let us range the valleys by limpid contemplation of eternal things, and so accomplish the third journey. Let us rise up early to fulfil the fourth by inebriating love of eternal things. Let us observe if the vines have flourished by the spreading revelations of eternal things, which corresponds to the fifth journey; and provide they, the flowers, bear fruits by the experimental foretaste of eternal things, according to the sixth journey; and that the harvest of virtue may clothe the hills by the uniform operation of eternal things, which completes the seventh journey. Thus man will enter the house of his eternity, in which there will be a manifest vision, full cognition, true love, undivided society, perfect similitude, and life blessed for ever and ever through all the eternal years. But the order and sweetness of these things being partly enjoyed with foretaste by the spiritual travellers, they run on quicker till at length they are dissolved and forever fixed in the eternal rest of that beatitude, to which house of eternity may His hand guide and conduct us, who is the one and true God, blessed forever."

Let us walk on this road of life with unfaltering steps under the guidance of the Holy Catholic Church. She will be to us as a cloud by day and a pillar of fire by night, safely conducting us amid the perils and fatigues of the desert places of life, guiding us, it may be, through a red sea of sorrows, sufferings and afflictions until we enter at last into the plenty, security and happiness of the promised land, yea, even God's eternal kingdom, the joys of which neither eye hath seen nor ear heard, nor hath it entered unto the heart of man to conceive.

> The land beyond the sea ;
> Sweet is thine endless rest,
> But sweeter far that Father's breast,
> Upon Thy shores eternally possest ;
> For Jesus reigns o'er thee,
> Calm land beyond the sea.—Faber.

Devotion to Jesus in His holy infancy is that which should be uppermost in our minds during this month. The mysteries of the Divine Infancy which the Church now commemorates contain for us lessons of the deepest import. In the feast of the Circumcision the Divine Child, shedding already His precious blood in expiation of human guilt and in obedience to a law which had no obligation for Him, but which He gladly obeyed, teaches us lessons of humility, obedience and mortification. We, in this age, are very delicate Christians. We shrink from pain, loath mortification, and think and act as if the way to heaven were a mere holiday excursion, and should be smooth and broad and lined with flowers and fruits, instead of being a narrow way to be trodden with bleeding feet. The first condition of the discipleship of Him who was born in a stable in cold and darkness and poverty, and who, even in His infancy, submitted to the knife of circumcision, is self-denial and mortification. "If any man," says Our Lord, "wishes to be my disciple let him deny himself, take up his cross daily and follow me." (Luke ix., 23.) "He that loveth his life shall lose it, and he that hateth his life in this world keepeth it until life eternal." (John xii., 25.) Self-denial, mortification, a spirit of penance and a willingness to suffer for sin must be the livery of the true Christian, and are the lessons taught by the Divine Child in His circumcision. The great Feast of the Epiphany occurs at this time. This feast was known in Ireland as "Little Christmas," because, as the birth of Our Lord was manifested to the Jews on Christmas Day, it was manifested to the Gentile world only on the Feast of the Epiphany. It occurred in this way: There appeared in Jerusalem three men whose dress and language and manners indicated that they had come from some far eastern land. And the story they told was strange and startling. They said that in their country there prevailed a cherished tradition, handed down from sire to son for many generations, that a Saviour would be born for the salvation of the world, and His birth would be announced to them by the rise of a new star flashing with unwonted brilliancy in their skies ; and that under the guidance of that star, and illumined by the interior light of Divine grace, they had come by many a winding river, over many a lofty mountain and far stretching plain until they arrived in Jerusalem. Being told by the chief priests that prophecy pointed to Nazareth as the birth-place of the new-born King, they resumed their journey under the guidance of the star until at Bethlehem they found the Divine Child in the arms of His virgin mother, and falling down they adored Him and they offered Him gifts—gold, frankincense and myrrh. In the persons of the eastern wise men the Gentile world has been called by God to the true faith. This vocation is one of heaven's greatest mercies, because the true faith is, as the Council of Trent declares, the beginning of human salvation, the foundation and the root of all justification, "without which it is impossible to please God." (Heb. xi., 6.) It is for this reason that the children of the Church have at all times prized the true faith as the greatest treasure upon earth. For it the Martyrs shed their blood, the Confessors professed it fearlessly before hostile tyrants and ferocious mobs. Virgins, overcoming the timidity of their sex, lived for it and died for it. For it our Irish forefathers suffered the loss of property and of life. They clasped the faith to their bleeding breasts and refused to surrender it but with their life-blood, handing it down to their children as a priceless legacy too precious to be lost. We are the inheritors of this glorious faith, and we should feel and say with good Father Faber :

"Faith of our fathers ; days of old,
   Within our hearts speak gallantly,
For ages thou hast stood by us,
Dear Faith ; and we will stand by thee.
   Faith of our fathers ; holy faith,
   We will be true to thee till death."

But the faith that will open heaven to us must be an active, living faith ; must be a faith working through charity. Such a faith will move us to offer Our Lord gifts symbolized by the gold, frankincense and myrrh offered Him by the Eastern Kings. The gold that our dear Lord prizes is the gold of our heart's love. He pleads with us for it ; He sweetly solicits us for it. He says

invitingly to each of us: "My child, give me your heart." That heart belongs to Him, it is made for Him; its unappeasable longings, its hunger and thirst after the sovereign happiness and supreme good can only be satisfied by the possession of God. The twofold love of God and of our neighbors is the magnet that draws the heart from the allurements of the passions and draws it to God, its centre and its home. As the heart panteth after the fountains of waters, so panteth my soul after Thee, O God, says the royal Psalmist. And St. Augustin exclaims :

"Thou hast made our hearts for Thee, O God, and they are not at rest until they repose in Thee."

We should offer Our Lord the frankincense of prayer. Incense is the symbol of prayer that mounts up with grateful fragrance before the throne of God. Prayer is the golden key that unlocks for us the gates of heaven. Offer to Him this incense, viz., the prayer of Adoration, by which we acknowledge Him as our God ; the prayer of Petition, by which to obtain the graces and mercies we so much need ; and the prayer of Thanksgiving ; by which we manifest our deepest gratitude for his unnumbered blessings and countless favors. Another gift remains for us to offer our beloved Saviour—the myrrh of self-denial and mortification. "For if," as St. Paul says, "you live according to the flesh you shall die, but if by the spirit you mortify the deeds of the flesh you shall live." And again: "They that are Christ's crucify the flesh, with its vices and concupiscences."

These are some of the salutary lessons taught us by the mysteries of the Divine Infancy. Let us ask of our new-born King to give us the grace to put them in practice. If in this way we spend the Januaries of our life, telling the beads of our days and months and years in prayerful spirit and with humble, contrite hearts, the end of this mortal pilgrimage will be for us but the beginning of an everlasting life of happiness in the beatific vision of God. Amen. Amen.

Day of Week.	Day of Month	Color.	CALENDAR	"Ring in the valiant man and free, The larger heart, the kindlier hand, Ring out the darkness of the land, Ring in the Christ that is to be "—*Tennyson.*	Sun. Rises.	Sun. Sets	Sun Slow	Moon Sets.
					H. M.	H. M.	M.	H. M.
Tuesday	1	w.	Circumcision of Our Lord. HolyDay of Obligation.		7 52	4 52	4	10 24
Wednesday	2	r.	Octave of St. Stephen.		7 52	4 53	4	11 27
Thursday	3	w.	Octave of St John.		7 51	4 54	5	A.M.
Friday	4	r.	Octave of the Holy Innocents.		7 51	4 55	5	0 29
Saturday	5	w.	Vigil of the Epiphany.		7 51	4 56	6	1 38

Epiphany of Our Lord.

Gospel, Matt , iii., 1-12 : The wise men from the East.

Sunday	6	w.	Epiphany of Our Lord.		7 51	4 57	6	2 49
Monday	7	w.	Within the Octave of the Epiphany.		7 50	4 58	7	4 4
Tuesday	8	w	Within the Octave of the Epiphany.		7 50	4 59	7	5 21
Wednesday	9	w.	Within the Octave of the Epiphany.		7 50	5 0	8	6 36
Thursday	10	w.	Within the Octave of the Epiphany.		7 49	5 2	8	7 42
Friday	11	w.	Within the Octave of the Epiphany.		7 49	5 3	8	rises.
Saturday	12	w.	Within the Octave of the Epiphany.		7 49	5 4	9	6 55

Sunday in the Octave of the Epiphany.

Gospel. Luke ii , 42-52: Jesus is found amongst the doctors

Sunday	13	w.			7 48	5 5	9	8 17
Monday	14	w.	St. Hilary, Bishop, Doctor of the Church.		7 48	5 6	10	9 37
Tuesday	15	w.	St. Paul, the Hermit		7 48	5 7	10	10 54
Wednesday	16	r.	St. Marcellus I., Pope and Martyr.		7 47	5 9	10	A.M.
Thursday	17	w.	St. Anthony, Abbot.		7 47	5 10	10	0 10
Friday	18	w.	St Peter's Chair at Rome		7 46	5 11	11	1 21
Saturday	19	r.	St. Canute, King and Martyr.		7 46	5 12	11	2 33

Second Sunday after the Epiphany.

Gospel, John ii., 1-11 : The Marriage of Cana.

Sunday	20	w.	Feast of the Most Holy Name of Jesus.		7 45	5 14	11	3 43
Monday	21	r.	St. Agnes, Virgin and Martyr.		7 45	5 16	12	4 50
Tuesday	22	r.	SS. Vincent and Anastasius.		7 44	5 17	12	5 51
Wednesday	23	w.	Espousals of the Blessed Virgin Mary,		7 48	5 18	12	6 43
Thursday	24	r.	St. Timothy, Bishop and Martyr.		7 42	5 19	12	7 26
Friday	25	w.	Conversion of St Paul.		7 41	5 21	13	sets.
Saturday	26	r.	St. Polycarp, Bishop and Martyr.		7 40	5 22	13	6 9

Third Sunday after the Epiphany.

Gospel, Matthew viii., 1-13: Christ heals the Centurion's Servant

Sunday	27	w.	Feast of the Holy Family, Jesus, Mary and Joseph.		7 39	5 23	13	7 12
Monday	28	w.	St. John Chrysostom, Bishop, Doctor of the Church.		7 38	5 24	13	8 14
Tuesday	29	w	St. Francis of Sales, Bishop, Doctor of the Church.		7 37	5 26	13	9 18
Wednesday	30	w.	St. Felix IV., Pope.		7 36	5 27	14	10 21
Thursday	31	w.	St. Peter Nolasco.		7 35	5 28	14	11 24

MOON'S PHASES.

	D	H.	M		D.	H.	M.
First Quarter	4	2	52 A.M.	Last Quarter	17	5	55 P.M.
Full Moon	11	1	50 A.M.	New Moon	25	4	26 P.M.

Month of the Holy Family.

AMONG the special devotions which have taken a firm grasp on the religious sentiments of the Catholic world, in the closing years of our century, none holds a more conspicuous place than that known as the Confraternity of the Holy Family. Though scarce five decades of years have elapsed since its establishment it has spread over the continent of Europe, enveloped the British Isles and established a lasting foothold in America. The aphorism God tempers the wind to the shorn lamb, if not true in the narrowest sense of the word, is accurate and expressive in a wider signification. God always provides a means for the end. He ever finds an instrument for His work. Such an instrument is the Confraternity of the Holy Family, and the work awaiting it is the reorganization of society through the family. Ever since Luther raised to the world the banner of revolt the cohesion of society has been loosening and crumbling away. He arrayed himself against ecclesiastical authority; a short step further, his adherents found themselves in contact with civil power; and from this point the incline was easy to the negation of parental authority. This triple negation we find embodied in that curse of our day—that monster, anarchy, the legitimate, uncouth offspring of the much-glorified reformation. He who would undertake the task of reconstituting society on a solid basis must begin by remodelling the family. Society is but an aggregation of separate families, as the stately structure is a harmonious combination of bricks and stones. If, therefore, individual families, which are the elements of society, be properly constituted and fashioned, if the authority residing in the parents be exercised with moderation and prudence, if obedience be prompt and cheerful, and not forced and churlish, if honesty and morality and unselfishness and religion dominate and direct the whole family, we may look to see the social fabric rise a graceful and harmonious structure. While elegant and stately, it will not sacrifice solidity for mere adornment, nor will it permit in any one portion undue weight or expansion to endanger or weaken the whole. It will be the ideal edifice outlined by Our Lord, secure alike against flood and tempest: "And the rain fell and the floods came, and the winds blew, and they beat upon that house and it fell not."— Matt. vii., 25.

We are told that object lessons are an efficient means of teaching truth. If so it will be readily admitted that the example of the model family—the Holy Family of Nazareth—must operate powerfully in forming families to be the safeguard of society. If it is at times difficult to obey, it is even more difficult to use authority justly. We cannot close our eyes to the fact that the abuse of authority has been the prolific parent of revolt—

"Man, proud man dressed in little brief authority
Plays such fantastic tricks before high heaven
As makes the angels weep."

Christ was forced to reprove the doctors of the law for imposing upon others intolerable burdens which they themselves would not touch with one of their fingers. Judas, too, used his position of trust to gratify his avarice. In civil administration men scarcely look for disinterestedness; they have almost come to believe that the legislator must be watched if he is to be kept honest; and although the admission pains us we think there is reason for the belief, for instances are all too numerous of politicians who make their position of trust subservient to their own personal ends. Small cause for wonder, then, if the erstwhile trusting elector, suddenly finding himself the dupe of villany, soon outstrips his master in the race of dishonesty, barters the franchise—man's birth-right—for personal gain, and ends by feigning to regard his fellow-man the knave he himself has turned out to be.

This disease in the higher branches is not local. The sap that nourished it has been drawn from a diseased root. The corrupt law-maker carried with him from the family nursery the germs of disease which in public life fostered and spread infection around about him. The evil, then, to be remedied must be treated first in the family. This appears to have presented itself to the founders of the Confraternity of the Holy Family with the force that brings conviction, as the following, taken from the Manual of the Confraternity, fully shows:

"It differs from other associations in not having been instituted for any one member of the family, taken separately; its graces are equally distributed to all who belong to it—to the son as well as the father; to the daughter as well as the mother; and although its special predilection may be for those who bear the greatest resemblance to the holy house of Nazareth, it denies admission to none, and all may share its benefits.

"Oh! we might enter the homes of the many unhappy families which exist and persuade them to seek at the true source the wealth which they are so eager to obtain. In placing themselves under the protection of Jesus, Mary, Joseph, what would soon be the result? These unfortunate households would be changed as by a miracle. The married would learn to imitate Mary and Joseph in their mutual relations, by a renewed fidelity and forbearance; parents would imitate Mary and Joseph in their relation to Jesus, by giving solid instruction, pious education to their children, in watching the companions they frequent, in preaching to them more by example than by words; children would imitate Jesus in His conduct towards Mary and Joseph, by the respectful affection, cheerful obedience and filial help they would render their parents. Under this triple patronage families would soon be transferred into so many sanctuaries of Nazareth. The incense of prayer would constantly ascend to heaven, and this prayer would draw down upon them heaven's choicest blessings, and procure the unspeakable sweetness of union and peace."

With the gradual diffusion among individuals of so many virtues, who can doubt that society itself would soon put on a changed appearance? Egotism, exposed in all its hideousness by the inculcation and practice of the beautiful virtue of charity, would be forever dissipated, religious indifference could find no place in lives fashioned after the sacred models of Nazareth, and feverish restlessness and discontent would give place to a resigned confidence in Almighty God and a cheerful acceptance of whatsoever lot Providence should see fit to mete out to us.

Day of Week.	Day of Month.	Color.	CALENDAR	O house of Nazareth ! Earth's Heaven ! Our households now are hallowed all by thee ; All blessings come, all gifts are given, Because of thy dear earthly Trinity.—*Faber.*	SUN. Rises.	Sets.	SUN Slow	MOON Sets.
					H. M.	H M.	M.	H. M.
Friday	1	r.	St. Ignatius, Bishop, Martyr.		7 34	5 29	14	A. M.
Saturday	2	w.	PURIFICATION OF THE B. V. M.		7 33	5 30	14	0 35

Fourth Sunday after the Epiphany.

Gospel, Matthew viii., 28-27 : Jesus stills the tempest.

Sunday	3	w.	St. Dionysius, Pope ; St. Blase.		7 32	5 32	14	1 42
Monday	4	w.	St. Andrew Corsini, Bishop.		7 31	5 34	14	2 59
Tuesday	5	r.	St. Agatha, Virgin and Martyr.		7 30	5 35	14	4 12
Wednesday	6	w.	St Hyacinthe of Mariscotti, Virgin.		7 29	5 36	14	5 20
Thursday	7	w.	St. Romuald, Abbot.		7 27	5 38	14	6 21
Friday	8	w.	St. John of Matha.		7 26	5 39	14	7 7
Saturday	9	w.	St. Zozimus, Pope.		7 25	5 40	14	rises.

Septuagesima Sunday.

Gospel, Matthew xx., 1-16 : The laborers in the Vineyard.

Sunday	10	v.	St. Scholastica.		7 23	5 42	14	7 9
Monday	11	w.	Our Lady of Lourdes.		7 22	5 43	14	8 30
Tuesday	12	r.	Prayer of Our Lord in the Garden		7 20	5 45	14	9 49
Wednesday	13	w.	St. Gregory II., Pope.		7 19	5 46	14	11 04
Thursday	14	w.	St. Agatho, Pope.		7 17	5 47	14	A. M.
Friday	15	r.	St. Martina, Virgin and Martyr.		7 16	5 49	14	0 19
Saturday	16	w.	St. Gregory X., Pope.		7 15	5 50	14	1 33

Sexagesima Sunday.

Gospel, Luke viii , 4-15 : The sower went out to sow his seed.

Sunday	17	v.			7 14	5 51	14	2 42
Monday	18	w.	St. Raymund of Pennafort.		7 12	5 53	14	3 47
Tuesday	19	r.	Commemoration of the Passion of Our Lord.		7 10	5 54	14	4 41
Wednesday	20	w.	St. Cyril of Alexandria, Bishop, Doctor of the Church.		7 8	5 56	14	5 27
Thursday	21	w.	Seven Founders of the Servites.		7 7	5 57	14	6 8
Friday	22	w	St. Peter's Chair at Antioch.		7 5	5 58	13	6 30
Saturday	23	v.	St. Peter Damian.		7 4	5 59	13	6 53

Quinquagesima Sunday.

Gospel, Luke xviii., 31-43 : Jesus gives sight to the blind man.

Sunday	24	v.	St. Matthias.		7 2	6 1	13	sets.
Monday	25	w.	St. Felix III., Pope.		7 0	6 3	13	7 11
Tuesday	26	w	St. Margaret of Cortona.		6 59	6 4	13	8 15
Wednesday	27	v.	ASH WEDNESDAY. Beginning of Lent.		6 57	6 5	13	9 19
Thursday	28	r.	St. Matthias, Apostle.		6 56	6 7	13	10 24

MOON'S PHASES.

	D.	H.	M.		D.	H.	M.
First Quarter	2	7	16 P.M.	Last Quarter	16	8	0 A.M.
Full Moon	9	0	23 P M.	New Moon	24	11	44 A M.

Month of St. Joseph.

THE month of March is called by Catholics the month of St. Joseph. The feast of the saint falling on the 19th of the month explains this fact. To the Catholic of even ordinary intelligence the name of St. Joseph is linked with associations the most sacred and consoling in the domain of our holy religion. Outside of our Blessed Lady no other human being was more intimately connected with the Redeemer, or had so much to do with the progress and development of the plan of Redemption. Doubtless nothing is impossible to God, and yet without St. Joseph one does not well see how the merciful designs of the Incarnate Word towards fallen humanity could have been successfully executed. In the scheme of Redemption St. Joseph was, in a sense, a necessary factor. We cannot contemplate the virgin mother apart from the guardian of that virginity, the champion of her spotless character. We cannot contemplate the young mother and her helpless infant without a bread-winner. We cannot contemplate the first Christian home and holy family without a head. High were the prerogatives and great the privileges which fell to St. Joseph. He is the chaste spouse of the Mother of God, the foster father of the Infant Saviour, the head of the first Christian family, and the model to all that come after him. His name is suggestive of office and prophetic of grace.

As in times past, under the old dispensation, God raised up Joseph for the salvation and protection of His people, so under the new dispensation God gives to the children of faith another Joseph. The peculiar notes of resemblance between these two patriarchs may have suggested to the late Sovereign Pontiff that step by which he proclaimed St. Joseph Patron of the universal Church. Long before, he had been chosen Patron of the Church in Canada. With these grounds on which to rest our claims we have every reason to hope that appeals made to St. Joseph for light, help and protection will not go unheeded.

If the first Joseph won favor with the King, and was thus in a position to succor his own people in the day of their distress, surely the second Joseph, styled in inspired language the just man, has found favor with the King his God —his foster child—whom he served so faithfully in life; and surely, too, he will not hesitate to wield that influence in our favor. St. Joseph is our patron. He is our model too. In all the paths of life he has gone before us and given us an example. If we have difficulties, so had he; if we have sorrows, his were deeper and fuller; if we have trials of faith and of obedience, his demanded greater sacrifices. If in life he is the model for all the faithful who would be perfect, so too is he in death. Jesus and Mary stood by him in his agony and received his parting sigh. He is invoked as the patron of a happy death, and to this end his name is invoked with the names of Jesus and Mary, as we find in the following ejaculation, to which the Church has attached rich indulgences:

Jesus, Mary and Joseph, I give you my heart and my soul.

Jesus, Mary and Joseph, assist me in my last agony.

Jesus, Mary and Joseph, may I breathe forth my soul with you in peace. Amen.

Day of Week.	Day of Month.	Color.	CALENDAR O Blessed St. Joseph, how great was thy worth, The one chosen shadow of God upon earth ; The father of Jesus—ah, then wilt thou be, Sweet Spouse of Our Lady,a father to me.—*Faber.*	Sun.		Sun Slow.	Moon
				Rises.	Sets.		Sets.
				H. M.	H. M.	M.	H. M.
Friday	1	r.	The Crown of Thorns of Our Lord.	6 54	6 6	12	11 35
Saturday	2	w.	St. Simplicius, Pope.	6 53	6 8	12	A.M.

First Sunday in Lent.

Gospel, Matthew iv., 1-11 : Jesus is tempted by the devil.

Sunday	3	v.		6 51	6 10	12	0 47
Monday	4	r.	St. Lucius I., Pope and Martyr.	6 49	6 11	12	2 0
Tuesday	5	w.	St. Casimir.	6 47	6 12	12	3 9
Wednesday	6	v.	Of the Feria. Ember Day. Fast.	6 45	6 13	11	4 8
Thursday	7	w.	St. Thomas of Aquin, Confessor, Doctor of the Church.	6 44	6 15	11	4 55
Friday	8	r.	Ember Day. The Lance and Nails of Our Lord. Fast.	6 42	6 16	11	5 33
Saturday	9	w.	St, Frances of Rome. Ember Day. Fast.	6 40	6 17	11	6 6

Second Sunday in Lent.

Gospel, Matthew xvii., 1-19 : The Transfiguration of Our Lord.

Sunday	10	v		6 38	6 18	10	rises.
Monday	11	w.	Of the Feria.	6 37	6 20	10	7 19
Tuesday	12	w.	St. Gregory I., Pope.	6 35	6 21	10	8 39
Wednesday	13	v.	Of the Feria.	6 33	6 22	9	10 58
Thursday	14	v.	Of the Feria.	6 31	6 23	9	11 14
Friday	15	r	The Winding Sheet of Our Lord.	6 29	6 24	9	A.M.
Saturday	16	v.	Of the Feria.	6 27	6 26	9	0 26

Third Sunday in Lent.

Gospel, Luke xi., 14-28 : Jesus casts out a devil.

Sunday	17	v	Feast of St. Patrick transferred to March 23.	6 25	6 27	8	1 35
Monday	18	w.	St. Gabriel, Archangel.	6 23	6 28	8	2 35
Tuesday	19	w	St. Joseph.	6 21	6 30	8	3 22
Wednesday	20	w.	St. Cyril of Jerusalem, Bishop, Doctor of the Church.	6 20	6 31	7	4 1
Thursday	21	w.	St. Benedict, Abbot.	6 19	6 32	7	4 33
Friday	22	r.	The Five Wounds of Our Lord.	6 17	6 33	7	4 58
Saturday	23	w.	St. Patrick.	6 15	6 34	7	5 18

Fourth Sunday in Lent.

Gospel, John vi., 1-15 : The miracle of the loaves and fishes.

Sunday	24	v.		6 13	6 35	6	5 36
Monday	25	w	ANNUNCIATION OF THE B. V. M. Lady Day.	6 11	6 37	6	5 54
Tuesday	26	v.	Of the Feria.	6 9	6 38	6	sets.
Wednesday	27	v.	Of the Feria.	6 8	6 39	5	8 16
Thursday	28	w.	St. Xystus III., Pope.	6 6	6 40	5	9 25
Friday	29	r	THE MOST PRECIOUS BLOOD OF OUR LORD.	6 4	6 41	5	10 38
Saturday	30	v.	Of the Feria.	6 2	6 42	4	11 49

Passion Sunday.

Gospel, John vii., 46-59 : The Jews try to stone Jesus.

Sunday	31	v.		6 1	6 43	4	A.M.

MOON'S PHASES

	D.	H.	M.		D.	H.	M.
First Quarter	4	7	40 A M	Last Quarter	18	0	32 A.M.
Full Moon	10	10	38 P M	New Moon	26	5	25 A.M.

Easter Month.

APRIL marks what, of old time, was called the newness of the year. It is the opening season, the month of springing life. Winter, the season of decay and death, is gone; mother earth thrills through all her frame, for life, exuberant and joyous, is coursing through her veins; all nature is made glad, and man, not less than the creation about him, hears and responds to the universal call to rejoice because that which was dead has come to life again.

Forcibly as this comes home to every one of us each succeeding spring, not less forcible is the analogous appeal made by the Church in this season of the Resurrection of Our Lord: "This is the day the Lord hath made; let us rejoice and be glad." Yes, Jesus is truly risen, as He foretold. Let us rejoice; again, I say, rejoice. Oh! who shall tell us the blissful hour, the blessed moment of His holy victory over death? O, beata nox! Blessed night, resplendent beyond the brightest day, that sawest the true Son of Justice rising and dispersing the gloom of night! Tomb, sacred abode of my Saviour's body, bed of His sleep, car of His triumph, thou hast no longer aught of sorrow or of sadness. Surrexit! non est hic: He is risen! He is not here. O death! where are thy arms? Where are thy fetters? Where is thy victory? We have conquered thee. We fear thee no more; for if our head and our God has destroyed thy power, we, His disciples and his friends, will conquer thee in our turn.

Arise then, brethren, arise, all ye who have lived upon the earth, arise and come to the tomb of the risen Jesus that you may learn the lesson of your grandeur. Behold here the cradle of your liberty, the field where life and death met and fought, humanity and Satan, heaven and hell. Surrexit! non est hic.

No doubt, though Jesus be risen, our bodies are still to be the victims of death, and sooner or later will be smitten by its chilling hand. But what matters it? I know that my soul, even as the soul of my Saviour, shall live purer and more perfect; I know that my body, even as the mortal body of my God, shall one day, after a brief hour of sleep in the tomb, awaken to the blare of the holy trumpets. I know it beyond the possibility of a doubt; for Jesus risen is my head, and could such a head fail to remember a member for which He endured such mortal pangs as His, especially if faithful in its love, it helped Him in His hour of trial and comforted Him in His suffering? I know it, because my flesh is the very flesh of Jesus; my blood, the very blood of Jesus; my life, His very life. I have been fed on His sacraments, His word and His grace; and can I die without hope? No. No!

Do your work then, fleet years! Run on, run on with all the speed you may! Bear away in your course earth and sky and all those lives of men, which are naught but ghosts and phantoms. What matters it whether this body perish by sword or flame? Whether it be honored or despised, loved or hated? It stands in the way of that real life which Jesus has won for us. Let it die that our souls may live more purely.

Besides, shall it not revive, no longer feeble and sickly, but strong, beautiful, luminous and immortal? Yes, such was holy Job's hope amidst the calamities which beset him, without, however, overmastering his unconquerable virtue. Such, too, ought to be ours, who have seen the Saviour's resurrection and the miracles it has wrought in the world. Let wiseacres talk as they may, philosophers, unbelievers, impious men; I believe in the resurrection of the body, and this faith is my strength, my comfort, my hope and my glory. Why shall the God who lifted Himself from out the grave be unable to rescue me from its grasp? Away, away with the vain sophisms of men! So long as the world refused to believe in the future life of souls and bodies, it was sceptical, materialistic, impious, given over to sensual delights. Once it admitted the Christian dogma, all was changed; life had a bridle, men knew remorse and virtue looked forward to a reward. Holy dogma of the Resurrection, thou hast done more for men than the books of all the philosophers; be thou forever blessed. Be thou, too, blessed, loved and adored, O risen Jesus, who, in this glorious Easter-season, confirmest our faith and our hope. We shall die; but a new spring will dawn, and we shall walk again in newness of life. "Rejoice, again I say, rejoice."

APRIL, 1895.

Day of Week.	Day of Month.	Color	CALENDAR Thrill, thrill with joy, O nations of the earth, And sing your grand hosannahs with the sky ; For God, by Calvary's pardon, interposed Between us and the thunders of Sinai. —*Frechette.*	Sun Rises.	Sun Sets.	Sun Slow.	Moon Sets.
				H. M.	H. M.	M.	H. M.
Monday	1	w.	Of the Feria.	5 59	6 44	4	0 59
Tuesday	2	w.	St. Francis of Paul.	5 57	6 45	3	2 1
Wednesday	3	w.	Of the Feria.	5 55	6 46	3	2 53
Thursday	4	w.	St. Isidore, Bishop, Doctor of the Church.	5 53	6 47	3	3 32
Friday	5	w.	Seven Dolours of the B. V. M.	5 51	6 48	3	4 4
Saturday	6	r.	St. Xystus I., Pope, Martyr.	5 49	6 50	2	4 31

Palm Sunday.

Gospel, Matthew xxvi. and xxvii.: The Passion of Our Lord.

Day of Week.	Day of Month.	Color		Sun Rises.	Sun Sets.	Sun Slow.	Moon Sets.
Sunday	7	v.		5 48	6 51	2	4 54
Monday	8	v.	Of the Feria.	5 46	6 52	2	5 14
Tuesday	9	v.	Of the Feria.	5 45	6 53	1	rises.
Wednesday	10	v.	Of the Feria.	5 43	6 55	1	8 45
Thursday	11	v.	HOLY THURSDAY.	5 41	6 57	1	10 4
Friday	12	b	GOOD FRIDAY.	5 39	6 58	1	10 17
Saturday	13	v.	Easter Eve. HOLY SATURDAY.	5 38	6 59	0	A M.

Easter Sunday.

Gospel, Mark xvi., 1-7 : The Resurrection of Our Lord.

Day of Week.	Day of Month.	Color		Sun Rises.	Sun Sets.	Sun Slow.	Moon Sets.
Sunday	14	w.		5 36	7 0	0	0 22
Monday	15	w.	Of the Octave.	5 34	7 1	0	1 16
Tuesday	16	w.	Of the Octave.	5 33	7 2	0	2 0
Wednesday	17	w.	Of the Octave.	5 31	7 4	0	2 35
Thursday	18	w.	Of the Octave.	5 29	7 5		3 1
Friday	19	w.	Of the Octave.	5 27	7 6		3 23
Saturday	20	w.	Of the Octave.	5 26	7 7	1	3 40

Low Sunday.

Gospel, John xx., 19-31: Jesus appears to His Disciples.

Day of Week.	Day of Month.	Color		Sun Rises.	Sun Sets.	Sun Slow.	Moon Sets.
Sunday	21	w.		5 25	7 9	1	3 57
Monday	22	r.	SS. Soter and Cajius, Popes and Martyrs.	5 23	7 10	2	4 13
Tuesday	23	r.	St. George.	5 21	7 11	2	4 32
Wednesday	24	r.	St. Fidelis of Sigmaringa, Martyr.	5 20	7 12	2	sets.
Thursday	25	r.	St. Mark, Evangelist.	5 18	7 13	2	8 26
Friday	26	r.	SS. Cletus and Marcellinus, Popes and Martyrs.	5 17	7 14	2	9 37
Saturday	27	w.	St. Anastasius, Pope.	5 15	7 16	2	10 50

Second Sunday after Easter.

Gospel, John x., 11-16 : The Good Shepherd.

Day of Week.	Day of Month.	Color		Sun Rises.	Sun Sets.	Sun Slow.	Moon Sets.
Sunday	28	w.	St. Paul of the Cross.	5 14	7 17	3	11 56
Monday	29	r.	St. Peter, Martyr.	5 12	7 18	3	A M.
Tuesday	30	w.	St. Catharine of Sienna.	5 11	7 19	3	0 51

MOON'S PHASES.

	D.	H.	M.		D.	H.	M.
First Quarter	2	4	28 P M.	Last Quarter	16	6	22 P M.
Full Moon	9	8	43 A M.	New Moon	24	8	11 P M.

The Month of Mary.

THE Church dedicates the month of May to the special service of the Blessed Virgin for many reasons. It is the most beautiful and charming month of the year, and as Mary is the most favored and exalted of God's creatures, she is entitled to receive from mankind tokens of love and veneration. At this season all nature revives from the deep sleep that was cast over it by winter and puts on a new garment of verdure and flowers. Everything proclaims the season of cold and frost as past, and nature begins to display the splendor of her riches. The trees are covered with their briliant foliage, the sun darts his rays into the heart of nature, and under his influence the birds fill the air with their joyful songs—in a word, all nature unites in contributing to make May the most pleasing and beautiful month of the year.

If you have a friend or benefactor to whom you are attached by the ties of love and gratitude, in order to prove your love and esteem, do you not strive to make an offering to him of the best you have, that the greatness of the value may express the extent and fervor of your esteem? After God, your Father; after Christ, your Redeemer; after the Holy Ghost, your Sanctifier, whom should you love more than Mary? For whom else should you entertain a nobler and more tender affection? Of all creatures the Blessed Virgin Mary is the most deserving of your love and veneration. Hence the Church recommends us to offer her our best and most precious gifts, and to consecrate ourselves to her service, especially during this lovely and charming month of May. Let us unite with nature in offering the treasures of this month to Mary; let us enhance Mary's delight by presenting her the crown of our virtues, the sweet perfume of our good works, and the melodious concert of our fervent prayers. During this month we should every day raise our hearts to her, to draw down some special favor that we need. We should unite with all the children of Mary throughout the world in celebrating her month with reverence and devotion, so as to obtain her powerful aid, that we may be enabled to imitate her virtues, and thereby please and honor her.

The sinners as well as the just gather round the altar of Mary and invoke her special intercession during this month; the former to seek through her aid the grace of conversion; the latter to obtain additional help to advance in piety and make sure of their election. She is the true Mother of Christians and Refuge of sinners, and she will assuredly protect and guide those who invoke her help.

The fruit of devotion to Mary is that sin is taken away, the soul is purified, and her servants advance in good works and the practice of virtue. Nothing pleases her more than to behold her followers striving to imitate her virtues by the purity and holiness of their lives.

Mary is likened to the fairest and most elegant objects in nature. She is compared to the cedar, because by her beneficent influence she puts to flight the evil spirit; to the cypress, because she inspires the fragrance of holiness; to the palm, because she makes us victorious over our passions; to the vine, because she leads us to produce the fruits of heavenly virtues; to the olive, because she brings peace to the soul; to the rose, on account of the divine love that she excites in our hearts; to the lily, because she breathes purity into the soul.

Practice then during this month some special devotion to Mary, so labor in the neglected garden of your soul that you may reap the abundant graces of this beautiful month of May.

To induce the Faithful worthily to celebrate the month of May, Pius VII. conceded:

1. An Indulgence of 300 days every day of the month to those who publicly or privately honor the Blessed Virgin by some prayers, good works, or other devout exercises.

2. A plenary Indulgence once during the course of the month, provided they communicate and pray to the Lord for holy Church, &c.

MAY, 1895.

Day of Week.	Day of Month.	Color.	CALENDAR — O Mary, all months and all days are thine own, In thee lasts their joyousness when they are gone; And we give to thee May, not because it is best, But because it comes first, and is pledge of the rest. —Newman.	Sun. Rises.	Sun. Sets.	Sun Slow	Moon Sets.
				H M	H. M.	M.	H. M.
Wednesday	1	r.	SS. Philip and James, Apostles.	5 9	7 20	3	1 34
Thursday	2	w.	St. Athanasius, Bishop, Doctor of the Church.	5 8	7 21	3	2 7
Friday	3	r.	Finding of the Holy Cross.	5 7	7 23	3	2 34
Saturday	4	w	St. Monica.	5 6	7 24	3	2 58

Third Sunday after Easter.

Gospel, John xvi., 16-22 : Sorrow shall be turned into joy.

Sunday	5	w.	Patronage of St. Joseph.	5 5	7 25	3	3 18
Monday	6	r.	St. John before the Latin Gate.	5 4	7 26	4	3 37
Tuesday	7	w.	St. Benedict II., Pope.	5 3	7 27	4	3 58
Wednesday	8	w.	Apparition of St. Michael the Archangel.	5 2	7 28	4	rises.
Thursday	9	w.	St. Gregory Nazianzen, Bishop, Doctor of the Church.	5 1	7 29	4	8 54
Friday	10	w.	St. Anthoninus, Bishop.	5 0	7 30	4	10 3
Saturday	11	r.	St. Alexander, Pope and Martyr.	4 59	7 31	4	11 4

Fourth Sunday after Easter.

Gospel, John xvi., 5-14 : Christ promises the Comforter.

Sunday	12	r.	SS. Nereus and Companions, Martyrs.	4 57	7 32	4	11 53
Monday	13	r.	St. Stanislaus, Bishop and Martyr.	4 56	7 33	4	A M.
Tuesday	14	w.	St. Paschal, Pope.	4 55	7 34	4	0 31
Wednesday	15	w.	St. Isidore, the Husbandman.	4 54	7 35	4	1 1
Thursday	16	w.	St. Ubaldus, Bishop.	4 53	7 36	4	1 26
Friday	17	r	St. John Nepomocene.	4 52	7 37	4	1 46
Saturday	18	r.	St. Venantius, Martyr.	4 51	7 38	4	2 4

Fifth Sunday after Easter.

Gospel, John xvi., 23-30 : Ask in the name of Jesus and it shall be given to you.

Sunday	19	w.	St. Peter Celestine, Pope.	4 50	7 39	4	2 20
Monday	20	w.	St. Bernardine of Sienna.	4 49	7 40	4	2 36
Tuesday	21	w.	St. Felix of Cantalicius.	4 49	7 41	4	2 53
Wednesday	22	w.	Vigil of the Ascension. St. Paschal, Babylon.	4 48	7 42	4	3 13
Thursday	23	w.	ASCENSION OF OUR LORD. HOLYDAY OF OBLIGATION.	4 47	7 43	3	3 40
Friday	24	w.	Our Lady, Help of Christians.	4 46	7 44	3	sets.
Saturday	25	w.	St. Gregory VII., Pope.	4 45	7 44	3	9 44

Sunday Within the Octave of the Ascension.

Gospel, John xv., 26-27 ; xvi., 1-4 : The testimony of the Holy Ghost.

Sunday	26	w.	St. Philip Neri.	4 44	7 45	3	10 42
Monday	27	r.	St. John I., Pope and Martyr.	4 43	7 46	3	11 28
Tuesday	28	r.	St. Urban I., Pope and Martyr.	4 42	7 47	3	A.M.
Wednesday	29	w.	St. Boniface IV., Pope.	4 41	7 48	3	0 9
Thursday	30	w.	Octave of the Ascension.	4 40	7 49	3	0 38
Friday	31	w.	St. Angela of Merici.	4 39	7 50	3	1 2

MOON'S PHASES.

	D.	H.	M.		D.	H.	K
First Quarter	1	10	44 P.M.	New Moon	24	7	46 A.M.
Full Moon	8	6	59 P.M.	First Quarter	31	3	48 A.M.
Last Quarter	16	0	44 P.M.				

The Month of the Sacred Heart.

DEVOTION to the Sacred Heart of Jesus is as ancient as the Church. Ever since our Divine Saviour shed His Precious Blood for the redemption of the world there have been privileged souls to whom Our Lord has disclosed the ardent love of His Heart. "But," in the words of the late Pius IX. in the decree of 'the beatification of Blessed Margaret Mary Alacoque, " to establish this pious devotion, so calculated to advance souls in virtue, so worthy in its object, Our Lord was pleased to choose a humble daughter of the Visitation." By wonderful and miraculous revolutions He made known His will to His chosen servant — revelations since recognized by the Church and eloquent of God's pure love. This was in 1673. Margaret Mary had been two years a nun in the Convent of the Visitation at Paray-le-Monial in France. " She was," says her biographer, " eminent in every virtue—in sanctity, humility and charity."

On one occasion, when the Blessed Margaret Mary was in an ecstasy of adoration before the Most Blessed Sacrament, Our Lord vouchsafed to show her in very truth His Heart saying: " Behold this Heart which has loved men so much, and which, to testify Its infinite love for them, is spent, and yet with love is ever consumed." Then having complained in the most pathetic terms of man's ingratitude Our Lord adds : " I ask of thee that the first Friday after the Octave of Corpus Christi be appointed a special feast to honor My Heart—that reparation and atonement may be made It—that Holy Communion be received to make expiation for the insults It has received while exposed on the Altar. I promise thee that My Heart shall dilate to pour forth yet more abundantly Its gifts of divine love upon all those who shall practice this devotion, or are instrumental in spreading such devotion. Go seek My servant, thy director (Father Colombiere, a very holy religious of the Society of Jesus), and tell him from Me to do all in his power to institute this devotion, and so bring joy to My Heart."

With fervor Father Colombiere obeyed this command. The Friday following the Corpus Christi (June 21st, 1675) he offered himself as a victim of love and reparation to the Adorable Heart of Jesus. He induced many devout persons to do likewise, and to observe faithfully the rules indicated by Our Lord to Blessed Margaret Mary respecting frequent Communion, particularly the Communion of Reparation on the first Friday of every month, as well as on the Friday following the Octave of Corpus Christi.

The fruits of this pious practice were wonderful. The Church from that time consecrated the glorious memory of these Revelations by honoring the Sacred Heart of Jesus with special devotions during the month of June, best known to-day by the beautiful name of The Month of the Sacred Heart.

It is thus the Church expresses her solemn Act of Thanksgiving for the abundant favors her Heavenly Spouse desires to lavish upon her as revealed in a vision to Blessed Margaret Mary when He bound Himself to fulfil the following promises :

1. I will give them (adorers of the Sacred Heart) all necessary graces for their station in life. 2 I will establish peace in their families. 3. I will console them in all their troubles. 4. I will be their safe refuge during life, and especially at their death. 5. I will pour down abundant blessings upon all their undertakings. 6. Sinners will find in My Heart the source and infinite ocean of mercy. 7. Tepid souls shall become fervent. 8. Fervent souls shall rapidly attain a great perfection. 9. I Myself will bless the houses where the image of My Sacred Heart shall be exposed and honored. 10. I will give to priests the grace of touching the most hardened hearts. 11. Those who spread this devotion shall have their names written on My Heart, and they shall never be effaced therefrom. 12. All those who receive Communion on the first Friday of nine consecutive months shall receive the grace of final perseverance and that of not dying under My displeasure nor without the Sacraments, and My Heart shall be their secure refuge at that last hour.

ASPIRATION. Jesus, meek and humble of heart, make my heart like unto thine. Indulgence 300 days.

PLENARY INDULGENCE may be gained on the Feast of the Sacred Heart by all who may communicate on that day and visit a church or public oratory where the feast is celebrated, praying according to the intent of His Holiness.

Day of Week.	Day of Month	Color	CALENDAR	Within Thy Saviour's Heart Place all thy care, And learn, O weary soul, Thy rest is there.—*Adelaide Procter.*	Sun Rises.	Sun Sets.	Fast	Moon Sets
					H. M.	H. M.	M.	H. M.
Saturday	1	w.	Vigil of Pentecost. Fast.		4 38	7 51	2	1 24

Pentecost, or Whitsunday.

Gospel, John xiv., 23-31 : The coming of the Holy Ghost.

Sunday	2	r.		4 37	7 52	2	1 44
Monday	3	r	Of the Octave.	4 36	7 53	2	2 4
Tuesday	4	r.	Of the Octave.	4 36	7 54	2	2 26
Wednesday	5	r.	Ember Day. Fast.	4 35	7 54	2	2 52
Thursday	6	r.	Of the Octave	4 35	7 55	2	3 18
Friday	7	r.	Ember Day. Fast.	4 34	7 56	1	rises.
Saturday	8	r.	Ember Day. Fast.	4 34	7 56	1	9 44

First Sunday after Pentecost.

Gospel, Luke vi., 36-42 : Even as you measure shall it be measured unto you again.

Sunday	9	w.	TRINITY SUNDAY. Gospel, Matthew xxvii., 18-20.	4 34	7 57	1	10 27
Monday	10	w.	St. Margaret of Scotland.	4 34	7 58	1	11 0
Tuesday	11	r.	St. Barnabas, Apostle.	4 34	7 59	1	11 27
Wednesday	12	w.	St. Leo III., Pope.	4 34	7 59	1	11 48
Thursday	13	w.	CORPUS CHRISTI.	4 34	7 59	0	A.M.
Friday	14	w.	St. Basil the Great, Bishop, Doctor of the Church.	4 34	8 0	slow	0 6
Saturday	15	w.	St John of St Facundus.	4 34	8 0		0 23

Second Sunday after Pentecost.

Gospel, Luke xiv., 16-24 : Parable of the Supper.

Sunday	16	w.		4 34	8 0	0	0 40
Monday	17	w.	St. Jane Francis Regis.	4 34	8 1	1	0 59
Tuesday	18	w.	St. Leo I , Pope, Doctor of the Church.	4 35	8 1	1	1 18
Wednesday	19	w.	St. Anselm, Bishop, Doctor of the Church.	4 35	8 2	1	1 41
Thursday	20	w.	St Juliana Falconieri, Virgin.	4 35	8 2	1	2 9
Friday	21	w.	Octave of Corpus Christi.	4 35	8 2	2	2 48
Saturday	22	w.	FEAST OF THE SACRED HEART OF JESUS. St. Paulinus, Bishop.	4 35	8 2	2	sets.

Third Sunday after Pentecost.

Gospel, Luke xv., 1-10 : Parable of the lost sheep.

Sunday	23			4 35	8 3	2	9 26
Monday	24	w.	ST. JOHN BAPTIST. Midsummer Day.	4 36	8 3	2	10 8
Tuesday	25	r.	St. Gallicanus, Martyr.	4 36	8 3	2	10 39
Wednesday	26	r.	SS. John and Paul, Martyrs.	4 36	8 3	3	11 5
Thursday	27	w.	St. William, Abbott.	4 36	8 3	3	11 26
Friday	28	w.	St. Leo III., Pope.	4 37	8 3	3	11 47
Saturday	29	r.	SS. Peter and Paul.	4 38	8 3	3	A.M.

Fourth Sunday after Pentecost.

Gospel, Luke v., 1-11 : The miraculous draught of fishes.

Sunday	30	w.	Commemoration of St. Paul, Apostle.	4 39	8 3	3	0 0

MOON'S PHASES.

	D.	H.	M.			D.	H.	M.	
Full Moon	7	6	0	A.M.	New Moon	22	4	51	P.M.
Last Quarter	15	6	28	A.M.	First Quarter	29	9	1	A.M.

Month of the Precious Blood.

"Christ loved us and washed us in His blood."

FROM the day Jesus Christ uttered the precept, "Do this for a commemoration of me," the Church, "which He founded in His Blood," faithfully obeyed, making a constant remembrance of His life, passion and death, and devoting all days to the honor and devotion of the saving Blood of her Divine Spouse and Redeemer. But as if this were not enough to satisfy her love and the love of her children, she consecrates the month of July, in a special manner, to this Divine mystery, and during its course celebrates a joyous festival to the praise, glory and adoration of the Most Precious Blood. It should always be remembered that the Precious Blood is the object of supreme adoration, because it is the Blood of God, because it is Jesus Christ the God-man, Our Lord and Master, our most loving and merciful Redeemer. In considering this mystery we behold the Son of God suffering, bleeding, dying, to the end that man may not suffer, may not die eternally, "but that he may have life, and have it more abundantly."

The shedding of the Precious Blood began in Our Lord's tender infancy, when he underwent the painful and humiliating ceremony of circumcision. Jesus Christ poured forth His Sacred Blood most lavishly for man's redemption during His ignominious Passion, and after His death His sacred body bled for us when His side was opened on the Cross by the spear of Longinus the Centurion. Although at the moment of the Resurrection Jesus Christ was clothed with immortality, "death has no more dominion over Him," yet wherever the Holy Mass is celebrated the sacrifice of Calvary is renewed, the Precious Blood flows in a mystical manner, and is offered to God on behalf of His people.

Upon consulting the Word of God we find that the Precious Blood is frequently the theme of the inspired writer, whether prophet, apostle or evangelist. Long ages before the coming of Christ the future effusion of His Blood was predicted by the great prophet Isaias. Listen to his words: "Who is this that cometh from Edom, with dyed garments from Basra, this beautiful One in His robe, walking in the greatness of His strength? Why, then, is Thy apparel red and Thy garments like theirs that tread the winepress." And the answer comes: "I have trodden the wine-press alone, and there is no man with me." The wine-press is used figuratively for the Passion of Our Lord which caused Him to shed that saving stream of His Precious Blood by which the human race was redeemed. If we wish to know what we owe to the Blood of Christ we have but to hearken to the words of St. Peter: "You were not redeemed with corruptible gold . . . but with the precious blood of Christ, as of a lamb unspotted and undefiled."

St. Paul is equally forcible and explicit on this subject. In his Epistle to the Hebrews he writes: "But Christ being present a high priest . . . by His own Blood obtained eternal redemp-

tion." In the same Epistle we find him saying: "Wherefore Jesus also, that He might sanctify the people with His own Blood, suffered without the gate." In the Epistle to the Colossians St. Paul writes: "Giving thanks to God the Father . . . who hath translated us into the Kingdom of His beloved Son, in whom we have redemption through His Blood, the remission of sins." In his first Epistle the Apostle St. John proclaims in no uncertain terms the power and efficacy of the Precious Blood, for he declares that "If we walk in the light, as He also is in the light, . . . the Blood of Jesus Christ His Son cleanseth us from all sin." Then how joyful and triumphant is His tone, in the Apocalypse, when he salutes the faithful saying: "Grace be unto you and peace from Jesus Christ, . . . who hath loved us and washed us from our sins in His own Blood." Further on he makes known that it is by virtue of the Precious Blood that the servants of God triumph over their enemy and gain eternal life. "And I heard a loud voice in Heaven saying, now is come salvation and strength, and the Kingdom of our God, and the power of His Christ; because the accuser of our brethren is cast forth, who accused them before our God day and night. And they overcame Him by the Blood of the Lamb. Blessed are they that wash their robes in the Blood of the Lamb, that they may have a right to the tree of life, and enter in by the gates into the city." The efficacy of the Precious Blood of Christ was foreshadowed in the time of Moses. When God was about to visit the land of Egypt with the tenth plague, the death of the first born of every family, Moses commanded the chosen people, then in bondage to Pharaoh, to sprinkle the transoms and door-posts of their houses with the blood of the paschal lamb. Behold the wondrous result of this act! The destroying angel saw the blood and dared not enter the dwellings thus marked, while in the darkness of that single night he slew the first born of every Egyptian family. The blood of the paschal lamb was merely the type of the Blood of Christ, yet it saved from death the first born of the Hebrew people. But if the figure was thus potent to save from temporal death, what will not be the power, the efficacy of the reality, the Precious Blood of Jesus Christ in saving from sin and from eternal death the souls of "them that believe in His name?" St. Augustine, St. John Chrysostom and St. Thomas Aquinas declare that the Precious Blood is the price which our Divine Master offered to God for the Redemption of the world. "By it," says St. Augustine, "we are watered, made white and beautiful." It is by virtue of the Precious Blood that men are regenerated in the Sacrament of Baptism, forgiven in the Sacrament of Penance, and nourished in the Holy Eucharist. In a word, it is from this source of grace that all the sacraments derive their power and efficacy.

Day of Week.	Day of Month	Color.	CALENDAR	Mine eyes upon Thy wounds are bent, Upon Thy streaming wo nds my weary eyes Wait like the parched earth on April skies. —*Keble.*	SUN Rises.	SUN Sets.	SUN Slow	MOON Sets.
					H. M.	A. M.	M.	H. M.
Monday	1	w.	Octave of St. John (Dominion Day.)		4 39	8 3	4	0 30
Tuesday	2	w.	Visitation of B. V. M.		4 40	8 3	4	0 57
Wednesday	3	w.	St. Paul I., Pope.		4 41	8 3	4	1 26
Thursday	4	r.	St. Irenaeus, Bishop and Martyr.		4 41	8 3	4	2 5
Friday	5	w.	St. Cyril and Methodius, Bishops.		4 42	8 2	4	2 54
Saturday	6	r.	Octave of SS. Peter and Paul.		4 43	8 2	5	rises,

Fifth Sunday after Pentecost.

Gospel, Matthew v,, 20-24 : First be reconciled with thy brother, then offer thy gift at the altar.

Sunday	7	r.	FEAST OF THE MOST PRECIOUS BLOOD.		4 43	8 2	5	9 1
Monday	8	w.	Blessed Eugene III., Pope.		4 44	8 1	5	9 30
Tuesday	9	w.	Prodigies of the Blessed Virgin.		4 45	8 1	5.	9 52
Wednesday	10	r.	Seven Brothers, Martyrs.		4 45	8 0	5	10 12
Thursday	11	r.	St. Pius I., Pope and Martyr.		4 46	8 0	5	10 28
Friday	12	w.	St. John Gualbert, Abbot.		4 47	7 59	5	10 44
Saturday	13	r.	St. Anacletus, Pope and Martyr.		4 48	7 59	6	11 0

Sixth Sunday after Pentecost.

Gospel, Mark viii., 1 9 : Jesus feeds the multitudes in the wilderness.

Sunday	14	w.	Dedication of the Churches.		4 49	7 58	6	11 19
Monday	15	w.	St. Bonaventure. Bishop, Doctor of the Church.		4 50	7 57	6	11 41
Tuesday	16	w.	Our Lady of Mount Carmel.		4 51	7 57	6	A.M.
Wednesday	17	w.	St. Leo IV., Pope.		4 52	7 56	6	0 1
Thursday	18	w.	St. Camillus of Lellis.		4 53	7 55	6	C 47
Friday	19	w.	St. Symmachus, Pope.		4 54	7 54	6	1 27
Saturday	20	w.	St. Jerome Æmilianus.		4 55	7 53	6	2 28

Seventh Sunday after Pentecost.

Gospel, Matthew vii., 15 21 : False prophets, by their fruits you shall know them.

Sunday	21	w.	St. Alexius.		4 56	7 53	6	3 40
Monday	22	w.	St. Mary Magdalene.		4 57	7 52	6	sets.
Tuesday	23	r.	St. Apollinaris, Bishop and Martyr.		4 58	7 51	6	9 6
Wednesday	24	w.	St. Vincent de Paul.		4 59	7 50	6	9 31
Thursday	25	r.	St. James, Apostle.		5 00	7 49	6	9 52
Friday	26	w.	St. Anne, Mother of B. V M.		5 1	7 48	6	10 13
Saturday	27	w.	St. Veronica Juliana.		5 2	7 47	6	10 36

Eighth Sunday after Pentecost.

Gospel, Luke xvi., 1 9 : Parable of the unjust steward.

Sunday	28	r.	SS. Victor, Nazarius and Celsus and Companions, Martyrs.		5 3	7 46	6	11 0
Monday	29	r.	St. Felix II., Pope and Martyr.		5 4	7 45	6	11 30
Tuesday	30	w.	St. Martha, Virgin.		5 5	7 43	6	A.M.
Wednesday	31	w.	St. Ignatius of Loyola.		5 5	7 42	6	0 4

MOON'S PHASES.

	D.	H.	M		D.	H.	M.
Full Moon	6	6	29 P.M.	New Moon	22	0	32 A.M
Last Quarter	14	10	31 P.M	First Quarter	28	3	36 P M

The Month of Perfection.

IN the Catholic yearly calendar August may be rightly called the Month of Christian Perfection. This may seem somewhat strange, for even practical Catholics are accustomed to consider August the month of religious relaxation: the month of picnics and garden parties, of excursions by land and lake, of seaside resorts and country outings, and of social enjoyment generally. This is all quite true, and perhaps it is just because it is true, because the world would have 'August the month of pleasure, that the Church would have it, in a special manner, the month of Christian and religious perfection. The Church never forgets the *one thing necessary*, and she would gently remind her children that even in the midst of their social enjoyments they have to save their souls. She would tell them that not only the time of penance, but also the time of pleasure should be considered the time of salvation; that the souls which are saved in Advent or Lent should not be lost or endangered, even in the month of August. Now the Church, like the wise and prudent Mother that she is, knows very well that the best way to inculcate a lesson, especially a lesson hard to learn, is by presenting attractive pictures and living models of the virtues she desires to teach. She knows, too, that if she would lead her children to the practice of Christian perfection, she must meet them half-way in their pleasures and accommodate herself to their ways. She accordingly invites them in summer time to come with her on a picnic to her houses of religious retreat. Convents and colleges seem to be all shut up during the holiday time, and perhaps even many Catholics may be surprised to find that these institutions of piety and learning are often more crowded during the summer months than during the scholastic year.

Other pupils indeed crowd them during vacation time—the pupils of Christian and religious perfection. Separating themselves from even their ordinary work, our religious teachers, men and women, go into the solitude and silence of retreat during the month of August to think only of their own eternal salvation. This most instructive fact is in itself sufficient to make ordinary Christians reflect. Here are religious men and women thinking of their salvation only, just at a time when other Christians are strongly tempted not to think of their salvation at all. These devoted souls give days and weeks to prayer and penance, when even practical Catholics hurry their daily devotions, and will have only the shortest, possible weekly Mass. The Church says to her children: "Look upon this picture and upon that," and she thinks the contrast should strike and instruct them. But besides presenting this striking picture of Christian perfection in houses of religious retreat, the Church would further impress her children by bringing in her Patron Saints for August. The Church's daily sermons are the lives of her Patron Saints. All Saints are models of Christian perfection, but the Patron Saints for August are teachers and models of Christian perfection in a very special manner.

First comes the soldier saint, Ignatius of Loyola, with his military "company" to capture the world by the fire of love and the sword of the spirit, and to lead men to relish " spiritual exercises " even in the summer months. Ignatius, indeed, is not a Saint of August, but he comes on the eve of August to usher in the month of perfection and set all men thinking of eternity by his startling meditation on THE END OF MAN. Nearly all the Saints of August are Founders of religious orders. St. Alphonsus, St. Dominic, St. Bernard, St. Augustine, St. Cajetan, St. Raymond, St Clare and St. Francis de Chantal. St. Alphonsus comes first with his Redemptorist Fathers to teach people and priests the practice of Christian perfection by their popular missions and ecclesiastical retreats. St. Dominic comes with his Rosary to tell the lovers of pleasure that when packing up for their outings they must not forget their Beads. And St. Bernard and St. Augustine come to sanctify summer schools and to tell men of science that God alone is great. St. Clare, the worthy companion of the gentle saint of Assisi, will teach Christian maidens how to perfect their lives in the cloister, and St. Francis de Chantal will show Christian mothers how to sanctify themselves and their families at home. Then that dear little amiable boy saint, St. John Berchmans, comes just in time to go on picnics with the Altar Boys, and indeed with all boys home for their holidays, and to show them how innocent play and pleasure may help to make boys good as long as they are accompanied by daily prayer and purity of life, and are such pleasures as Saints can join in. The girls, too, at their summer resorts have their sweet little Rose of Lima to teach them that fashion is fickle and beauty is vain, and that modesty, meekness and humble self-sacrifice will make them more pleasing to God and more attractive to men. And even the politicians have their patron in this month of universal perfection, the illustrious St. Louis, King of France, who lived the maxims his saintly mother taught him : " Death before dishonor, and the only dishonor a man should fear is the dishonor of deliberate sin."

To complete and crown all this teaching the Queen of all the Saints comes right in the middle of the month on the Feast of her glorious Assumption, to show her clients that Christian perfection is easy and within the reach of all, for it consists in humble conformity to the will of God.

ASPIRATION : Sweet Heart of Mary, be my salvation. *Indulgence—300 days.*

AUGUST, 1895.

Day of Week.	Day of Month.	Color.	CALENDAR	The skies with dazzling glory beaming, Before thy heart's bright lustr · pale, The sun with peerless splendor gleaming By thee, seems covered with a veil.	Sun. Rises.	Sun. Sets.	Sun Slow.	Moon Sets.
					H. M.	H. M.	M.	H. M.
Thursday	1	w.	St. Peter's chains.		4 6	7 41	6	0 52
Friday	2	r.	St Stephen I., Pope and Martyr.		5 8	7 40	6	1 44
Saturday	3	r.	Finding of the relics of St. Stephen.		5 9	7 40	6	2 45

Ninth Sunday after Pentecost.

Gospel, Luke xix., 41·47 : Jesus weeps over Jerusalem, and casts out of the Temple those that sold therein.

Sunday	4	w.	St. Dominic.		5 . 0	7 39	6	3 51
Monday	5	w.	Our Lady of the Snow.		5 12	7 38	6	rises.
Tuesday	6	w.	Transfiguration of Our Lord.		5 13	7 37	6	8 17
Wednesday	7	w.	St. Cajetan.		5 14	7 35	5	8 35
Thursday	8	r.	St. Cyracus and Companions, Martyrs.		5 15	7 33	5	8 52
Friday	9	r.	St. Æmidius, Bishop and Martyr.		5 16	7 32	5	9 9
Saturday	10	r.	St. Laurence.		5 17	7 30	5	9 26

Tenth Sunday after Pentecost.

Gospel, Luke xviii., 9 14 : The Pharisee and the Publican.

Sunday	11	r.	St. Xystus II., Pope and Martyr.		5 18	7 29	5	9 44
Monday	12	w.	St. Clare, Virgin.		5 19	7 27	5	10 7
Tuesday	13	w.	St. Alphonsus Ligarii.		5 20	7 26	5	10 37
Wednesday	14	w.	St. Hormisdas, Pope.		5 22	7 25	4	11 17
Thursday	15	w.	ASSUMPTION OF OUR LADY.		5 23	7 23	4	A.M.
Friday	16	w.	St. Roch.		5 24	7 21	4	0 6
Saturday	17	r.	Octave of St. Laurence Fast.		5 25	7 19	4	1 14

Eleventh Sunday after Pentecost.

Gospel, Mark vii., 31·37 : Jesus cures the deaf and dumb man.

Sunday	18	w.	Solemnity of the Assump. St. Joachim, Father of the B.V.M.		5 26	7 17	3	2 32
Monday	19	w.	B. Urban II , Pope		5 28	7 16	3	3 52
Tuesday	20	w.	St. Bernard, Dr of the Church.		5 29	7 14	3	sets.
Wednesday	21	w.	St. Jane Francis de Chantal.		5 30	7 12	3	7 54
Thursday	22	w.	Octave of the Assumption.		5 31	7 10	2	8 14
Friday	23	w.	St. Phillip Benitius.		5 32	7 9	2	8 38
Saturday	24	r.	St. Bartholomew, Apostle		5 33	7 7	2	9 2

Twelfth Sunday after Pentecost.

Gospel, Luke x., 23 37 : The good Samaritan.

Sunday	25	w.	Feast of the most pure Heart of Mary.		5 34	7 5	2	9 31
Monday	26	r.	St. Zephyrinus, Pope and Martyr.		5 35	7 3	2	10 5
Tuesday	27	w.	St. Joseph, Calasanctius.		5 36	7 2	1	10 47
Wednesday	28	w.	St. Augustine, Bishop, Dr. of the Church.		5 37	7 0	1	11 39
Thursday	29	r.	Behending of St. John the Baptist.		5 38	6 58	1	A.M.
Friday	30	w.	St. Rose of Lima.		5 39	6 57	0	0 38
Saturday	31	w.	St. Raymund Nonnatus.		5 40	6 55	0	1 42

MOON'S PHASES.

	D.	H.	M.		D.	H.	M.
Full Moon..............	5	8	51 A.M.	New Moon.............	20	7	56 A.M.
Last Quarter ....:..	13	0	18 P.M.	First Quarter.........,	27	0	43 A.M

Our Lady of Sorrows.

ONE of the greatest mysteries of religion is the close alliance between godliness and suffering. The nearer and dearer to God, the greater the share man has to take of the cross. The greatest loss a man can sustain is the loss of God, and a noble and high-strung, sensitive nature will be nearly rent in twain by the very fear of such a possible loss. This anguish is commensurate to the degree of love for God which a soul possesses.

Of all the mortals none loved nor could love God more intensely than His Mother, in whom the love of the Queen of all Saints was blended with the instincts of maternal love. Hence no mortal could feel suffering as keenly, or bear more of it, than the Mother of God, and such in fact was her lot in life. The Queen of Saints was to be likewise the Queen of Martyrs. But whilst the torments of martyrs were those of the body, buoyed up by the secure hope of a speedy recompense, and whilst these torments lasted but a short time, often but a few hours, Mary's sufferings were of a different nature, sufferings of the heart, more excruciating than any that can be inflicted upon the body, and sufferings which lasted uninterruptedly through a space of 48 years They change in appearance, yet they are the same in essence; it is the anguish of a mother's heart asked to give up freely that which is much dearer to her than her own life and happiness, to sacrifice her Son for others, and for such sinners, and by such a death.

And this Son is at the same time her God, her life, her all. He is not wrested from her by brutal force, he is not snatched away by the accidents of war and disease, he does not die away from her. He gives Himself willingly, and He expects His Mother to share in this voluntary sacrifice. His Incarnation was dependent on her free consent; she is asked also to freely consent to His death and her incumbent separation from him. Was ever mother asked before to give, as it were, the death-warrant of an innocent son, to make herself, as it were, an accomplice in His death? O, ye all, who pass by the way, behold and see if there is sorrow like my sorrow!

This sorrow commences the same hour in which, with feelings of love and tenderness, she presents her first-born to His Eternal Father in the temple. The first sword pierces her virginal heart when she learns that her child is set not only for the Redemption, but also for the fall of many in Israel The prophecies of the old law in this moment gain for her an appalling distinctness. She trembles.

Soon the *second* sword presents itself. "He came unto His own, and His own would not receive Him." They go further, they seek His life, and the Saviour of Israel is bound to flee, to abide amidst idolators in a foreign country and endure all the privations of poverty amongst strangers. What did the loving Mother suffer by

these reflections and her own banishment from home? Yet she still possessed her only treasure, her Divine Child. But before the hard exile in Egypt can vanish from her mind the *third* sword pierces her most keenly: she loses her child. For three days her soul is consumed by the anxious question: Is my Jesus alive yet, or has His expiatory death taken place unknown to me? And when she finds Him it is only to learn that He must be about His Father's business, that consequently he lives not for her but for the world. Now for the first time she realizes the heroic magnitude of the sacrifice demanded of her, she experiences what it is to live without her Jesus. This sting transfixes her heart, and forever after it remains fixed there.

Years pass; they may somewhat dull the edge of this pain, they cannot efface it; the cross is everlastingly looming up before her agonized eyes. It gathers clearness, the enemies of her Son grow more numerous, their hatred intensifies, the persecutions increase, and at last hell seems to conquer; her Son is condemned to death, painfully dragging His heavy cross, disfigured by the cruelties practised upon Him, and thus He meets His afflicted Mother The poignant pain of this meeting surpasses the preceding swords, and but for the extraordinary assistance of God His Mother could not receive this thrust and live. Yet the valiant woman follows the awful procession, for love is stronger than death. In rapid succession she receives three more swords: she sees her Son expire, she holds His inanimate body in her arms rendering to it the last offices of charity, she sees this body laid into the sepulchre, and this closed. Disconsolate she turns homewards. What she dreaded so long is accomplished: she is deprived of Him who was Her life, and in whose love she lived She that begot Him without labor in Bethlehem, gave birth to Him for the world beneath the cross. Can a merely human mind fathom the horror of these sorrows, can the dolorous Mother herself ever forget her sacrifice?

Is it, therefore, to be wondered at when we find that Mary shows herself partial to those who have a great devotion to her sorrows, that she selected places almost innumerable where she wished to be venerated as the Mother of Seven Dolors, and that there are proofs without number that when invoked under this title, so dear to her and her Divine Son, she is always ready to help and to borrow, so to say, the omnipotence of her Son in behalf of her devotees. Hence we cannot direct our prayers this month more auspiciously than to Our Lady of Sorrows, and whenever our prayer is accompanied by a feeling of sympathy with and gratitude for the sacrifices Mary brought for us we may rest assured that our petitions will be granted.

An indulgence of 100 days can be gained each time a person recites the "Stabat Mater" with devotion, to honor the dolors of Our Blessed Lady.

SEPTEMBER, 1895.

CALENDAR

Hush ! and with rev'rent sorrow still
Mary's great anguish share ;
And learn, for the sake of her Son Divine,
Thy cross, like His, to bear.
— *Adelaide Procter.*

Day of Week.	Day of Month.	Color		Sun Rises. H. M.	Sun Sets. H. M.	Sun Fast. M.	Moon Sets. H. M.
			Thirteenth Sunday after Pentecost.				
			Gospel, Luke xvii., 11-19 : The ten lepers made clean.				
Sunday	1	w.	St. Elizabeth of Portugal.	5 41	6 54	0	2 48
Monday	2		St. Philomene.	5 42	6 52	1	3 54
Tuesday	3	r	St. Rose of Viterbo	5 43	6 50	1	4 58
Wednesday	4	w.	St. Lawrence Justinian.	5 44	6 49	1	rises.
Thursday	5	w.		5 45	6 47	2	7 13
Friday	6		B Adrian III., Pope.	5 46	6 45	2	7 32
Saturday	7	w.		5 48	6 43	2	7 51
			Fourteenth Sunday after Pentecost.				
			Gospel, Matthew vi , 24-33 : To seek first the kingdom of God.				
Sunday	8	w.	Nativity of B V. M.	5 49	6 42	3	8 12
Monday	9	w.	St. Sergius I., Pope.	5 50	6 40	3	8 39
Tuesday	10	w.	St. Hilary, Pope.	5 51	6 38	3	9 14
Wednesday	11	w.	St. Nicholas of Tolentnio.	5 52	6 36	3	9 59
Thursday	12	w.	Of the Octave of the Nativity.	5 53	6 34	4	10 54
Friday	13	w.	Of the Octave of the Nativity.	5 54	6 32	4	A. M.
Saturday	14	r.	Exaltation of the Holy Cross.	5 55	6 30	5	0 5
			Fifteenth Sunday after Pentecost.				
			Gospel, Luke vii., 11-16 : Jesus brings back to life the son of the widow of Naim,				
Sunday	15	w.	The most Holy Name of Mary.	5 56	6 28	5	1 25
Monday	16	r.	SS. Cornelius and Companions, Martyrs.	5 58	6 27	5	2 50
Tuesday	17	w.	Stigmata of St. Francis.	5 59	6 25	6	4 12
Wednesday	18	w.	St. Joseph of Cupertino. Ember day. Fast.	6 0	6 23	6	sets.
Thursday	19	r.	SS. Januarius and Companions, Martyrs.	6 1	6 21	6	6 37
Friday	20	w.	St. Agapitus I , Pope. Ember Day. Fast.	6 2	6 19	7	7 2
Saturday	21	r.	St. Matthew, Apostle. Ember Day. Fast.	6 3	6 18	7	7 28
			Sixteenth Sunday after Pentecost				
			Gospel, Luke xiv , 1-11 : Jesus heals the man that had the dropsy.				
Sunday	22	w.	Seven Dolours of the B. V. M.	6 4	6 16	7	8 1
Monday	23	r.	St. Linus, Pope and Martyr.	6 5	6 14	8	8 41
Tuesday	24	w.	B. V. M. de Mercede.	6 7	6 12	8	9 32
Wednesday	25	r.	SS. Eustache and Companions, Martyrs.	6 8	6 10	8	10 30
Thursday	26	r.	St. Eusebius, Pope and Martyr.	6 9	6 8	9	11 33
Friday	27	r.	SS. Cosmas and Damian, Martyrs.	6 10	6 7	9	A. M.
Saturday	28	r.	St. Wenceslaus, King and Martyr.	6 12	6 5	9	0 38
			Seventeenth Sunday after Pentecost.				
			Gospel, Matthew xxii., 35-46 : The greatest commandment. Jesus confounds the Pharisees.				
Sunday	29	w.	St. Michael. Michaelmas Day.	6 13	6 3	10	1 44
Monday	30	w.	St. Jerome, Doctor of the Church.	6 14	6 1	10	2 49

MOON'S PHASES.

	D.	H.	M.			D.	H.	M.	
Full Moon	4	0	55	A. M.	New Moon	18	3	55	P M.
Last Quarter	11	11	51	A M	First Quarter	25	1	23	P M.

Month of the Guardian Angels.

ANGELS are pure spirits employed by the Creator to direct His other creatures and to carry out His orders. God, in His great love for man, has not only delegated His holy angels to be the protectors of cities, provinces and kingdoms, but He has also given to each human being in particular a prince of the heavenly court to guide him on the path of life, to relieve his wants and to protect him from his enemies. This protector is the Guardian Angel.

What tenderness and what solicitude God shows to us! He has commissioned one of those heavenly spirits to accompany us at all times and in all places, day and night, at home and abroad; to be with us constantly, even when we commit sin, at which he shudders, when we are unfaithful to his inspirations and rebel against his guidance. What goodness on God's part! What an honor for us! And at the same time what an advantage such a companionship is for us!

This angel's mission is to guard our interests as he would his own, and to do for us a thousand acts of kindness. When we pray he bears our bequests to God, and brings back God's gifts to us. When we are in sorrow he consoles us with the good thoughts he pours into our souls. No matter what state we are in he watches over us as over a brother; he bears us in his arms as a loving mother does her child; snatches us from the perils of life and finds a way for us out of the most difficult situations; he is for us what the guide is for the traveller, the physician for the sick man, the shepherd for his sheep, the father for his children, the faithful friend for the one he loves.

Whence come those lights which enliven our faith, those movements which impel us to do good, those blissful moments when the heart feels the need of giving itself all to God? Ah! that is the work of God's angels, and when they have been successful they rejoice in Heaven. In the "Dream of Gerontius" the angel sings a song of thanksgiving when the soul entrusted to his care has been faithful to the end.

My work is done,	My Father gave
My task is o'er;	In charge to me
And so I come,	This child of earth,
Taking it home,	E'en from its birth,
For the crown is won,	To serve and save.
Alleluia!	Alleluia!
For evermore.	And saved is he.

We should then accept most gladly the kindnesses of the angels, listen to their good inspirations, and dread, as a great misfortune, resistance to them.

If the Guardian Angels have a mission to fulfil towards us, we in turn owe duties to them.

We should respect our Guardian Angel. The great ones of this world and holy men and women have a right to our respect; how much more then ought we to respect the princes of Heaven and the officers of God's house. How grievous a fault it is to be heedless of their presence. How much more grievous to do before them what we would not do before a respectable person. Since our good angel is with us everywhere, we should remember it everywhere; and that thought should keep us within the bounds of duty and make us avoid every word and every deed that would be unworthy of so august a presence. We should love our Guardian Angel. And why not love such a benefactor, such a friend so devoted, so holy, so perfect? Why not declare to him a thousand times a day our love? Why not thank him for his company, for his kindness, for the good thoughts he gives us and for the good sentiments with which he inspires us.

We should speak to him. When we really love a friend and have the happiness to live with him, we salute him and speak to him; we tell him of our joys and sorrows, we pour our heart into his. We do not love our Guardian Angel if we pass whole days and nights and do not speak to him, or lay our hearts open to him, or pay our respects to him; or, again, if we do not salute him in the morning on waking, or in the evening before going to sleep, to ask him to love and adore God during the night in our stead; if in our difficulties and in our moments of languor and vexation, in our struggles and our illnesses, both of mind and body, we do not call on him for aid; if, finally, in our journeys we do not salute the Guardian Angels of the places through which we pass, and in our dealings with others do not perform some act of honor to their Guardian Angels.

We should imitate our good Angel: at church we should imitate his profound reverence before the tabernacle; at prayer his recollection and piety; at work his union with God; in our temptations his glorious combats against the evil one; in the practice of charity his support of the wrongs and of the defects of our neighbors, his patience, his sweetness, his eagerness to render service, his devotedness in all things; his conformity to the will of God, his rectitude of intention, his purity and spotlessness of life.

Indulgenced Prayer.—O Angel of God, who, through Divine goodness and charity, has been constituted my guardian, enlighten and protect, direct and govern me. Amen.

Day of Week.	Day of Month.	Color.	CALENDAR — Angels of light, spread your bright wings and keep Near me at morn ; Nor in the starry eve, nor midnight deep, Leave me forlorn.—*Procter*	Sun Rises.	Sun Sets.	Sun Fast.	Moon Sets.
				H. M.	H. M.	M.	H. M.
Tuesday	1	r.	St. Gregory, Armenian, Bishop and Martyr.	6 15	6 0	10	3 52
Wednesday	2	w.	Angels, Guardian.	6 17	5 58	11	4 55
Thursday	3			6 18	5 56	11	rises.
Friday	4	w.	St Francis of Assisi.	6 19	5 54	11	5 57
Saturday	5	w.	St. Galla.	6 20	5 53	12	6 17

Eighteenth Sunday after Pentecost.

Gospel, Matthew ix., 1-8: Jesus cures the man sick of the palsy.

Sunday	6	w.	The Most Holy Rosary of the B. V. M.	6 22	5 50	12	6 42
Monday	7	w.	St. Mark, Pope.	6 23	5 49	12	7 15
Tuesday	8	w.	St. Bridget.	6 24	5 47	13	7 55
Wednesday	9	r.	St. Dionysius and Companions, Martyrs.	6 25	5 45	13	8 49
Thursday	10	w.	St Francis Borgia.	6 26	5 43	13	9 51
Friday	11	w.	B John Leonard.	6 27	5 42	14	11 5
Saturday	12			6 28	5 40	14	A. M.

Nineteenth Sunday after Pentecost.

Gospel, Matthew xxii., 2-14 : The parable of the Marriage Feast.

Sunday	13	w.	Maternity of the Blessed Virgin Mary.	6 29	5 38	14	0 24
Monday	14	r.	St Callistus, Pope and Martyr.	6 30	5 37	14	1 45
Tuesday	15	w.	St. Teresa.	6 31	5 35	14	3 5
Wednesday	16	w.	B. Victor III., Pope.	6 32	5 33	14	4 25
Thursday	17	w.	St. Hedwig.	6 34	5 31	15	5 47
Friday	18	r.	St. Luke, Evangelist.	6 35	5 29	15	sets
Saturday	19	w	St. Peter of Alcantara.	6 36	5 28	15	5 56

Twentieth Sunday after Pentecost.

Gospel, John iv . 46-53 : Jesus cures the son of the ruler at Capharnaum.

Sunday	20	w.	Purity of Blessed Virgin Mary.	6 37	5 27	15	6 33
Monday	21	w.	St. Hilarion, Abbot.	6 39	5 25	15	7 21
Tuesday	22			6 41	5 25	16	8 16
Wednesday	23	w.	Most Holy Redeemer	6 43	5 22	16	9 20
Thursday	24	w.	St Raphael, Archangel.	6 44	5 21	16	10 26
Friday	25	w.	St. Boniface I , Pope.	6 45	5 19	16	11 34
Saturday	26	r.	St. Evaristus, Pope and Martyr.	6 46	5 18	16	A. M.

Twenty-First Sunday after Pentecost.

Gospel, Matthew xviii., 23-25 : The parable of the king taking an account of his servants.

Sunday	27	r.	Commemoration of all the Holy Roman Pontiffs.	6 48	5 16	16	0 40
Monday	28	r.	SS. Simon and Jude, Apostles.	6 49	5 15	16	1 42
Tuesday	29			6 50	5 14	16	2 44
Wednesday	30			6 51	5 12	16	3 47
Thursday	31	w.	St. Siricus, Pope. Vigil of All Saints. Fast.	6 52	5 11	16	4 51

MOON'S PHASES.

	D.	H.	M.		D.	H.	M.
Full Moon	3	5	46 P.M.	New Moon	18	1	10 A M.
First Quarter	11	9	34 A.M.	First Quarter	25	6	4 A M.

Month of the Holy Souls.

"Weeping she hath wept into the night; there is none to comfort among all them that were dear to her."—*Lamentations*, I., 2.

THERE is in suffering something sadder than the suffering itself; there is abandonment. To suffer and to find a kindred soul that remembers us and compassionates is to suffer but half; but to suffer and to know that no one enters into our sorrow, that no one blends his tears, his sighs with ours, is to multiply grief by grief. It was this which wrung from Job in his misery, and from Jeremias weeping over the fall of Jerusalem, their most grief-laden sighs. It is this fact which lends to the sufferings of the souls in Purgatory a sovereign interest, and calls most eloquently on our compassion. They above all others have a right to cry out in the terrible reality of their abandonment, "You have heard the voice of our groanings, and amongst you there is found none to console us." The poets of Paganism tell us that the dead, after leaving this life, drank, in a river called Lethe, forgetfulness of the living. This is a fiction; but it is a sad reality that the living forget the dead.

Have you ever reflected upon this phenomenon so mortifying to the dead, so humiliating to ourselves, the forgetfulness of the dead? When the face of man has been taken away before our eyes, his remembrance quickly fades out of our soul. When we hold in our hand the hand of our dying brother, when he looked into our eyes and said, "You at least will not forget me," we told him that we would not, that we would rather die than forget him. But what a traitorous heart is ours! The days wear on and our dead wear out of our minds; and new friendships germinating in our hearts, complete the work which advancing time has begun.

And yet the dead are not wholly forgotten. There is one heart in which they ever abide; Mother Church forgets not one of her children. Hearken to her, as on the day of the Commemoration of all the dead, she cries aloud: "Be consoled, dear souls, your mother forgets not. If all your friends forget you, if they pray no more for you, I will always pray, I will never forget. I will call into my house your sisters and brothers that they may weep and pray, that they may soothe your pain and hasten the hour of your deliverance I will send my priests to them; I will put into their voice the accents of mine, and I will tell them: Go and move the hearts of your living brethren to compassion for the dead. Speak loudly to them, for deep is the silence which encompasses my dead; speak strongly to them, and fear not to tell them that their conduct is inhuman, is opposed to all brotherly love."

Thus speaks Mother Church, and that she does well to qualify our conduct as inhuman, this one proof will suffice. The souls in Purgatory, so pain-stricken, so utterly forgotten, are absolutely powerless to help themselves. On the earth, even in our hour of supremest agony, we have no idea of such a situation. The wretch abandoned by all can find in himself a last resource; if his right hand fail him, he can call upon his left; and if both fail him, he has, in his own heart, a refuge where God awaits him to succor and to save him.

But to suffer and to know that our sufferings are barren; to shed tears of fire and to know that this burning dew is powerless to bring forth aught save pain superadded to pain until the day when justice, after counting the hours and weighing the punishment, shall say: It is enough; this is the pain of pains, the punishment of punishments. Poets and romancers who strive to arouse our sympathies by the spectacle of great misfortunes, have over chosen lone, barren, wave-beaten rocks to be the scene of the calamities they depict. There they set down abandoned creatures and picture them reaching out towards passing vessels their suppliant hands and sending up, amidst the noises of the wind and the sea, the cry of their extreme distress. These inventions, which have often brought tears to our eyes, are not even a shadow of the sufferings of the souls in Purgatory. There is a place more barren than all the deserts of the world, there is a rock more arid than ever poet's fancy dreamt of, a rock blazing with the fires of justice, a rock upon which our brethren have been cast by the shipwreck of life. Erect upon this desolate shore, with arms turned towards this world, they lift up their tear-laden voices, they cry out to us from amidst the darkness which encircles them: "Oh, all you who sail upon the sea of life whereon we so lately rode, oh pause and see if there be any suffering like our suffering." And the voices that come to us are the voices of fathers and mothers, of husbands and wives, of brothers and sisters, of friends made dear by a thousand ties. Do we, like thoughtless, heartless sailors, pass on and heed them not? It is not as if we were unable to succor. Within reach of our hands are the gifts, many and sovereign, which will relieve their sorrowings and hasten their deliverance. Prayers, fasts, abstinences, alms deeds, communions, masses, the countless indulgences placed by the Church within our reach—these are some of the fountains of mercy whose cooling waters we can bring to bear upon the penal fires of Purgatory.

Surely the Master who said: I was hungry and you gave me not to eat, I was thirsty and you gave me not to drink, therefore are you cast out from before my face, will visit with rigorous punishment the cold, heartless Christian who has refused to bestir himself and bring relief to his suffering brethren in Purgatory. And just as surely will His hand be reached out in mercy to him who has not forgotten his dead, but with prayer, and indulgence, and communion, and Mass has lightened their burden and shortened their pain and hastened the hour of their deliverance, of their arrival in that fatherland where pain is not, nor sorrow, but joy eternal in the company of God and His saints.

Day of Week.	Day of Month	Color.	CALENDAR	O Father, give them rest— Thy faithful ones, whose day of toil is o'er, Whose weary feet shall wander never more O'er earth's unquiet breast. —*Harriet M. Skidmore.*	SUN Rises.	SUN Sets.	SUN Fast.	MOON Rises.
					H. M.	H. M.	M.	H. M.
Friday	1	w.		ALL SAINTS, DAY OF OBLIGATION.	6 53	5 9	16	4 23
Saturday	2	b.		All Souls.	6 55	5 8	16	4 46

Twenty-Second Sunday after Pentecost.

Gospel, Matthew xxii., 15-21 : Giving tribute to Cæsar.

Sunday	3	w.			6 56	5 7	16	5 16
Monday	4	w.	St. Charles Borromeo.		6 58	5 5	16	5 54
Tuesday	5	w.	Of the Octave.		7 0	5 4	16	6 44
Wednesday	6	w.	Of the Octave		7 1	5 3	16	7 45
Thursday	7	w.	Of the Octave.		7 2	5 2	16	8 57
Friday	8	w.	Octave of All Saints.		7 3	5 0	16	10 13
Saturday	9	w.	Dedication of St. John Lateran.		7 5	4 59	16	11 30

Twenty-Third Sunday after Pentecost.

Gospel, Matthew ix., 18-26 : Jesus raises the ruler's daughter to life.

Sunday	10	w.	St. Andrew Avellinus.		7 6	4 58	16	A.M.
Monday	11	w.	St. Martin of Tours.		7 7	4 57	16	0 44
Tuesday	12	r.	St. Martin I., Pope and Martyr.		7 8	4 56	16	2 2
Wednesday	13	w.	St. Nicholas I., Pope.		7 9	4 55	16	3 20
Thursday	14	w.	St. Deusdedit, Pope.		7 10	4 54	16	4 39
Friday	15	w.	St. Gertrude.		7 11	4 53	16	6 0
Saturday	16	r.	St. Josaphat, Bishop and Martyr.		7 13	4 52	15	sets.

Twenty-Fourth Sunday after Pentecost.

Gospel, Matthew xiii., 31-35 : The parable of the grain of mustard seed.

Sunday	17	w.	St. Gregory Thaumaturgus.		7 15	4 51	15	5 8
Monday	18	w.	Dedication of the Basilicas of SS. Peter and Paul.		7 16	4 50	15	6 1
Tuesday	19	r.	St. Pontianus, Pope and Martyr.		7 18	4 49	14	7 3
Wednesday	20	w.	St. Felix of Valois.		7 19	4 48	14	8 11
Thursday	21	w.	Presentation of B. V. M.		7 20	4 47	14	9 20
Friday	22	r.	St. Cecilia, Virgin and Martyr.		7 21	4 47	14	10 25
Saturday	23	r.	St. Clement, Pope and Martyr.		7 22	4 46	13	11 30

Twenty-Fifth Sunday after Pentecost.

Gospel, Matthew xxiv., 15-35 : The abomination of Desolation.

Sunday	24	w.	St. John of the Cross.		7 24	4 45	13	A.M.
Monday	25	r.	St. Catharine, Virgin and Martyr.		7 25	4 45	13	0 34
Tuesday	26	w.	St. Sylvester, Abbot.		7 26	4 44	12	1 34
Wednesday	27	w.	St. Elizabeth of Hungary.		7 27	4 44	12	2 37
Thursday	28	w.	St. Gregory III., Pope.		7 28	4 44	12	3 41
Friday	29	w.	St. Gelasius I., Pope.		7 29	4 44	11	4 47
Saturday	30	r.	St. Andrew, Apostle.		7 30	4 43	11	5 57

MOON'S PHASES.

	D.	H.	M.			D.	H.	M.	
Full Moon	2	10	18	A.M.	New Moon	16	0	11	P.M.
Last Quarter	9	6	7	P.M.	First Quarter	24	2	19	A.M.

The Immaculate Conception.

DECEMBER, the last month of the civil year, is the first month of the ecclesiastical year, because around the first of December falls the first Sunday of Advent, which is the first day of the ecclesiastical year. Advent is that solemn time immediately preceding Christmas, instituted by the Church in order that we should prepare ourselves in a proper manner for the coming of Christ.

While spending the season of Advent, according to the spirit of the Church, preparing our hearts for the birth of the Divine Child, we are called upon at the outset of this holy time to celebrate a feast in honor of the Immaculate Mother of this Divine Child. This feast of Mary comes at a fitting time. For, whilst our thoughts are directed to Him who came in the fullness of time, and for whom the patriarchs and prophets longed, we are drawn towards her of whom was born the Messiah. She, after Jesus, was immediately comprised in the decree of the Divine Incarnation, and from eternity predestined to be the most august Mother of the Son of God.

It may be instructive to know what we understand by the Immaculate Conception of her who gave human nature to the Son of God.

This dogma of faith has been defined recently. But it was always believed, for the Church does but *define* what was ever believed by the Church, and confer on that belief an obligatory character which was wanting to it: so that it is the belief which gives rise to the decree, and not the decree to the belief. "Hence in 1854," to quote the words of the author of a recent work entitled, "The Hail Mary," "when the Immaculate Conception was defined by Pius IX. the Church did not create a new article of faith, nor approve solemnly any miracles which, according to some authors, attended the conception of Mary; nor teach that Mary's conception took place in any other than the usual way; nor that she was born in any other than the usual mode. The dogma of the Immaculate Conception has nothing to do with the physical events in the birth of Mary, in the natural order, as regards the origin of human *life* in her *body*. The dogma treats solely of the time of the origin of sanctifying *grace* in her *soul*. It teaches:

(1) That all children of Adam contract, and must contract, original sin at the moment when their souls are, by God's creative act, united with their bodies in the course of formation—Jesus only excepted, as holiness by nature;

(2) That to become a child of God this stain must subsequently (at various times in various persons) be removed by the grace of God, merited for man by the blood of Jesus;

(3) That Baptism removes this stain *since* Christ, as faith did *before* Christ;

(4) That from some souls this stain has been removed, anticipatedly, before birth, as in St. John the Baptist and in Jeremiah the Prophet;

(5) That in Mary this anticipation was earlier. That in her this outpouring of grace, this application of the Blood of Jesus and the sanctification resulting from it, took place at the first moment of union between her soul and body in the process of formation;

(6) That in her case, conception, the beginning of bodily, the union of soul and body, and the sanctification of the soul, were all concurrent events happening all at one and the same time. Thus, in her the physical life of the human being composed of body and soul, and the spiritual life of grace and union with God began together by a spiritual Baptism administered at that first moment by God in the foreseen Blood of Jesus;

(7) That consequently she was altogether prevented by God's act, through the foreseen and fore-applied merits of Jesus Christ, from ever incurring that stain of original sin, which, but for this anticipated action of God, she would otherwise have incurred. Jesus, alone sinless by nature, made His mother sinless by His special gift, saving her by His own Blood from ever having, for even one moment, the stain of sin or evil on her soul.

This is a great, glorious and unique privilege conferred by God's pure bounty on our dear Mother Mary, rendering her more than all other human beings under obligation to Jesus. It was given to her for the honor and glory of her Son Jesus more than for her own, for it was bestowed on her for the purpose of making her the worthy Mother of Jesus, the All-holy One."

ASPIRATION : Blessed be the Holy and Immaculate Conception of the Blessed Virgin Mary! *Indulgence—100 days.*

Day of Week	Day of Month	Color.	CALENDAR Christ is coming ! From thy bed Earth-bound soul, awake and spring, With the sun now-risen to shed Health on human suffering. —Newman.	SUN. Rises.	Sets.	SUN Fast.	MOON Rises.
				H. M.	H. M.	M.	H. M.

First Sunday in Advent.

Gospel, Luke xxi., 25-33 : Signs of the coming of the Son of God.

Sunday	1	v.		7 31	4 42	11	3 52
Monday	2	r.	St. Bibiana, Virgin and Martyr.	7 32	4 42	10	4 37
Tuesday	3	w.	St. Francis Xavier.	7 33	4 42	10	5 35
Wednesday	4	w.	St. Peter Chrysologus.	7 34	4 42	9	6 45
Thursday	5	w.	St. Stanislaus Kostka.	7 35	4 42	9	8 2
Friday	6	w.	St. Nicholns	7 36	4 42	9	9 21
Saturday	7	w.	St. Ambrose, Bishop, Doctor of the Church.	7 37	4 42	8	10 37

Second Sunday in Advent.

Gospel, Matthew xi., 2-10 : John hearing of Christ's works sends his disciples to Him.

Sunday	8	w.	IMMACULATE CONCEPTION B. V. M.	7 38	4 42	8	11 54
Monday	9	r.	St. Eutychianus, Pope and Martyr.	7 39	4 41	7	A M.
Tuesday	10	w.	Translation or the Holy House of Loretto.	7 40	4 41	7	1 9
Wednesday	11	w.	St. Damascus I., Pope.	7 41	4 41	6	2 23
Thursday	12	r.	St. Melchiadis, Pope and Martyr.	7 42	4 42	6	3 41
Friday	13	r.	St. Lucy, V M.	7 43	4 42	6	4 59
Saturday	14	w.	St. Leonard of Port Maurice.	7 44	4 42	5	6 17

Third Sunday in Advent.

Gospel, John i., 19-28 : John answers the questions of the priests of the Jews.

Sunday	15			7 44	4 43	5	7 30
Monday	16	r.	St. Eusebius, Bishop and Martyr.	7 45	4 43	4	Sets
Tuesday	17	v.	Of the Feria.	7 45	4 43	4	5 52
Wednesday	18	w.	Expectation of B. V. M. Ember Day. Fast.	7 46	4 43	3	7 1
Thursday	19	w.	B. Urban V., Pope.	7 46	4 44	3	8 10
Friday	20	v.	Vigil of St. Thomas. Ember Day. Fast.	7 47	4 44	2	9 16
Saturday	21	r.	St. Thomas, Apostle. Ember Day. Fast.	7 48	4 44	2	10 20

Fourth Sunday in Advent.

Gospel, Luke iii., 1-6 : John preaches the Baptism of Penance.

Sunday	22	v.		7 49	4 45	Slow	11 23
Monday	23	v.	Of the Feria.	7 49	4 45		A M.
Tuesday	24	v.	Vigil of Christmas. Fast.	7 50	4 46		0 24
Wednesday	25	w.	CHRISTMAS. HOLYDAY OF OBLIGATION.	7 50	4 47	1	1 25
Thursday	26	r.	St. Stephen, Protomartyr.	7 50	4 48	1	2 29
Friday	27	w.	St. John, Apostle and Evangelist.	7 51	4 49	2	3 37
Saturday	28	v.	Holy Innocents.	7 51	4 50	2	4 48

Sunday within Christmas.

Gospel, Luke ii., 33-40 : The Prophecy of Simeon.

Sunday	29	r.	St. Thomas of Canterbury, Bishop and Martyr.	7 51	4 50	3	5 59
Monday	30	w.	Of the Octave of Christmas.	7 52	4 50	3	7 5
Tuesday	31	w.	St. Sylvester, Pope.	7 22	4 51	4	8 5

MOON'S PHASES.

	D.	H.	M.		D.	H.	M.
Full Moon	2	1	38 P M.	First Quarter	24	0	23 A.M.
Last Quarter	9	2	9 A.M.	Full Moon	31	3	31 P.M.
New Moon	16	1	30 A M.				

SISTERS ADORERS OF THE PRECIOUS BLOOD.

Foundation of the Order—Dress—Mother Catharine—Jubilee Celebration—Mother St. Joseph—First House in Toronto—Present Monastery—Industries— Boarders—Retreatants—Reception—Chapel for Public— Hours of Services—When Members May be Seen.

"Jesus—thrice blessed be His most Holy Name!—is all our own, neither can we spare anything of Him. Yet it was not precisely His soul which was to redeem us, nor the Passion of His Body which was to be exactly our expiation. It was the shedding of His Blood which was to cleanse us from our sins. The remedy of the Fall was precisely in the Saviour's Blood. All the sorrows of His life grew up to the shedding of His Blood, and were crowned by it; and His shedding the last few drops of it after He was dead was significant of the work it had to do. The soul and the Body and the Blood lay separate, and the sacrifice was thus complete." Precious Blood.—*Faber.*

SOME twenty years ago the writer was brought to Toronto to enjoy the privilege of a retreat in a convent in preparation for First Communion. There were friends in the different communities established in the city to be seen, that their prayers might be solicited for the young aspirant. One of these visits has ever remained a happy recollection. We rang the door-bell of a house of very modest pretensions—after the large institutions we had been visiting—and my mother began telling me that she expected to see here a nun who had been her music teacher long ago in St. Hyacinthe, Que., and whom she had not seen since she left school; how this teacher had joined a most severe order, contemplative, founded by one who had been a daily visitor at the convent in St. Hyacinthe, and upon whom all looked with awe and wonder as a remarkably holy and privileged person; how it was whispered among the girls that she never partook of any food, yet was she always joyous, cheerful, delightful; how the wonderful manifestations of her election by Almighty God to honor in an especial manner the Precious Blood had moved the Bishop of St. Hyacinthe and her director to assist her in the arduous labor of establishing a community devoted to the Precious Blood; how continued manifestations showed the Divine complacency in her work; and how inestimable would be the privilege of seeing the beloved foundress, Aurelie Caouette—Mother Catharine Aurelie du Precieux Sang.

Duly impressed and in very great awe I waited for the opening of the door. How immaculate the simple, austere interior, how visible the extreme poverty of the nuns! But my mother's friend comes in and they have much to say, and as the conversation is all in French I have plenty of opportunity to note the peculiar dress of the order—the habit or tunic of white serge, sleeves very full and long enough to completely cover the hand; the long red scapular worn over this reaching to the bottom of the skirt; the linens apparently in but two pieces—the forehead band one, the cap and guimpe the other; the veil black, with a small red cross stitched on over the centre of the forehead; the red girdle with red pendant, upon which are represented the instruments of the Passion; the usual rosary terminating in a tiny skull attached to the girdle; a silver cross containing relics hangs from the neck, a silver ring is on the third finger. I learned later an additional long white mantle of serge is worn in the chapel.

A bevy of convent girls now come, fill the small parlor and overflow the hall. We learn for the first time that Mother Catharine is visiting the house and is to receive the convent girls. We are so favored as to be received with them.

Mother Catharine is short and plain-looking, but possessed of a wonderfully attractive personality. One brings away a fixed idea of loveliness in her—it must be the loveliness of the soul that shining through makes us forget all else. Her manner is warm and affectionate, her sympathy quick and unfailing, her strong faith a refuge for the weakest. Her energy is shown in the personal foundation of houses at Toronto (1869), Montreal (1874), Ottawa (1887), Three Rivers (1880), Brooklyn, N. Y. (1889), Mount Thabor, Oregon (1892). In Brooklyn, N.Y., a fine monastery was completed and taken possession of May, 1894. These convents Mother Catharine visits from time to time in the spirit and wisdom of another Teresa.

Mlle. Aurelie Caouette founded the Congregation of the Sisters Adorers of the Most Precious Blood in her own home at St. Hyacinthe, Que., September 14, 1861, with the approbation and assistance of his Lordship Mgr. La Rocque, and in conjunction with the Rt. Rev. Mgr. Raymond, whom the Sisters term their co-founder.

Three young ladies with Mother Catharine formed the struggling community; of these four but Mother Catharine and Mother St. Joseph— the latter superior of the Toronto house—remain.

But how many have been received and added to the Sisters Adorers of the Precious Blood! The community in Toronto alone numbers 38. How it has pleased God to multiply those souls so eager to gather up every drop of that Precious Blood spent so lavishly ; so jealous for its proper recognition, its praise, honor and adoration ; so ambitious to share for very love in the sufferings that sent the Redeeming Stream.

As early as 1869 the first mission, consisting of six Sisters, with Mother St. Joseph superior, was sent from the Mother House to Toronto at the earnest solicitation of His Grace the late Archbishop Lynch, who was convinced that their advent among his people —their holy life of contemplation, prayer and penance, joined to their arduous labors, would bring down upon his people God's blessings. They arrived in Toronto on the Feast of the Nativity of the Blessed Virgin, September 8, and so celebrated their twenty-fifth anniversary this year ('94). A solemn High Mass, at which His Grace Archbishop Walsh and many of the clergy assisted, was offered up by the chaplain, Very Rev. Father Marijon, Provincial of the Basilians, for the benefactors of the Community. This date marks also the jubilee of Mother St. Joseph, who has been superior in Toronto of the community ever since its foundation, whose fostering care has nursed and cherished its infancy, and whose wise government directs its flourishing maturity.

MONSIGNOR J. S. RAYMOND.

The Rule of the Community has been submitted to Rome and was approved for five years. This term of five years expires in December, 1894, when the Sisters expect final approbation. It was a cause of great joy among these holy nuns that their severe rule suffered so little alteration.

The first home of the Order in Toronto was in the old Loretto Convent on Bathurst street. Within a year four of the six died. The building was found damp and unhealthy.

Through much poverty and much privation this heroic community, happy in sufferings, struggled. Kind friends helped them, and in 1872 they moved to a more comfortable home on the corner of St. Joseph and St. Vincent streets, where the writer first saw them. Here they were given work and thus relieved from utter destitution.

In 1879 the Novitiate was opened, and the house becoming too small the community, through the timely gift of a generous benefactor, were enabled to purchase a larger one farther west on the same street. To this a very large addition was made, the corner stone being laid by His Grace Archbishop Walsh May 28, 1891, and in this Monastery of the Precious Blood, built to suit the cloister, the Sisters are at last in a home where their health does not suffer from overcrowding, and where they can live their life in accordance with the rules and directions of their Institute.

True, they are laden down with a heavy debt—the improvements costing $24,000—but even as they are generous in their offerings for our souls, so can they hope for a like generosity from us in their needs. The building possesses a handsome exterior, is built of red brick with stone facings. High up over the principal entrance is a statue of the Blessed Virgin, a gift from Mr. John Murphy of Guelph—father of one of the nuns ; two niches on either side are still vacant, awaiting like thoughtful and generous benefactors.

In the middle of the summer of '92, knowing that soon the new building would be finished, and desirous to see once more without the grate a friend, I visited the new Monastery and was shown through all the building, out even to the garden, with its useful and ornamental vegetation, whose limits are the nuns' out-of-door world. It is kept in a high state of cultivation, being cared for entirely by the nuns, whom I have seen doing all kinds of labor in it—a straw hat, looking oddly over the veil, protecting them from the hot sun.

Let me tell you what I saw and a little of what I learned in the intimate and unconstrained chat with my friend, a Sister Adorer of the Precious Blood.

The Convent may be divided into two parts, that portion open to the public outside the cloister, and the cloister. Outside the cloister are the parlors separated by a grate from the corresponding parlors, the dining-room for guests, the rooms for the chaplain or visiting priest, and the exterior chapel where the public are free to attend and join in the nuns' devotions.

Above these, reached by a separate staircase, are the rooms for strangers visiting the city and preferring the seclusion and privacy of the Convent to the publicity of a hotel or boarding-house, or for those who may desire to spend quietly a few days in recollection and prayer, or for any who may wish to make a retreat either under the direction of a confessor or the Sisters. These are the north and west sides of the building. On the east side, corresponding with the chapel, is the entrance to the procuratrix's office. Here are transacted business dealings with the outside world. A revolving shelf is in the grate large enough to hold a barrel of flour, though provisions are usually received through the grate within the kitchen-door in the basement.

From the hall of the main entrance we pass through the door of the cloister, which opens into a similar hall. We enter first the Nuns' refectory to the left, a large airy room with long pine tables painted and grained; the reader's desk is at the far end of the room, and behind it a serving pantry with opening at either end, from which the meals are conveyed by two sisters as they are passed in from the kitchen. In the tables are drawers, each containing plate, cup and saucer, knife, fork and spoon, with a square of coarse linen. These pieces of linen, spread before each nun, take the place of a tablecloth. "It must be a labor attending to so much dishwashing." "It is quite simple. A basin of water and towel are passed down the table and each cleanses her own dishes." "They are not easily broken?" and I am laughingly handed for my inspection the granite plate and the heavy delf. "The dishes upon which meat is served of course go to the kitchen." "The duties are changed every week, and the dignified appellation of Dishwasher occurs opposite each nun's name in turn, as do all the different duties." "Then you have no lay nuns?" "Yes, but that does not dispense the choir nuns from such labor. Our foundress insists upon labor—that is our ordinary penance; the choir nuns sweep, cook, wash, iron, scrub; there is no distinction in the labor." "Why lay nuns then?" "That necessary duties may not suffer from the interruptions consequent on the recital of the Divine Office. The lay nuns who, by the

MONSIGNOR LA ROCQUE.

way, wear a black habit, do not recite the Office, neither is a superior education required of them, nor is a dowry exacted from them."

"Do you ever have recreation at your meals?" "No, that is an offering we made to St. Joseph that he might help us in our temporal needs."

We cross the hall to the laundry, where I see the apparatus used in washing, drying, ironing and mangling. The engine and furnace room is beyond the laundry. Above is the attendant's room with separate entrance and staircase, the meals being passed in from the cloister through a window.

"We laundry nearly all the altar linens in the city. We make, too, the altar breads for the diocese." This industry has since grown to large dimensions. Boxes are specially made to hold the different sizes, and are sent often great distances, the Sisters' make being popular even outside the diocese.

We then crossed to the kitchen on the east side, where a large revolving shelf is in the grate to receive supplies. At this wicket the Sisters are solicited by all kinds of necessity, and too often idleness, for meals. Some are grateful, others bold and impudent, loudly clamoring for better food than is known to the Convent table. "But there are places especially provided for such people; you with your own pressing needs should not be taxed in this way?" "We cannot turn the hungry away so long as we have anything to feed them," is, as I think, the too magnanimous reply.

We now pass upstairs, and leaving the linen room enter a workroom where soutanes are made. The Sisters' work gives universal satisfaction, the soutanes, even for the altar boys, being properly fitted, and the work of the neatest description. Single orders are sometimes given by parents proud to have a child serving on the altar, and often contracts are filled for the sanctuary boys of a particular church. We pass the procuratrix's office I mentioned before, and then I get my first and last view of the chapel as seen from within the cloister. The interior and exterior chapel form an L, with the altar situate in the angle facing the longer arm, which is the Nuns' chapel. The windows are on the side next the street, their colored lights proclaiming the "dim religious" interior, while the chanting of the Nuns floating through may arrest for a moment's thought the heedless passer-by.

Again we go up, and I am all interest to see the community room and the noviciate. They are pleasant, airy rooms, the woodwork painted in a light creamy tint used throughout the building in accordance with the directions of the Rule. There is the Crucifix with the Bleeding Saviour prominent in this as in all the rooms, and the first object to meet the eye. There are work tables and chairs, with shelves holding the Sisters' library, whose books I am afraid would not be found of thrilling interest to the modern woman of the world.

Then was forcibly brought home to me the beautiful simplicity of that life which never loses sight of the reason of its creation. Small apertures in the wall looked down into the chapel, and any not able to attend Mass or devotions in the chapel can assist here—the infirmaries being on the same flat. There is also a private parlor adjacent to the Superior's room, where a like provision is made. From here on Holy Thursday the Nuns enjoy their only full view of the Repository, which has always faced the people's chapel. Rev. Mother Catharine especially commended these arrangements for the sick. Near the infirmaries is a carefully stocked pharmacy.

And now, still remaining within the cloister, we go up another flight of steps to the Nuns' cells. Here are wide and long corridors with doors on either side opening into the diminutive rooms termed cells. Many are glanced into; one attracts me very much; it is situate in one of the towers, and so of irregular shape, and perhaps a little larger than the others, high enough up to give the occupant a magnificent view. "What a view! How you must enjoy it!" There is an amused smile on the Sister's face. "You don't mean to say that mortification goes so far with you that you do not let yourself enjoy the world from this vantage point?" "That might be a distraction—we do not look out of the windows, neither would it be prudent in a large city." I silently turn to examine the furnishings of the room, which consist of a small cabinet, a bed—not, O reader, what you and I would call a bed, for chancing to knock against it I satisfied myself as to its construction. Over the plain boards a sheet is spread and a hard pillow is at the head. A white counterpane covers this again—all looking so sweet and restful in its spotless white—but that chance examination of the condition of things below quenched all desire to test the hospitality of the austere cell. A priedieu before a crucifix completes the room. As everyone knows, the Sisters chant the Divine Office, rising at midnight to sing matins and lands. "How do you ever get into your elaborate costume in time?" I am rude and curious enough to ask. "That is not difficult—there is nothing elaborate about it. It is easier than your modern dress. See, one string fastens all this—veil and face

linens come right off. Our scapular is buttoned over the shoulder. It is all very simple." Are not your long flowing sleeves very awkward when working? How do you manage when washing, baking, or say blackleading a stove?" "The sleeves are turned back thus and kept in place by a tighter sleeve above; for work requiring further protection we wear over-sleeves. We are not handicapped in any way. I can reach as far and as easily as a Delsarte devotee." So was proved to me the convenience of a costume I till then had thought of only as emblematic and picturesque.

"What if you are sick and not able to attend chapel?" "We turn the card on our door." Then I noticed on the door of each cell a card, all bearing different mottoes, chosen by the occupant of the cell; when ill the reverse is turned, which bears the words: "I sleep, but my heart watcheth." "Do you always assemble in order when you go to the chapel?" "Yes, we take our ranks in the hall outside the chapel door, except—" "Ah, there is one exception!" "We begin the year a little differently. The anniversary of the first shedding of the Precious Blood is a great day with us—a day of special fast and reparation—when the bell rings at midnight all hurry and try each to be first in the chapel to wish Our Lord a Happy New Year, and to resolve to do all in our power by prayer and penance to make some reparation for the neglect, the outrages daily offered that Precious Blood shed so superabundantly for us."

There is yet another flight of stairs that takes us to yet more cells and workrooms partitioned off here by temporary canvas-halls. In one of these latter the industry of what, think you? shoemaking is carried on—and splendid wearing shoes the Sisters make, for I know this same Sister who is my guide capable of wearing out the "store article" in a month, and the Sisters' manufacture lasts her really years. In another workroom the habits are made.

The Sisters make also birettas, soutanes, bourses for the Blessed Sacrament, veils, stoles, vestments, scapulars of all kinds, rosaries and chaplets, and mend them also ; paint statues and crucifixes, and make habits for the dead. This last work, I am told, is not as well known among the people as is desirable, or there would probably be more patronage. Of course I was practical enough to ask prices, and learned scapulars could be obtained from 10c. to $1 ; rosaries, chaplets from 10c up ; habits for the dead from $4 to $12.

The Sisters also publish a beautiful prayer book, called the Book of the Elect, price 50c. and higher for better styles of binding.

Yet another room we enter called the paint-room, and here I learn that every particle of painting, graining and varnishing, even the first coat of the new building has been done by the Sisters themselves, and it is done so beautifully —just see it and satisfy yourself. "But who is painting the fence?" I ask. "The Sisters; they rise very, very early and do it when no one is stirring." I shall come some fine morning and witness that sight, I thought, but it was not easy to rise as early as the Sisters do.

We come down the stairs again, leaving the cloister after the second flight to pass into the rooms reserved for transient boarders and retreatants. They are often taken by pious people who wish to enjoy to the full the privilege of frequent visits to the chapel on Exposition Days (first Sunday of the month), or the Forty Hours Adoration, which occurs three times a year. They can be secured for a day, ten days or longer according to the disposition of the applicant. Such pleasant rooms as they are, so conveniently fitted up and commanding such a pretty view. They are entered from a spacious hall, in the large sunny window of which I noticed many cages with beautiful singing canaries. "Whose are all these?" "Those are looked after by Sister Jane. She is very successful in raising birds and has them for sale." Sister Jane, I think, is better known to outsiders than any other member of the community. For very many years she was the only tourière, and even before she entered as a novice was the first to offer the over-taxed Nuns the much-needed assistance of willing hands and feet. It was no light task to even answer the door in those early days when troops of visitors—the curious, along with those whose devotion and charity led them—called on the nuns in their bleak, draughty house. I have heard Sister Jane say how many, many times she has gone to the market unable to buy more than a single pound of coarse meat for the Nuns, and no skilled French chef could have done more with that one pound than did excellent Sister Jane, for it was stewed and fried and hashed and just made go round. There was much stern privation in those days and more fasts than were obligatory. Sister Jane tells how the Superior, being very ill, she was asked by a Sister could she make some little biscuits with which the appetite might be tempted. "Why, certainly; will you give me a little butter?" "There is none." "No, we have none." "Milk or eggs, then?" Another negative. "A little sugar, perhaps?" "No, I can give you nothing." I'm afraid Sister Jane's biscuits under the circumstances did not prove tempting to the invalid. But Sister Jane's reminiscences deserve a chapter, and another time justice can be done them. Meanwhile, my young friends, if you are on the lookout for a pet patronize Sister's little household, and perhaps you will learn something more than just how to take care of your pets.

At the east end of the corridor are Miss Hoskin's rooms. She is inseparably connected by all Catholics with the foundation of the Precious Blood community in Toronto. It is through her indefatigable efforts, her unfailing energy and courage that the Nuns have prospered in Toronto and been justified in putting up the fine monastery they now occupy. Her life is devoted to the service of the Precious Blood Nuns.

A private staircase leads down to the chapel. Another staircase leads to the parlors in the basement.

The grates in the Monastery are of wood in the prevailing light creamy tint; the floors are painted.

We go on to the exterior chapel. Here I noticed, in addition to the sanctuary lamp, seven others hanging before the altar, some lighted. These are votive lamps which the piously disposed may burn before the Blessed Sacrament—the cost being a dollar a month. The number of the lamps represents the Seven Sheddings of the Precious Blood. For a long time the Sanctuary lamp has burned at the expense of a friend of the Institute—an enviable reward for the devotion that prompted so sweet a charity. There are also votive lamps before the statues of the Blessed Virgin, St. Joseph and the Sacred Heart. The candelabras, of which there are two, for votive candles are the only ones I have seen that are in keeping with their surroundings and worthy of the service they render. They were specially designed by a friend of the institution for the purpose, and one's æsthetic ideas are satisfied as well as one's devotion when slipping in the unobtrusive little box the five cents that entitles one to burn a candle on the candelabra.

As I mentioned before, the altar faces the interior chapel, which is separated from the sanctuary by the grate. A small square in it is swung open to administer Holy Communion. There is a door also in the grate. I was present in July, 1894, at a reception and profession when the idea of the cloister was materialized by the click of the spring lock as the newly-professed, having expressed their desire to model their lives on the rule of the Sisters Adorers of the Precious Blood and Daughters of Mary Immaculate, pronounced in the Sanctuary before the Blessed Sacrament exposed on the altar the vows of Chastity, Poverty and Obedience, and passed through into the cloister.

I found the solemn ceremony intensely interesting, the forms observed instructive. Two tourière Sisters were professed—their vows are renewed from year to year, they are not cloistered, being the Sisters' means of communication with the world. Their habit is of black serge—a black cape taking the place of the white guimpe; a cap with fluted frill fits closely the face, and is covered all but the frill with a black veil; the other parts are the same as the cloistered nuns.

The postulants were presented by Assistant-Sister St. Stanislaus and the Mistress of the Novices, Sister M. Teresa to the officiating priest, Very Rev. Father Marijon. Kneeling in the sanctuary they petitioned him for the habit. He questioned them regarding their determination to adopt the life—blessed the habit, handing the different parts to the kneeling postulant, who was assisted in their adjustment by her Superiors. The sweetest English hymns were sung by the Nuns' choir. This I did not expect, but the community here in Toronto. I learn, is composed almost entirely of English Nuns—with English the language of the house.

The rules of the order ask for Exposition of the Blessed Sacrament the first Sunday of every month. For many years the Nuns had to forego this privilege on account of the cost of the candles —it would be in the neighborhood of $3 for each exposition. A friend of the community mentioned this to other friends, and they immediately volunteered each to bear the cost in turn of the candles. It seems to me there are many who, if they knew how timely and acceptable such offerings are, would be glad to share this privilege, for the Nuns give a special intention to the provider or providers of the candles. The Forty Hours Adoration is another devotion practised three times a year in the Convent, beginning on

the first day of the year—the Circumcision. Here is another opportunity for the busy Martha to leave a cheerful witness of her pie'y and affection, while also a reminder to the willing Sisters' victims of reparation, of her spiritual needs. All through the night the Nuns adore the Blessed Sacrament—the Forty Hours being consecutive.

Surely 'tis a wonderful chapel where one catches the pervading spirit of devotion ; prayer comes without effort, self-sacrifice seems possible.

The Convent chapel is open every day from 5.30 a.m. till dark. Mass is celebrated daily at 6.3) a.m., and Benediction of the Blessed Sacrament every day during the months of May, July and October, also the Wednesdays and Fridays of Lent and Advent, the Feasts of Our Lord, the Blessed Virgin and the Apostles, at 5.30 p.m. On Sundays the hour for Benediction is 4.30 p.m.

The Sisters may receive visitors in the morning from 10 to 11.30, and in the afternoon from 2 to 3 and from 4 to 5.30.

NIGHT WATCHES.

To The Order of Sisters Adorers.

Written for the Catholic Almanac of Ontario.

Throughout the silent hours of the night,
    When crime runs deep,
Rise, Sisterhood, and watch with prayerful hearts—
    The angels weep.

Like faithful sentinels of virtue join
    The spirit band ;
Into the brooding shadows upward lift
    A pleading hand.

Still from the burdened cross a mystic stream—
    The Saviour's blood—
Pours through the rocky, sin obstructed land
    Its saving flood.

Work, gentle hands, these rocks of sin to lift,
    The stream to free
And set afloat God's pinioned souls to life
    And liberty.

        JESSIE WILLIS BROADHEAD,
Sunday, June 17th, 1894.   Detroit, Mich.,

A BALLAD OF GREEN TREES AND THE MASTER.

Into the woods my Master went,
    And He was all forespent ;
Into the woods my Master came,
    Forespent with love and shame;
But the olives, they were not blind to Him,
    The little gray leaves were kind to Him,
    As into the woods He came

Out of the woods my Master went,
    And He was well content ;
Out of the woods my Master came,
    Content with death and shame.
And when death and shame would woo Him last,
    'Twas from under a tree they drew Him last,
    'Twas on a tree they slew Him last,
    When out of the woods He came.

        SIDNEY LANIER.

THE CASUISTRY OF THOMAS PLAYFAIR.

Written for the Catholic Almanac of Ontario.

THOMAS PLAYFAIR, chubby, rubicund, was unusually cheerful after his fourth confession. He experienced a spiritual consolation which was inclined to show itself exteriorly in the breaking of things.

However, as he walked homeward. there happened to be nothing breakable convenient; so Tom was fain to content himself with drawing a stick rapidly along the iron rods of a fence. His fullness of happiness, however, was tempered by regret for his drum at home.

Tom, you may be sure, had made a good confession; and he had resolved, among other things, to avoid fighting. Such a promise at this interesting period of his life meant much.

As it happened, it meant a great deal on this

very occasion. One square beyond the church, and in a very unfashionable quarter, stood a saloon, fronted at the edge of the sidewalk by a large watering-trough. Beside this trough, as Tom came near, were several very dirty little boys, prominent among whom, for dirt and size, was a dark-eyed, black-haired, unwashed son of Italy. This youth had been knocking his followers about quite freely. His fists were clenched, his scanty shirt was open at the throat, and he was breathing heavily. Two others of the group were rather the worse for battle.

Tom paused.

"If I try to pass that Dago," he reflected, "just as like as not he'll want to fight; I've heard about him. Anyhow, he's not more than my size, and—"

At this stage of his thought Tom shook his head violently. Here he had been actually planning a fight.

"I think I'd better turn and go the other way," he continued to himself, as he slacked his pace.

Now it so happened that the young bully perceived Tom's hesitation. Instantly the fire of battle flashed from his eyes, and he bawled out:

"Halloa, dude!"

Poor Tom! To turn now would seem to be a confession of cowardice. To go on? Yes, Tom would go on; but he would *not* fight, in any event.

The Italian youth met him half-way, advancing with doubled fists and a strut which would have passed muster in the Bowery.

"For two cents I knock your head off."

Tom was anxious, but collected. He put his hand in his pocket, drew out a nickel, and said:

"Here's five cents not to do it."

The bully took the five-cent piece, while a tide of emotion bore down upon him. For the moment he was dumbfounded, while Tom passed on, demure, serene; and all the world, that is the youngsters by the water-trough, wondered.

On coming to himself the young swash-buckler pocketed the nickel, then gave a yell and made after Tom with intentions that could not be misunderstood.

And Tom! Tom took to his heels.

This, I believe, was the beginning of his career as a hero. He ran well, too, and reached home panting, breathless, and, it must be confessed, in a very uncomfortable frame of mind.

"He'll be on the lookout for me again," Tom muttered to himself, "and it won't do to keep running away all the time. It's too hard, and, besides, it will make things worse. All those fellows will want to fight me. I wish I could see my way out. I won't fight, anyhow. It's a conundrum."

Then Tom went out to a sand-pile in the street, and there enjoyed himself in the artless fashion peculiar to boys of his tender age. Meanwhile his mind sustained a process of hard thinking.

Suddenly, hands and feet sent the sand flying into the air, and Tom, with a happy smile, dashed into the house.

He came out presently, giving evidence in his improved appearance of having bestowed unusual attention upon his person. One hand was in his jacket pocket, the other, as he walked, described three-quarter circles in the air. There was no hesitation in his step now, as he retraced at a dignified walk the path of his recent flight.

"Immense," he muttered, as he came in sight of the saloon and perceived the group still lingering beside the horse-trough.

The young Italian seemed to look upon the situation in the same light. He whispered a few words to his admirers, and, putting his arms a-kimbo, stationed himself midway on the pavement.

Tom, ineffably serene, continued to advance. "Yoy come-a to fight?" called out the bully.

"No," answered Tom affably. "It's against my precepts to fight."

The word "precepts" had occurred in Tom's last catechism lesson. It was the nearest word to "principles" that suggested itself.

"I'll knock your 'ead off," continued the Italian, still keeping his arms a-kimbo.

Tom came on with steady pace until he was within a yard of the enemy.

Then, quick as a flash, out from the pocket came the hand clasping a bar of soap. At the same instant Tom threw his arms about the Italian, and with one sudden and vigorous swing had his head in the trough.

There was a gurgling, a coughing, a quick motion up and down of the hand that held the soap, a few lusty kicks upon Tom's insensible shins, and presently the Italian's face came up, clean, dripping, terrified, awe-stricken. His face had never been thus treated within its owner's memory. The few kicks which he had distributed upon Tom's legs at first were the beginning and the end of his resistance. The washing had acted upon him as blinders upon a horse.

His following was standing at a safe distance. "There now," panted Tom, "I've given your face a good washing. It needed it. It was *virtuous* to wash it. Next time you bother me *I'll wash your neck too.*"

With which horrible threat on his lips Tom walked away unmolested. Tom was not bothered again.

He went away, taking himself quite seriously. Perhaps the angels were amused at Tom's solution—of that I am not certain; but I am convinced, at any rate, that his application of soap upon the young bully was imputed to him by the angels' chancery unto justice.

FRANCIS J. FINN, S.J.

THREE CHRISTMAS EVES.

Written for the Catholic Almanac of Ontario.

DEAR Old Quebec! Who that has ever seen the quaint old city can forget it? Who that has ever dwelt there but loves every crooked street, every rugged, break-neck pathway that serves to lead the unwary stranger in the opposite direction to that he set out for? Quebec, the picturesque, is never more beautiful than in winter when covered with her deep, thick mantle of snow. Piles upon piles of beautiful snow everywhere; on the streets, upon the houses, on the fences—where there are any; one might say over the fences, for they are frequently buried out of sight; on the river, up and down and away across to the other side, over the Citadel, down the sides of the rocks; and beyond, where the view is arrested by the mountains, nothing but snow, sparkling like diamonds under the winter sun. Nowhere is the cold so cheering and bracing; bright, clear, crisp, sunshiny cold. One loves to be out and feel the invigorating breath of a winter's morning, and hear the dry, powdery snow crunching under the feet.

On just such a morning as this Mary Dawson looked out of the window after breakfast, up and down St. Louis street. The sun was tempting, the snow looked as though it would crunch beautifully, the cold was sharp and keen.

"This is Christmas Eve; I think I'll run up to see Katie Wilson, mother; she always goes to midnight Mass; they have it every year, you know, in the Catholic churches and convents. I have often thought I would like to go to the service at the Ursuline Convent. They say it's beautiful there; the nuns and girls sing behind the grate; it must be lovely. If you don't want me this morning, mother, I'll run up and ask Katie to take me to-night. May I?"

"I don't want you particularly this morning, my dear," replied Mrs. Dawson, "but I hardly know what to say about your going to this midnight service. you are such an enthusiastic girl. What if you should be fascinated by these Catholic doings?"

Mary laughed a merry, light-hearted laugh.

"Mother, mother dear, what *are* you thinking of? I fascinated, or even yielding to fascination in matters of religion! No, no! I should want solid proof, and where can I find that but in my own faith, the Church of England? Katie Wilson is a dear, good girl, so is her brother Harry—well, of course, he isn't a girl; you know what I mean; you needn't laugh; I was going to say it's a pity Katie doesn't go to our church, she is so sweet and lovely, Well, may I go, mother ? "

" "I suppose so," answered her mother, "but, if you go to this affair to-night, how will you get there and home so late ? "

" Oh, that's easily managed, and quite proper too, little mother. Mrs. and Mr. Wilson always go, I know, and as they have to pass here on the way to the convent they can call for me going and leave me returning, without going a step out of their way."

Mary Dawson was just twenty years of age; her birthday had been celebrated with great rejoicing on the 8th December. Surely the Immaculate Mary would take this little namesake under her protection! Let us hope it was not merely a coincidence that she was born on that beautiful feast and named after the Queen of Heaven.

Mrs. Dawson had been a widow for five years. Mary, her youngest born, a married daughter living in Montreal and three sons constituted her family Two of her sons were also in Montreal practising law, and the youngest, two years older than Mary, who had just taken his degree in medicine, was about to begin to practise in Quebec.

Mary was a gentle, amiable girl; she had been carefully brought up and educated chiefly at home by governesses. Mrs. Dawson had a dread and dislike of convents, and could not bear the thought of sending her little girl to a distance to a Protestant school. Thus Mary knew very little of convents, which may seem strange for a Quebec girl.

Two years before she had formed a friendship for Katie Wilson, who was one year her junior, and who had been educated at the Ursuline Convent. Katie had but one brother—Harry three years older than herself, upon whom she looked as her hero, and was proud to own him for her brother. He certainly was a fine, handsome young man, and as good as he looked; an earnest Catholic, attentive to all his duties, spiritual and otherwise. He had been for about three months junior partner in a law firm.

At twenty minutes to twelve the Wilsons stopped before the Dawson house, and Mary, who had been watching for them, joined them noiselessly, for her mother and the rest had retired. (The absent ones had come home that evening).

Their house was only a few minutes' walk from the convent (one is never far from anywhere in Quebec), so they were soon walking down Parloir street, facing the ancient, historic pile which for over two centuries has sheltered the daughters of St. Ursula.

The church, which is devoted to the public, was very nearly filled when they entered, but Harry had gone early and secured a seat near the front for our party on the right-hand side,

close to the grate, behind which is the Nuns' chapel, concealed usually from curious eyes by a curtain drawn across the grate. But Mary thought she could see the faces and white veils of one or two pupils, where the curtains gaped a little apart, as she looked curiously over while her friends were engaged at their devotions.

How she longed to have a peep into that mysterious interior ; she wondered what they looked like, those black - robed nuns and young girls hidden away behind that jealous grate and curtain. Good breeding forbade her to gaze long at that division in the curtains, though she felt sure if she craned her neck ever so little she could see farther into the chapel ; but she must restrain herself; perhaps the curtains would be drawn aside some time during the services.

What a quaint old church it was ; plain, with no pretension to architectural beauty. How fat and puffy were those angels' faces looking down with bulging eyes from cornices and ceiling. Montcalm was buried here, she had heard ; how ancient it must all be. She wondered whether it was just as it used to be ; were the walls and benches, the carved angels and the altar all the same ? Ah ! the altar, that was beautiful ! Hundreds of lights, it appeared to the young girl, were reflected in the crystal and brightly burnished ornaments upon the altar. And what was the other altar, to the left, facing the Nuns' grate ? It appeared to be beautifully decorated, but was not yet lit up, and a curtain concealed it from view. Was that the crib, she wondered; she had seen it once or twice in Catholic churches; this one must be beautiful.

Mary's eyes rested upon the congregation around her. How devout they all looked, how silent it was; the opening and closing of the door as people entered was done with as little noise as possible; no one seemed to speak, no one looked about. She glanced at her own friends; they were all occupied with their devotions; even Harry seemed to pay no attention to his surroundings, but had his eyes bent devoutly upon a prayer book. The priest had not yet come out; the service had not commenced; how strange they should be all praying beforehand. Why was it? She saw no harm in sitting at ease and looking around a little if one were early for church, or even in a whispered word or two; though, of course, after the services had commenced, none would be more decorous and devout than was Mary Sunday after Sunday in their pew at the Anglican cathedral. Mary soon saw she was the only one gazing around, and immediately drew her eyes to the front.

On the stroke of midnight the priest entered, preceded by his acolytes. This was the white-haired, gentle-faced priest Mary had frequently seen passing their house. From her earliest childhood she remembered him, and had always been attracted by his kind, benevolent expression. Katie had often told her of dear Pere Le Moine, the chaplain at the convent, so beloved by the pupils.

There is a gentle rustle as all go on their knees; a faint rustle comes also from behind the grate. The priest stands at the foot of the altar and Mass begins.

It seemed a little tame at first to Mary; she could not understand what was going on, and wondered at those around her, whose devout attitudes and rapt attention showed a perfect comprehension and sympathy.

But, hark! what heavenly singing! Where does it come from? Mary could not refrain from looking up; there she saw, high above the heads of the people, a grate similar to the one below, but smaller. Evidently the organ loft was there, inside the cloister.

How exquisitely they sang! The children's choruses were enchanting. "Gloria in excelsis Deo."

That must be a nun; what a voice; how sweet, how lovely! "Gloria in excelsis Deo!" Mary was herself a sweet singer and enthusiastic about music.

By and bye a little bell is rung at the foot of the altar; the silence becomes, if possible, more intense: a devout look of expectancy is upon every countenance. Mary remains seated, but attentive. She fancies she hears a little motion behind the curtains; they seem to shake a little. Ah! they are drawn slowly apart. Mary can see a veiled nun kneeling beside the curtain; before she can look further the little bell rings again, and instantly every head is bowed. As Mary

looks now into the chapel she sees row upon row of benches occupied by pupils, but all are bowed in adoration; she can see nothing but snowy billows of white veils; the stalls on each side of the chapel are occupied by the nuns, who are also bending low, their veils concealing them completely from Mary's curious eyes. She turns to look at the worshippers around; they are in the same attitude of adoration; a breathless silence reigns; every head but hers is bent. A feeling of loneliness, of desolation comes over her; she feels as though all had gone somewhere and left her behind. She looks at the altar; what is it? The gentle-faced priest she had seen so often was holding something aloft. A majesty, a dignity she had never before observed seemed to invest him. What is it?

Mary sank upon her knees and bowed her head; she knew not why. A whisper came into her heart: "What if after all I should be wrong." Oh! the agony of that thought. "God help me! can it be that this is truth, and I am outside the pale? O! God, no! this is only a temptation!" While these thoughts were passing through her mind her exterior was calm; no one guessed her mental excitement. She continued to observe what was going on. After the elevation two acolytes approached the side altar, and while one lit the candles around the shrine the other drew aside the screen which concealed the crib. A beautiful representation of the Infant Jesus lying in the manger was revealed; near by stood a statue of Our Blessed Lady. Mary looked first at the sweet little Babe, then at the Mother, that dear Mother of Mercy and Love who was as yet a stranger to this other suffering Mary. As she gazed upon the tender countenance of that dear Mother she exclaimed, "O! if you have any power in Heaven exert it for me now, I am so miserable." She was conscious of a stir around her; people were advancing towards the sanctuary railing; it was time to receive Holy Communion. It took a long while to administer Holy Communion there. First the priest went to the grate, where the nuns and pupils all received. Then he returned to the sanctuary railing, and nearly all the congregation went forward in turn. The Wilsons went, and Mary again felt left out. An intense longing to partake of that mystic Communion seized upon her. As she watched the priest passing down the line the same sensation she experienced at the Elevation came over her "What is it?" she breathed. "My God, what is it?"

At length Mass was over; a few left at once, but nearly all remained for at least a quarter of an hour in silent adoration. Mary had time to compose herself; it would never do to let the Wilsons see her agitation. When they were outside Katie said:

"How did you like it, Mary?"

"Oh, it was beautiful," answered Mary, drawing in her breath. "The singing was lovely; who sang that 'Gloria in excelsis Deo!'"

" That was one of the nuns; has she not a beautiful voice?"

"Beautiful, indeed," assented Mary. "I should like to learn that, but here we are at our door. Good night, and thank you all."

"Good morning, rather," broke in Harry. "And Merry Christmas, Mary."

"Merry Christmas, Harry," sang out Mary as she disappeared.

———

A year had quickly rolled away. Christmas Eve had come around again; people were assembling for Midnight Mass in the Church attached to the Ursuline Convent. The bench occupied by our friends last year has been secured by them again. Mr. and Mrs. Wilson are there, Kate looking tearfully happy, Harry looking grave but evidently well pleased; and who is this maiden all in white enveloped in a cloudy veil? Can this be our Mary? Even so, this is Mary; no looking around now, no wondering what it all meant, no question, no doubt; nothing but joy—calm, sweet, heavenly joy.

It looks as though the little church would be taxed to its utmost to-night, for all Quebec has heard that pretty, merry Mary Dawson was received into the Church that morning by Pere Le Moine, and is to receive her First Holy Communion at Midnight Mass.

It is not our intention to enter upon any controversy in this short relation, nor to give Mary Dawson's reasons for the step she took. Suffice it to say that she set about to seek the truth; above all she prayed; and God, who hears every earnest prayer, set her upon the right path, which she followed faithfully. Six months before she implored Father Le Moine to give her conditional Baptism; but he, usually so mild and gentle, was inexorable; she could not obtain her mother's consent, therefore she must wait until she would be of age. The probation would do her good, he maintained; it would strengthen her character, and show whether she was possessed of perseverance.

Mrs. Dawson, naturally enough, felt what she considered her daughter's defection keenly; she could not give her consent to the step Mary desired to take, but she did not treat her harshly. Her sorrow was trial enough for Mary, who suffered as a warm-hearted girl cannot but suffer when she knows her duty to God clashes with the tender love she bears her parents; but when God calls we must obey, no matter at what cost. Mary came of age on the 6th December, but her Baptism was deferred until Christmas Eve. Pere Le Moine performed the ceremony in the morning about 10 o'clock in the little Ursuline church. None were present but Mr. and Mrs. Wilson, who were the sponsors, Katie shedding floods of happy tears, and Harry, who looked happy and very serious.

She was to receive her First Holy Communion at Midnight Mass; fervently she prayed for the grace of a good Communion, and as the sweet voice of last year sang out " *Gloria in excelsis Deo*" a heavenly smile lit up her lovely countenance, while she thanked God for the gift she had received since last she heard that glorious hymn. At the Elevation she bowed her head to adore the God who had revealed Himself to her. At the Holy Communion—but we must draw a veil over her feelings at that sacred moment; we may only hear her murmur in her joy and gratitude to God resting upon her heart: "I am all Thine, my Jesus; do with me as Thou wilt; I give myself to Thee."

———

For a third time we must visit the little church of the Ursulines on Christmas Eve for Midnight Mass. It looks as usual; one would think it was last year or the year before, so little has anything changed. Shall we find the Wilsons where we are accustomed to see them? Yes; here are Mr. and Mrs. Wilson with Katie and Harry, but where is Mary Dawson? We miss her, she is not with them, she is not in the little church. Pere Le Moine, as before, is the celebrant and Mass is in progress.

" *Gloria in excelsis Deo!*" rings out from the cloistered choir. The soloist is not the sweet-voiced nun we heard before; we thought her voice sweet and lovely; so it was, but this is different, it is richer, fuller, more melodious, more of heaven, if we may so speak " *Gloria in excelsis Deo!*" The singer seems to be singing her heart right up to God.

Katie, as the notes burst out, puts up her handkerchief to stifle a little sob. A look of pain passes over Harry's face, and he turns pale; he buries his face in his hands and prays earnestly, fervently until he is calm and resigned. Mr. and Mrs. Wilson turn a little uneasily and settle themselves to pray with increased devotion. They all recognize the voice of their dear little friend Mary Dawson. She has now consecrated that voice and all her talents to the service of God. On the 8th December she received the habit of an Ursuline novice after three months' probation as postulant. She is known now as Mother Mary of the Immaculate Conception.

M. H.

THE CURE OF A TUMOR BY THE MEDAL OF ST. BENEDICT.

Written for the Catholic Almanac of Ontario.

BEING well acquainted with the lady in whose favor this remarkable cure was wrought, I offer to your Almanac a brief history of the cure. I have the details from my friend herself.

I. In July last year, while I was residing at Sacred Heart Retreat, Louisville. I received a message from a friend to call and see her at SS. Mary and Elizabeth Hospital, whither she had come for treatment. I was surprised to find her in Louisville, having been away from there myself for several weeks, and not having heard from her the while.

When we met I was much pained to learn that she had been suffering from a tumor on the breast. She had first noticed it on the first of June, and had straightway written to her doctor in Cincinnati, who had given her in reply the consoling opinion that the tumor was nothing serious, and that the remedy he sent would soon disperse it. However, the swelling grew worse every day, and on the 14th of June this same doctor wrote advising my friend to see some good surgeon.

This counsel she delayed to follow, from sheer dislike of submitting to surgical treatment. And meanwhile the tumor kept increasing in size and became tender and painful.

On the 6th of July she began applying hot poultices, and continued this till the 10th. But, finding that only aggravated the tumor, she wisely gave it up. The Sisters of the hospital advised her to consult without further delay a celebrated surgeon in the city. Accordingly she went that very afternoon, in company with one of the Sisters, to the office of this eminent doctor. He examined the tumor, and said that "it must come out, and soon too."

"What do you mean by soon?" she asked.

"In three or four days," he replied.

"Why, you don't think it a cancer?"

"Yes, I do."

"But there's none in the family," she urged.

"That's nothing," he answered

Then, enquiring into her general health, he decided that she needed medical treatment, and that before he could fix the date of the operation he must await the result of the treatment.

Next morning, July 12th, the surgeon came out to the hospital, and brought with him another distinguished member of his profession. The latter gentleman examined the patient's heart, and then the tumor, remarking that the tumor was very near the skin and about the size of two lemons. It had been a hard tumor from the first.

II. Now comes in the supernatural. A priest who was staying with the Trappists at Gethsemane, and to whom my friend had written to secure the prayers of the monks, called to see her the next day (July 13th) and brought with him a medal of St. Benedict, telling her that the good Trappists had said she was to put the medal in water and to drink the water, a little every day, for nine days; and that they would go to Holy Communion for her. But she hesitated to pray for a miraculous cure, having made up her mind to offer the pain of the tumor, and even death itself, for a certain favor she had long been asking of God. The priest suggested that she should petition for the cure with entire submission to God's will; that perhaps it was not His will to accept her sacrifice. But she concluded to think the matter over first.

The following day she went into the city to ask the surgeon an important question. The jolting of the street cars caused her great pain, but she felt quite justified in taking the journey. She begged the doctor to tell her candidly what were her chances for life and what for death, after the operation, remarking that she was not afraid to die, not having lived for this world; but that, in case she would be likely to die, she wished to have her daughter with her—a Sister of Charity, then at Nazareth. The doctor replied: "Well, to be candid, you have ten chances to live and ten to die." "Why, then," she demanded, "undergo the operation?" "Because," replied the doctor, "you would suffer such agony you would have to be kept under the influence of morphia." She then requested him to postpone the operation till after the 19th, as the community where her daughter was were in retreat till that date. He assented; and they settled it between them that the operation should be performed on the 25th.

She now decided to try the novena, putting St. Benedict's medal in water and drinking a little of it daily. She asked Our Lord to cure her, only if it would be for His greater glory, and began to take the water at noon on Wednesday, July 20th.

Up to this time the pain of the tumor had gone on increasing. The poor lady could get very little sleep, and lie only on her back; could not even sit in a chair for long, nor stoop, nor use her arm without great pain. Such was the state she had been brought to when she began using the water. Kneeling first, with her arms in the form of a cross, she said an Our Father and a Hail Mary in honor of St. Benedict; then asked God in her own words to hear the intercession of His servant in her behalf, if it would be for His own greater glory.

She wrote to the Trappists that she had begun the novena, and received a consoling reply, with the promise that they would all go to Communion for her twice, besides offering several Masses.

III. Thursday, the 21st, though my friend had used the water but one day, *there was a perceptible decrease in the tumor.* So that when her daughter arrived from Nazareth to stay with her the Sister was greeted with very unexpected good news.

Next day our patient's friend, the doctor whom she had first consulted, himself a distinguished man in his profession, arrived from Cincinnati and examined the tumor. The pain and tenderness had ceased, and the skin was no longer drawn tightly over the swelling. She asked the doctor to tell her the size of the tumor, and he said, "About that of a fair-sized apple."

This doctor being a Catholic my friend told him what she was doing for a cure, and with what results. "Then you must put off the operation," he said. She replied that she did not know how to manage the surgeon who was to perform it. "Leave that to me," said her friend.

The Cincinnati physician then held a consultation with the surgeon. On returning to the patient the Louisville surgeon said : "You will be ready, then, on Monday, Mrs. ——." "Well, doctor," she began, but her Cincinnati friend took up the unfinished sentence and informed his colleague that she wished to postpone the operation for three or four days more.

"Oh, I wouldn't do that !" said the operator; "it ought to be out now ' " Well, doctor," said the other, "give her four days. She wants to see the result of a certain matter first." "Very well," was the rejoinder; "but I wouldn't postpone it long." "No, doctor," said the patient; "I will telephone you when I'm ready."

She continued taking the water each day, and each day the tumor grew smaller and smaller. Friday, the 29th, brought the novena to a close. This was the fourth day after the one first fixed upon for the operation. The tumor had now decreased to the size of a silver dollar, and sank so far from the skin as to be quite buried in the flesh. Moreover, instead of being round, like an apple or a lemon, it was quite flat, like a dollar. The eminent operator arrived that morning. The four days of grace were over. A Sister brought him to the room. "Well, when will you be ready for the operation, Mrs.   ?" My friend saw that now she could conceal her secret no longer. "Doctor," she said, "we Catholics believe a great many things you don't. I have a medal of

St. Benedict, sent me by the Trappists—" Here the Sister interrupted with "Have you ever been out to their monastery, doctor ? " "No," he said; "but tell me if they have cured that " (pointing to the patient's breast) "I will go and see them."' He then made an examination of the tumor. For a minute or two he did not speak. Then said abruptly : "The root's there, anyway, and will have to come out. But we'll postpone the operation till the Fall. The weather will be cooler then, and you will be better able to bear it."

IV. My friend now began a second novena, taking the water daily as before. The tumor went on decreasing : from the size of a dollar to that of a half-dollar, and then to that of a quarter, until, by the end of the second novena, it was gone—completely gone !

She then took two of the Sisters with her to the doctor's office. As soon as he saw her the surgeon exclaimed : "Well, is it gone ? " She asked him to examine and see. He did so, and said : "It's gone—sure ! "

Of course she enquired how the doctor accounted for the disappearance of the tumor. He replied that he didn't believe in miracles, but that he was quite unable to account for the singular fact which he had witnessed. Then, at his patient's request, he wrote a statement to the effect that he had found a hard tumor nearing the skin, and had advised operation, but that the tumor had *spontaneously* disappeared. He was mistaken, he said, in his diagnosis of it as malignant.

"But, tell me, doctor," rejoined my friend; "allowing you were mistaken in your diagnosis, did you ever know a tumor of the kind you now claim mine to have been to disappear in that length of time ? " "Never," he replied. "Is there anything on record in medical science to account for it ? " "Nothing." "Then, why is it not a miracle ? " "I do not believe in miracles." "Then, how do you account for this extraordinary cure ? " "I cannot account for it."

My friend, however, got the doctor to promise that he would wear a medal of St. Benedict on his watch chain, and sent him one blessed by the Trappists at Gethsemane. She has heard from the Sisters that he still wears it, and tells everyone that that medal cured a lady patient of his of a tumor, and that she gave it to him. That he is thrown out of his buggy and all manner of misfortunes happen to him, and that he has never been hurt since he has been wearing that little medal. One day he came into the hospital holding up the medal, and said : "Look, Sister ! the wheel came off my buggy, and I didn't get a scratch ! "

Let us hope that St. Benedict will soon work a greater miracle than the cure of the tumor—by obtaining for the soul of this eminent surgeon the grace of conversion to the Faith.

August, 1894.   EDMUND HILL, C.P.

SOCIETY OF ST. VINCENT DE PAUL.

THE SOCIETY OF ST. VINCENT DE PAUL is a Society of men associated together for mutual encouragement in the practice of a Christian life. The first object is the sanctification of its members, and as the best means of doing so is to love God and one's neighbor, they try to be friends of the poor—visiting them in their homes and relieving them in their necessities, instructing them in religion, visiting hospitals, prisons and similar institutions, distributing wholesome reading, conducting libraries, teaching catechism and night schools, and giving such kinds of help as may be required. It is a primary rule that no work of charity is foreign to the Society.

Members are active or honorary. An active member is required to attend the weekly meetings of the Conference, at which there is a voluntary and secret offertory, and to visit the poor families to whom he is assigned. Honorary members incur no obligation, but the contribution of a fixed sum annually or otherwise to the Society's funds. All men are eligible as members provided they are in a position to contribute anything, howsoever small, to the Society's funds, and are so far practising their religion that they may be expected to edify their fellow-members, and be edified by them.

The Society was founded in Paris in 1833 by six students, from 19 to 22 years of age, and Mr. Bailly, a man of 40, whom the young men, in their modesty, put at their head to guide their inexperience. Of the six Frederick Ozanam was one of the most zealous, and attained most renown, and his name is always connected with the foundation. Gatherings of students for the discussion of literary or other subjects connected with their studies were in those days called "conferences," and when Ozanam and his young comrades decided to form a society for practical works of charity they called it "The Conference of Charity," and the name has always been retained. They placed the first Conference under the protection of the Blessed Virgin, and later under that of the Apostle of Charity—St. Vincent de Paul, whose name they took for the Society.

The need and popularity of the Society was soon recognized, and in two years it spread to different parts of France, and a few years later reached other countries. At present wherever the Church flourishes the Society is represented, and Conferences are multiplying every year. As the Conferences increased the officers of the first Conference were formed into a Council General for the direction of the whole Society; and as necessities arose the Council General instituted other Councils to aid it in this work of direction. In the order of their authority they are Superior Councils, having supervision over the Conferences of a country or province; Central Councils, over one or several dioceses; and Particular Councils, over a city where there is more than one Conference. Thus the Society, whilst giving to its local Conferences the fullest liberty of action, has the strength and power that come from a solidly united body under one authority dictating a combined plan of action and work.

In 1845 the Society received the Apostolic sanction of the Holy See, and was granted many precious indulgences. The Sovereign Pontiff, Gregory XVI., in conceding these indulgences to the members of the Society, sanctioned its Rule, and gave the Council General the right of allowing to participate in these favors the faithful whom it admits into the Society, whether admitted directly or through the mediation of the Councils it has instituted or the Conferences it has aggregated. Each Conference must therefore receive formal authority from the Council General, whose seat is in Paris.

This authority is expressed by a document under the seal of the Council, signed by its officers, and called "Letters of Aggregation." The members of the Conference are then entitled to participate in all the favors and indulgences granted to the Society by the Church. With these spiritual treasures she has endowed it, with a most lavish hand. On reading the briefs of the Sovereign Pontiffs we must conclude that they did not wish to leave a single act of the charitable life of a member of the Society without a reward. Every attendance at a meeting, or at the funeral of a poor person; every visit to a poor family, to a hospital, to a prison, to a school, or any other work in the spirit of the Society, has an indulgence attached to it, and these spiritual favors are even extended to those who are connected with the members—their fathers, mothers and wives.

The Society was introduced into Canada in 1846, when a Conference was formed in Quebec, and that city now possesses the Superior Council of Canada, which has jurisdiction over the whole Dominion.

On the 10th November, 1850, the Conference of Our Lady of Toronto—the first in Ontario—was organized with the approval of the Chief Pastor, Bishop de Charbonnel; and there are now in the Province five Particular Councils, thirty-three Conferences aggregated and four Conferences awaiting aggregation. The Report of the

Superior Council of Canada for 1893 contains the following statistics of the Society in Canada It is composed of a Superior Council and ten Particular Councils, having jurisdiction over one hundred Conferences, besides works of patronage and other associations of the same kind. There are 4,804 active members, and they relieved 3,071 families. The receipts for the year amounted to $54,814.67, and the expenses to $43,526.40.

The Councils and Conferences of Ontario are as follows :

Toronto—Particular Council—President, J. J. Murphy.
  Conference of Our Lady—Pres., M. Keilty.
  Conference of St. Paul—Pres., J. J. Mallon.
  Conference of St. Mary—Pres., Martin J. Burns.
  Conference of St. Basil—Pres., J. F. Kirk
  Conference of St. Patrick—Pres., Wm. Burns.
  Conference of St. Peter—Pres., John Rodgers.
  Conference of the Sacred Heart—Pres., P. Jobin.
  Conference of Our Lady of Lourdes—Pres., Patrick Hughes.
  Conference of St. Helen—Pres., V. P. Fayle.
  Conference of St. Joseph (not aggregated) — Pros., James Pape.
  Hospital Board—Pres., Patrick Hynes
Ottawa — Particular Council—Pres., John Gorman.
  Conference of Our Lady—Pres., James Carroll.
  Conference of St. Joseph—Pres., Adrian Clancy.
  Conference of St. Patrick—Pres., Wm. Kearns.
  Conference of St. Mary—Pres., J. W. White.

  Conference of St. Patrick (Aspirant)—Pres., E. L. Sanders.
  Particular Council of St. Louis—Pres., A. Potvin.
  Conference Notre Dame—Pres., J. A. Doetaler.
  Conference Ste. Anne—Pres., J. P. M. Lecourt.
  Conference St. Jean Baptiste—Pres., N. Larochelle.
  Conference Sacre Cœur—Pres., A. Potvin.
  Conference La Salle School—Pres., A. Davis.
London — Particular Council—Pres., J. M. Keary.
  Conference of Our Lady—Pres., D. Labelle.
  Conference Sacred Heart—Pres., James Hurley.
Hamilton—Particular Council—Pres., H. Arland.
  Conference of Our Lady—Pres., T. Walsh.
  Conference of St. Patrick—Pres., John Ronan.
  Conference of St. Lawrence (not aggregated)—Pres., M. Brackin.
Almonte—Conference of St. Mary—Pres., John O'Reilly.
Barrie — Conference of Our Lady of the Sacred Heart (not aggregated)—Pres., John Devine.
Brantford—Conference of Our Lady—Pres., Wm. Cutmore.
Collingwood—Conference of St. Mary—Pres., J. J. Long.
Guelph—Conference of Our Lady—Pres., J. E. McElderry.
Lindsay—Conference of Our Lady—Pres., P. J. Hurley.
Newmarket—Conference of Lady of Lourdes—Pres., (vacant).
Orillia—Conference of Guardian Angels—Pres., Wm. Thomson.
Pembroke—Conference of St. Patrick—Pres., Michael Howe.
Peterboro'—Conference of St. Peter—Pres., A. Vinette.
Stratford—Conference of St. Joseph—Pres., D. J. O'Connor.
Windsor—Conference of St Alphonsus (not aggregated)—Pres., Joseph DeGurse.

THE CATHOLIC MUTUAL BENEFIT ASSOCIATION.

THE CATHOLIC MUTUAL BENEFIT ASSOCIATION was organized at the village of Niagara Falls, N.Y., in July, 1876, and was incorporated by the Legislature of the State of New York in 1879.

The organization of this Association was first suggested by the Right Rev. S. V. Ryan, Bishop of Buffalo, and by its members he is referred to with pride and affection as the "Father of the C. M. B. A." His name, with many other distinguished prelates and a large number of the reverend clergy throughout the United States and Canada, adorns its rolls.

The mother branch, No. 1, of New York State, was organized at Niagara Falls, N.Y., July 3rd, 1876, by Rev. Father Moynahan, the parish priest, and fourteen other zealous Catholics.

The First Grand Council Convention was held in October, 1877. Bishop Ryan was present, and in his address said : "So far as I can judge I see nothing in the C. M. B. A. but what is deserving of my warmest support."

The Association is sanctioned by His Holiness Pope Leo XIII., and has received the approbation of His Eminence Cardinal Taschereau, and the Archbishops and Bishops of Canada. The Association is composed of a Supreme Council, Grand Councils and Branches. In the United

States the Supreme Council is the chief governing body.

The first branch in Canada was organized at Windsor, Ontario, in February, 1878. The Grand Council of the C. M. B. A. of Canada was organized also at Windsor, Ont., February 10, 1880. At that date there were but six branches in Canada, viz.: No. 1, Windsor; No. 2, St. Thomas; No. 3, Amherstburg; No. 4, London; No. 5, Brantford, and No. 6, Strathroy, with an aggregate membership of 224.

The charter-members and first officers of the Grand Council were :

  Grand Spiritual Adviser—Rt. Rev. John Walsh, Bishop of London (now Archbishop of Toronto).
  Grand President—Thomas A. Bourke, Windsor, Ont.
  First Vice-President—J. H. Barry, Brantford, Ont.
  Second Vice-President—John Doyle, St. Thomas, Ont.
  Grand Treasurer—M. J. Manning, Windsor, Ont.
  Grand Secretary—Samuel R. Brown, London, Ont.
  Grand Marshal—C. W. O'Rourke, Amherstburg, Ont.
  Grand Guard—C. W. O'Rourke Amherstburg, Ont.
  Grand Trustees—Rev. J. P. Molphy (Strathroy, Ont.), C. W. O'Rourke, J. Doyle, T. A. Bourke and J. H. Barry.

The installation was conducted by Supreme Deputy J. T. Keene, of Detroit.

The Grand Council was incorporated in Ontario January 18, 1890 ; registered in Ontario August 22, 1892, and incorporated in the Dominion of Canada in March, 1893. On 31st December, 1892, the C. M. B. A. of Canada was formed into a Separate Beneficiary Jurisdiction, and there is now complete financial separation from the United States. In Canada the Grand Council is the governing body and is termed the Association, incorporated for the following purposes and objects:

(a) To unite fraternally all persons entitled to membership under the constitution and laws of the Association; and the word "laws" when hereinafter used shall include general laws and by-laws.

(b) To improve the social, intellectual and moral condition of the members of the Association, and to educate them in integrity, sobriety and frugality.

(c) To establish, manage and disburse a mutual benefit and a reserve fund from which, within sixty days after the receipt at the office of the Secretary of the Association of satisfactory evidence of the death of a member of the Association who has complied with its lawful requirements, a sum not exceeding two thousand dollars shall be paid by the Association to the widow, orphans, dependents or other beneficiary whom the deceased member has designated, or to the legal representatives of such deceased member.

In each Province in which the Association transacts business it appoints an agent under a power of attorney bearing the seal of the Association and signed by the President and Secretary, to receive service of process in all suits and proceedings against the Association in the Province in which said agent resides.

Applicants for membership must be practical Catholics not under 18 years of age nor over 50 at date of initiation; must pass a medical examination, be approved by the Supervising Medical Examiner, the Board of Trustees, and elected by ballot of the Branch to which application is made before they can be admitted to membership.

Three grades of policies are issued, viz., a $2,000, a $1,000 and $500.

As a measure toward the perpetuation of the Association, and for the protection of its members from the effects of epidemics or heavy death rate, when assessments might be more numerous than members would be able to pay, a Reserve Fund has been established, being the safest and most reliable safeguards for its protection. It is accumulated by setting apart five per cent. of each assessment collected. It will from time to time be invested in the safest of interest-bearing securities, and neither principal nor interest can be drawn upon until MORE than twenty-four assessments would be necessary to be levied on the membership of the Association in any one year; or, until said fund shall have reached the sum of $125,000, which is the limit under the present law of the Grand Council of the C. M. B. A. of Canada.

This fund at present amounts to about $40,000, and was only established on 1st July, 1887.

Since organization the Association has had 394 deaths in its ranks, and has paid $723,000 to the heirs of deceased members in Canada. Who can calculate the great help the receipt of this money has been to widows and orphans, at a time too when most needed?

The beneficiary on the death of a member is paid promptly within the time fixed by the Constitution to the person or persons legally entitled to the same, and is exempt from execution or liability for the debts of a deceased member.

The Grand Council of the C. M. B. A. of Canada has organized 237 Branches, with a membership at present of about 10,000. The officers for the ensuing term are:

BRANCHES—(CONTINUED).

No.	LOCATION.	MEETING NIGHTS.	WHERE HELD.
55	Petersburg,O	2d and last Sat	John Nell, sec
56	Hamilton, O	....	C M B A Hall
57	Orillia, O	....	Jas Patton, sec
58	Ottawa, O	1st and 3d Tues	Kennedy's Hall
59	Ottawa, O	....	Ed Lemie ix, sec
60	Dublin, O	1st and 3d Wed	C M B A Hall
61	Merriton, O	....	W A G Hovey, sec
62	Canaad River, O	....	O Reaume, sec
63	St. Mary's, O	2d and 4th Thur	A O H rooms (Guest Bl)
64	North Bay, O	....	P McCall, sec
65	Ayton, O	....	A O'Farrell, sec
66	Mattawa, O	....	John McKevk n, sec
67	Pembroke, O	2d and 4th Wed	C M B A Hall (Foster's Bl)
68	Hull, Q	1st and 3d Tues	St Joseph's Hall
69	Demerton, O	1st and 3d Satur	Geo Goldinger, sec
70	Mildmay, O	....	K Weller, sec
71	Trenton, O	1st and 3d Wed	C M B A Hall
72	Formosa, O	1st and 3d Frid	Austett'sHall
74	Montreal, Q	2d and 4th Mon	Sarsfield school
75	Penetanguishe, O	2d and 4th Thur	Gendrvies' Hall
76	Belleville, O	....	W A G Hardy, sec
77	Lindsay, O	1st and 3d Tues	Catholic Lit rary Society
78	Oshawa, O	Once a month	O F Kinneard, sec
79	Gananoque, O	1st and 3d Wed	Gananoqua
80	Tilbury Centre, O	Alternate Tues	C M B A Hall
81	Smith's Falls, O	....	P Delaney, sec
82	Kingsbridge, O	1st and 3d Frid	Kintail
83	Montreal, Q	2d and 4th Mon	51 Montcalm st
85	Toronto, O	2d and 4th Tues	Beacon Hall
86	Deseronto, O	Sum'er, alt Wed	
		Winter ev'y Wed	C M B A Hall
87	Montreal, Q	1st and 3d Wed	Gareau's Hall
88	Orangeville, O	2d and 4th Mon	R C Presbytery
89	Perth, O	....	J H Kehoe, sec
90	Picton, O	2d and 4th Tues	Gregor 's Hall
91	Alliston, O	1st and 3d Mon	C M B A Hall
92	Teeswater, O	....	H Campbell, sec
93	Renfrew, O	1st and 3d Satur	De La Salle
94	Ottawa, O	1st and 3d Mon	C M B A Union Hall
95	Lachine, Q	2d and 4th Frid	Hall No. 4 Town Hall st
96	Levis, Q	2d and last Wed	Hall No. 7 Eden st
98	Campbellford, O	....	P J Anderson, sec
99	Westport, O	1st and 3d Wed	Hazelton's Block
100	Haden, O	....	F Dehl, sec
101	Three Rivers, Q	1st and 3d Frid	No. 28 St. Joseph st
102	Richmond, Q	Friday evening	C M B A (Separate school)
104	Waterloo, O	2d and last Tues	Killer's Block
105	London, O	1st and 4th Mon	School house
106	Parry Sound, O	1st and 3d Satur	C M B A Room
107	Cobourg, O	1st and 3 1 Tues	55 Division st
108	Qu bec, Q	....	43 Artillery st
110	Quebec, Q	1st and 3d Tues	S . Sauveur
111	Toronto, O	2d and 4th Tues	St Helen's school
112	Merrickville, O	2d Thursday	Church's Block
113	Waterloo, Q	1st and 3d Tues	Waterloo
114	Niagara, O	1st and 3d Tues	Worden's Block
115	Chepstow, O	2d and 4th Thur	J T Lacey's Hall
116	Fergus, O	2d and 4th Tues	C M B A Hall
117	Joliette, Q	....	C H G Beaudolin, sec
118	Sherbrooke, Q	1st and 2d Wed	McMannan's Block
119	Welland, O	2d Tuesday	C M B A Hall, Morwood's
120	Fort Colborne, O	2d and 4th Tues	
		(winter only)	C M B A Hall
121	Sudbury, O	....	F F Lemieux, sec
122	Sandwich, O	1st and 3d Tues	S C A A Hall
123	Dunnvil e, O	....	John Flannigan, sec
124	Biddulph. O	2d and 4th Frid	School house
125	Lauzon, Q	....	D Nolin, sec
126	Calgary, N W T	2d Tuesday	School hous
127	Windsor Mills, Q	1st and last Wed	Dr H H Prefontaine, sec
128	Parkhill, O	....	Jas Phealan, sec
129	Granby, Q	1st and 3d Thur	C M B A Hall
130	Bathurst, N B	1st and 3d Tues	B thurst
131	North Sydney, NB	1st and 3d Frid	C M B A rooms
132	Halifax, N S	1st and 3d Frid	A sociation rooms
133	St. John, N B	Every Mon	eve St. Patrick's Hall
134	St. John, N B	Every Tues	eve Furlong Building
135	St. Hyacinthe, Q	1st and 3d Wed	City Hall
136	Fort Erie, O	2d and 4th Mon	Town H ll
140	Montreal, Q	1st and 3d Tues	asem't Sacred Heart Ch
141	Chapleau, O	....	J E Jackman, sec
142	Montreal, Q	2d and 4th Wed	Basem't of St J B Church
143	Montreal, Q	1st and 3d Wed	390 Laval ave
144	Toronto, O	2d and 4th Mon	Vest. of Our L of l ourdes
145	Toro to, O	1st and 3d Tues	St. Basil's Church
146	Drummondville, Q	1st and 3d Mon	Belguon Hall
147	Portage du Fort, Q	2d and last Wed	C M B A Hall

No.	LOCATION.	MEETING NIGHTS.	WHERE HELD.
148	C lumet Island, Q	....	R McNally, sec
149	La Salette, O	1st and 3d Satur	Separate school
151	Brechin, O	....	John Malone, sec
152	Whitby, O	....	Jas Long, sec
153	Midland, O	1st and 3d Frid	Branch Hall, Midland
154	Eganville, O	1st and 3d Frid	C M B A Hall
156	St. Catharines, O	....	P J Brennan, sec
157	Fletcher, O	....	P G Murphy, sec
158	St. Vin. de Paul, Q	1st and 3d Mon	St Vincent de Paul
150	Ottawa, O	2d and 4th Mon	Central Hall
160	Halifax, N S	2d and 4th Tues	C M B A Hall
161	Carleruhe, O	1st and 3d Tues	Branch Hall
162	Moncton, N B	Every Thursday	C M B A Hall
163	Winnipeg, Man	1st and 3d Mon	170 Austin st
164	Nicolet, Q	....	J E Belcourt, sec
165	Cardinal, O	....	P K Leacy, sec
166	Rock Island, Q	2d and 4th Mon	St Joseph's Hall
167	Dorchester, N B	Wednesday	eve II J McGrath, sec
168	Amherst, N B	Monday evening	St Charles Hall
169	Shediac, N B	Tuesday evening	Ouel tte's Hall
170	Elgin, O	2d and 4th Wed	C M B A Hall (Main st)
171	St. Laurent, Q	....	Rev J M Demers, sec
172	Collingwood, O	2d and 4th Thur	Jas Cornett, sec
173	Belle River, O	1st and 3d Thur	C M B A Hall
174	Kinkora, O	2d and 4th Mon	C M B A Hall
176	Ottawa, O	2d and 4th Wed	240 Church st
177	Newcastle, N B	Tuesday evening	Over P J McEvoy's store
178	Memramcook, NB	Saturday even'g	C M B A Hall
179	Fox Creek, N B	Twice a month	C M B A Hall
180	Yarmouth, N S	1st and 3d Tues	Horton's Block
181	Hespeler, O	1st and 3d Tues	Sunday school at church
182	Wolfe Island, O	1st and 3d Mon	C M B A Hall
183	Snyder, O	2d and last Satur	Parsonage Hall
184	Fairville, N B	....	John Gillis, sec
185	Caraquet, N B	1st and 3d Frid	Caraquet
186	Victoriaville, Q	2d and 4th Mon	P H Ouay, grocery store
187	Sturgeon Falls, O	....	J Michaud, sec
188	Carlton Place, O	2d Wednesday	Mr Cliff's Hall
189	Sydney, N S	Tuesday evening	County Hall
100	Montreal, Q	1st and 3 1 Wed	No. 7 Rue Claude
191	Montreal, Q	2d and 4th Thur	321½ Notre Dame st
192	Antigonish, N S	Friday evening	Branch Hall
193	St. Jean Bap., M	1st and 3d Satur	St Joan Baptiste
194	Valcourt, Q	1st and 3d Tues	C M B A
195	Petit Rocher, N B	1st and 3d Thurs	M H Levasseur, sec
196	Montreal, Q	1st and 3d Wed	Basement St Joseph's Ch
197	Trout Creek, O	1st and 3d Frid	K Lynett, sec
198	Maribank, O	1st and 3d Satur	Fitzgerald Hall
190	E monton, NWT	....	C M B A Hall
200	Toronto, O	2d and 4th Wed	St Ann's Hall
201	Alexandria, O	....	Separate school
202	Chatham, N B	Tuesday evening	St Patrick's Hall
203	Caneo, N S	1st and 3d Wed	C M B A Hall
204	Parrsboro', N S	Monday evening	Gillespie & Son's Hall
205	Stoco, O	1st and 3d Tues	Wm J O'Brien, sec
206	West Pubnico,NB	....	H D Le Blanc
207	Montreal, Q	....	573 Lorimer st
208	Dartmouth, N S	2d and 4th Thur	St Peter's C T A So'y rooms
209	Louisville, Q	2d and 4th Mon	Town Hall
210	Grand Falls, N B	1st and 3d Wed	C M B A Hall
211	Bat Portage, O	1st and 3d Mon	Basement of church
212	Owen Sound, O	2d and 4th Mon	St Mary's school room
213	St Ours, Q	....	
214	Alberton, P E I	Alter. Thursday	Vestry Sacred Heart Ch
215	Summerside, PEI	....	C M B A Hall
216	Charlotte'n, PEI	....	S P Paoli, sec
217	L'Assomption	Q 1st and 3d Thur	F D Genuin's office
218	Soroi, Q	....	A P Vanasse, sec
219	White River, O	2d Saturday	Vestry R C church
220	Schreiber, O	1st and 3d Frid	Provencher Hall
221	Woodslee, O	1st and 3d Frid	Woodslee Separate school
222	Gravenhurst, O	1st and 3d Mon	St Satur W J Moore, sec
223	Spring Hill, N S	Wednesday e en	C M B A Hall
224	Murray Bay, Q	1st & 16th month	Murray Bay village
225	Arthabaskavil e, Q	2d and 4th Mon	H Laurier, sec
226	Coten St. Paul, Q	2d and 4th Frid	Basement of church
227	Fort William, O	1st and 3d Mon	Vestry of St Patrick's ch
228	Port Arthur, O	2d and 4th Tues	At rooms
229	Dalhousie, N B	2d and 4th Thur	Office of President
230	St. Boniface, M	....	J O E Levesque, sec
231	Simcoe, O	....	St Mary's church
232	Montreal, Q	....	217 St Huebert st
233	Matapangenor, O	....	Joe Belanger, sec
234	Hamilton, O	....	P J McGowan, sec
235	Ridget wn, O	....	John J Hugan, sec
236	Champlain, Q	....	H Marchand, sec
237	Buctouche, N B	....	J H Bourke, sec

ANCIENT ORDER OF HIBERNIANS.

The organization known as the ANCIENT ORDER OF HIBERNIANS had, as the name implies, its origin in Ireland. About the year 1700, while the Penal Laws in their most malignant form were still rampant, a body of men banded themselves together for the special purpose of guarding the Catholic priesthood and keeping watch while they offered the Holy Sacrifice of the Mass in the glens and caves of that country. No nobler duty could the youth and manhood of Ireland devote themselves to; and never was duty discharged more faithfully, as the history of the Order fully attests.

The A. O. H. is known in Ireland as the "Board of Erin," and under that name is still the governing body of the Order both at home and abroad. In 1836 the Order was established in New York City by an envoy specially commissioned and vested with the necessary power of the home authorities.

The Society soon took root among the exiled Irish in America and spread, not alone in the city and state of New York, but in many other states of the Union, till to-day the Order is recognized as one of the largest, most influential and beneficent in the wide domain of the Republic.

The history of the Ancient Order of Hibernians in Canada is of recent date, the first Division having been founded at Hamilton, Ontario, in 1880, by John Lalor. He was the Division's first President, and held subsequently the offices of County and Provincial Delegate. In the same year Division No. 1 was organized in Toronto, in which city there are now five Divisions of the Order. St. Mary's, Ontario, followed, in which there is one Division. Next came Stratford; then Kingston, St. Thomas, Clifton and Dixie. Several applications from other places are now in the hands of the Provincial President, who is making the necessary arrangements for organizing the Order in each, and putting it in active operation.

NATIONAL OFFICERS.

At the last biennial session of the Ancient Order of Hibernians, held in Omaha, Nebraska, U. S., May, 1894, the following officers were elected:

Grand Chaplain—Right Rev. John S. Foley, Bishop of Detroit, Michigan.
National President—P. J O'Connor, Savannah, Georgia
Vice-President—J. C. Weadock, Bay City, Michigan.
Secretary—M. J. Slattery, Albany, N Y.
Treasurer—T. J. Dundon, Columbus, Ohio.

PROVINCIAL OFFICERS.

The Order in Ontario held its biennial convention at Stratford, June, 1894, at which the following officers were elected for the term of two years:

Grand Chaplain—Very Rev. Dr. Kilroy, Stratford, Ont.
Provincial President—Hugh McCaffrey, 83 Wellington avenue, Toronto
Vice-President—John Dillon, Stratford, Ont.
Provincial Secretary—John Falvey, Deer Park P.O., Toronto.
Provincial Treasurer—Michael Guerin, Box 43, Stratford, Ont.
Insurance Secretary—Thomas O'Dowd, 137 Simcoe street East, Hamilton, Ont.

YORK COUNTY.

County President—P. W. Falvey, Deer Park P.O., Toronto.
Division No. 1 meets 1st and 3rd Sunday each month, Temperance Hall, Temperance street.
President—Thomas McKeague, 239 Berkeley street.
Vice-President—John Travers, 53 Blair avenue.
Recording Secretary—W. F. Ryan, 177 Claremont street.
Financial Secretary—J. E. Dillon, 5 Morrison street.
Treasurer—Frank Hizgins, 13 Massey street.
Division No. 2 meets 1st and 3rd Mondays each month, Red Lion Block, Yonge street.
President—M. J. Lenihan, 29 Queen's Park, Toronto.
Vice-President—J. Falvey, Deer Park.
Recording Secretary—M. J. Ryan, 574 Yonge street.
Financial Secretary—M. F. Hyland, 114 Scollard street.
Treasurer—T. Dorgan, 102 Bloor street east.
Division No. 3 meets every alternate Thursday each month.
President—William Moore, 131 Lippincott street.
Vice-President—William Dawson, 174 Richmond street west.
Recording Secretary—Geo. J. Owens, 225 Farley avenue.
Financial Secretary—Patrick J. Lowe, 49 Hackney street.
Treasurer—George Moore, 267 Niagara street.
Division No. 4 meets 2nd and 4th Sunday of each month in Reid's Hall, corner of King and Berkeley streets.
President—James Findley, 510 Queen street east.
Vice-President—John Foley, 194 Duchess street.
Recording Secretary—Joseph Coady, 136 Spruce street.
Financial Secretary—P. D. McDonald, 106 Sherbourne street.
Treasurer—Arthur Stuart, 583 King street east.
Division No. 5 meets every 2nd and 4th Wednesday in each month at Dingman's Hall, corner of Queen street and Broadview avenue.
President—Hugh Kelly, 260 Logan avenue.
Vice-President—Michael Burns, 104 Sackville street.
Recording Secretary—Joseph Russell, 223 Sumach street.
Financial Secretary—Ambrose McTernan, 101 Jarvis street.
Treasurer—John Kane, 228 Ontario street.

PEEL COUNTY.

County President—F. J. Goulding, Summerville P.O.
President—Patrick McCartney, Summerville P.O.
Vice-President—Patrick Heary, Summerville P.O.
Recording Secretary—P. J Lamphier, Burnhamthorpe P.O.
Financial Secretary—Francis Hickey, Summerville P.O.
Treasurer—Francis Lamphier, Burnhamthorpe P.O.

WENTWORTH COUNTY.

County President — Maurice Foley, 199 Walnut street, Hamilton.
President—M. J. Allen, 330 Victoria avenue north.
Vice-president—W. Magill, 342 Wilson street.
Recording Secretary—Thomas O'Dowd, 137 Simcoe St. East.
Asst. Recording Secretary—P. J. McGowan, Strachan St. East
Financial Secretary—W. J. Mulvale, 61 Clark s'reet.
Treasurer—P. F. McBride, 340 John street north.

WELLAND COUNTY.

County President—James Abbott, Niagara Falls, Canada.
President—James S. McDonough, Erie avenue.
Vice-President—Patrick Griffin, Erie avenue.
Recording Secretary—Simon J Glynn, Ellis street.
Financial Secretary—Daniel J. Mahoney, Morrison street.
Treasurer—Patrick McGrail, Morrison street.

ELGIN COUNTY.

County President—P. J. Handley, Box 1,168, St. Thomas.
President—P. J. McManus, St. Thomas.
Vice-President—John McCaffery, St. Thomas.
Recording Secretary—James McManus, St. Thomas.
Financial Secretary—B McCaffery, St. Thomas.
Treasurer—Ed Moylan, 98 Thomas.

PERTH COUNTY.

County President—John Hoy, Stratford.
Division No. 1—President—M F. Burns, St. Mary's.
Vice-President—James Graham, St. Mary's.
Recording Secretary—Jain s Fleming, St. Mary's.
Financial Secretary—M. Fleming, St. Mary's.
Treasurer—D. Currie, St. Mary's.

THE IRISH CATHOLIC BENEVOLENT ASSOCIATION OF CANADA.

THIS Association, as its name implies, is intended for practical Catholics, age limit 15-45 years, who in sickness and in trouble help one another, paying a weekly benefit, usually $4.00, to sick members and in case of death a funeral benefit of $100. It is the ambition of the Association to have a branch in every parish so that a member can find, everywhere, brothers ready to help him in sickness and to give his remains Christian burial in death.

A system of Travelling and Withdrawal Cards exists in the Association which ensures to members everywhere the rights and privileges of membership in all branches. These cards are recognized by the branches of the I. C. B. U. and the German Roman Catholic Central Union in the United States.

The object and aims of the Association, which was incorporated in 1883, are thus set forth :

" To form a union of the Catholic people of Canada for their common interests; also for the establishment of libraries and lectures, and to counsel and direct the members of the Association in the way best calculated to ensure to them a firm, lasting and independent position in this country ; and while doing so to instil within them an everlasting love for the birthplace of their forefathers ; and to always remind them of the love and veneration which we owe to Holy Mother Church, and at all times and under all circumstances to assist a fellow Catholic in the hour of affliction."

Conventions are held yearly; that for 1895 will be in Toronto, Monday, May 13th. At the last Convention held in Cobourg, 1894, the following officers were elected for the ensuing year :

Grand President and Solicitor—C. J. McCabe, B.A., Toronto.
1st Vice-President—P. Delanty, Cobourg.
2nd Vice-President—Miss M. Harling, Toronto.
Grand Treasurer—Wm. Lavoie, Paris.
Grand Secretary and Organizer—P. Shea, Toronto. (P. O. Box 805).
Assistant Secretary—Mrs. E. M. Brown, Toronto.
Auditors—E. J. Maguire and J. J. McCarthy, Toronto.

LOCAL BRANCHES.

Irish Catholic Beneficial Association, Toronto, organized Jan., 1869, meets 1st and 3rd Tuesday in I.C.B.A. Hall, corner King and Jarvis sts., at 8 p.m. Secretary, H. J. McQuillan, P. O. Box 395.
Catholic Celtic League, Toronto, April, 1886. Alternate Mondays at 8 p.m., in I.C.B.A. Hall, Bathurst st. Secretary, Owen Lynch, 69 Mitchell ave.
St. Agnes Beneficial Society, Toronto, January, 1894 (Ladies). 1st and 3rd Mondays in I.C.B.A. Hall, corner King and Jarvis sts. at 8 p.m. Secretary, Mrs. Greer, 3 Widmer st.
Our Lady of Good Counsel Beneficial Society, Toronto, April, 1894—alternate Tuesdays at 8 p.m., in I.C.D.A. Hall, Bathurst st. Secretary, Miss Susie Kelly, 37 Defoe st.
St. Patrick's Beneficial Society, Hamilton, September, 1888. Secretary, John Rankin, corner King and Dundurn sts.
Emerald Beneficial Society, Cobourg, July, 1890. Secretary, J. J. Gormely.
St. Mary's Beneficial Society, Cobourg, August, 1894 (Ladies). Secretary, Miss E. O'Connor.
O'Connell Beneficial Society, Port Hope, November, 1890. Secretary, M. J. O'Neill.
St. Patrick's Beneficial Society, Galt, June, 1890. Secretary, T. P. Skelly.
Sacred Heart Beneficial Society, Paris, November, 1888. Secretary, E. J. Stapleton.
Young Irishmen's Catholic Beneficial Society, Kingston. Secretary, P. Miln, care of Canadian Freeman.
St. Gertrude Beneficial Society, Kingston (Ladies). Secretary, Miss M. O'Neill, Sydenham st.

EMERALD BENEFICIAL ASSOCIATION OF CANADA.

THE EMERALD BENEFICIAL ASSOCIATION was conceived, founded and formed by the Rev. A. D. Finan, of St. Peter's Church, Reading, Penn., in 1864, and three years later it was organized in the City of Hamilton, Ontario. "The object and design of said Association, as a beneficial and literary organization, is to promote the spread of the great fundamental principles of Faith, Hope and Charity, and brotherly love, and the advancement of literature, science and virtuous practices amongst its members." The E. B. A. is a strictly Catholic Association composed of respectable Catholics of all Nationalities and Races between the ages of 17 and 50 years (male and female) regardless of social rank or intellectual capacity of applicants for membership. It provides free medical attendance and medicine to members who are sick and a Funeral Benefit at death. It also provides an Insurance payable in case of total disability or death.

The Grand Branch was organized in the City of Hamilton, Nov. 22, 1876. At the annual Convention held in the City of London, Ont., May 4 and 5, 1892, it was decided to withdraw from the International Grand Branch and make the Association a Canadian Organization, and in compliance with the Insurance Act of Ontario the Grand Branch was Registered in 1892 and Incorporated in 1893 under the name and title of the Grand Branch of the Emerald Beneficial Association of

Canada. The Conventions of the Grand Branch are held annually, the date and place of next meeting being arranged then. The last Convention was held in the Town of Peterboro , May 1, 2and 3, 1894, when the proposition to form Ladies' Circles in affiliation with the Branches was unanimously adopted. The next Convention will be held in Toronto on the 6th of August, 1895. Subordinate Branches elect their officers annually at the first Branch meeting in December.

The present officers are: Chaplain, Right Rev. Monsignor F. P. Rooney, V.G.; President, David A. Carey; Vice-President, Thomas F. Gould; Secretary, W. Lane.

SUBORDINATE BRANCHES.

Sarsfield No, 1—Organized 1872, President, J. R. Ball ; Secretary, N. T. Curran, 41 Wood st. E. ; meets 2nd and 4th Monday in C.M.B.A Hall, Hamilton.

O'Connell No. 2—Organized 1874, President, P. J. Crotty ; Secretary, W. Donnelly, 33 Carr st , To onto; meets 2nd and 4th Thursdays.

St. Patrick's No 7—Organized 1878, President, M. Madden ; Secretary, M J. Madden, 241 Farley ave. ; meets 1st and 3rd Sunday in E.B.A. Hall, Farley ave , Toronto.

St. Paul's No. 8—Organized 1880, President, A. McDonald ; Secretary, J. Cleary, 32 Louisa st. ; meets 4th Sunday in I C.B.A. Hall, Toronto

Davitt No. 11—Organized 1882—President, D. Shea; Secretary, W. Lane, 17 Hamburg ave ; meets 1st and 3rd Tuesdays in Hall corner Sheridan ave., Toronto.

St. Patrick's No. 12—Organized 1882, President, J. J. Moloney ; Secretary, W. P. Murphy, 83 Tecumseth st. ; meets 2nd and 4th Wednesdays in Hall corner McCaul and Queen sts., Toronto.

St Peter's No. 21—Organized 1888, President, T. Lynch ; Secretary, J. Hickey, Peterborough ; meets 2nd and 4th Thursdays in C.M.B.A. Hall, Peterborough.

St. Peter's No. 23—Organized 1880, President, T. F. Gould; Secretary, M. Quirk, South London ; meets 2nd and 4th Wednesday in I. O. F. Hall, London.

St. Mary's No. 24—Organized 1889, President, R. McGregor; Secretary, C. E. Loaney, Almonte ; meets 2nd and 4th Thursdays in E.B.A. Hall, Almonte.

St. Joseph's No. 28—Organized 1891, President, A. McPhee ; Secretary, E. J. Knelil, Stratford ; meets 2nd and 4th Mon days in C.M.B.A. Hall, Stratford.

Sarsfield No. 28—Organized 1893, President, R Brankin ; Secretary, A. Morell, 79 McKay st. ; meets 2nd and 4th Tuesdays in St. Patrick's Hall, Ottawa

St. Cecilia No. 29—Organized 1893, President, M. Mahoney ; Secretary, H. T. McDonald ; meets 2nd and 4th Friday, West Toronto, I.C.T.

St. Patrick's No. 30—Organized 1893, President, T. Coughlin ; Secretary, T. E. Brown, Kinkora ; meets 1st and 3rd Friday, Kinkora.

LADIES' CIRCLES.

St. Patrick's No. 1—Organized Dec. 6, 1893, President, Miss Henley ; Secretary, Mrs. J J Nightingale, 26 Orde st.; meets 1st and 3rd Wednesday in Hall corner McCaul and Queen sts., Toronto.

St. Helen's No. 2—Organized March 19, 1894, President, Miss Brennan ; Secretary, Miss Marchman, 36 Defoe st., meets 1st and 3rd Mondays in Hall corner Sheridan ave., Toronto.

St. Cecilia No. 3—Organized June 10, 1894, President, Mrs. Kelly ; S cretary, Miss Boylan, Annetta st. ; meets 2nd and 4th Friday at West Toronto Junction.

CATHOLIC ORDER OF FORESTERS.

THE practice and cultivation of that virtue peculiar to Christians, that virtue which Our Lord's life upon earth exemplified—Charity —is the object of the Catholic Order of Foresters, whose watchword. in the words of the Constitution, is " Friendship, Unity and True Christian Charity."

The Society was founded on the 23d of May, 1883, in the Sodality Hall of the Holy Family Church, Chicago, by Mr. Thos. Taylor in conjunction with a few other earnest gentlemen. They drew up a constitution and submitted it to His Grace Archbishop Feehan, who graciously gave his approbation.

In this Order membership is confined exclusively to Catholics only who are faithful in the discharge of their religious duties and obligations. The members of the various Courts of the Order are called together twice a month in regular meetings, when, after the transaction of necessary business, greetings are exchanged, acquaintances made and union cemented among them. The three great calamities so common, and so prolific of misery in the world, are loss of employment, loss of life and loss of health. The efforts of the Order are directed to alleviate those evils, and minimize the sorrow flowing from them. The names of Brothers out of employment are read out at each meeting and efforts made to secure them

employment. In cases of sickness the Brother is not only visited by his fellow-members, but is provided, in most cases, with a sum from $4 to $7 per week during illness, whilst, if death should overtake him, his Funeral expenses are borne by his Court, and in addition, his family receive a beneficiary of one thousand dollars.

During the first five years of its existence the Order established 88 Courts, with a membership of 5,000, and since has expanded and increased rapidly. In 1892 there were 228 Courts. On April 30, 1894, the end of the official year, the Courts numbered 445, having a total membership of 26,579.

In Canada 157 of these Courts are located, the membership reaching 8,372; the others are distributed through the United States.

The headquarters of the Order are in Chicago, and the present Executive officers are :

Thos. H. Cannon, High Chief Ranger, Chicago.
T. J. Callen, High Vice-Chief Ranger, Milwaukee.
Theo. B. Thiele, High Secretary, Chicago.
Michel Cyr, High Treasurer, Chica o.
Dr. T. F. O'Malley, High Medical Examiner, and also a Board of five Trustees.

The Government of the Order is carried on through the Annual Session ; to this, each Court is entitled to send one delegate. In the Session or Convention of 1894, held at St. Paul, Minn., a radical change in the representation at the Annual Session was made, by the formation of a Grand Council in each State or Province. These

Councils are to meet annually and govern their various constituencies, and will elect a representative for every 500 members or fraction thereof, as delegates, who, with the High Court officers, will form and compose the High Court Annual Session.

We give the locations, &c., of the Canadian Courts :

ONTARIO COURTS.

Kingston No. 150—Meeting night, 1 and 2 Thursday, Hall, Brock street.

Westport No. 187—Meeting night, 1 and 3 Saturday, Cobram Hall.

Toronto No. 201—Meeting night, 1 and 3 Thursday, Temperance Hall.

Ottawa No. 203—Meeting night, 2 and 4 Thursday, St. Patrick's Hall.

Ottawa No. 213—Meeting night, 2 and 4 Thursday, Hall, Catholic Lyceum

Sudbury No. 221—Meeting night, 2 and 4 Wednesday.

Sarnia No. 223—Meeting night, 1 and 3 Tuesday, C.M.B.A. Hall.

Pembroke No. 225—Meeting night, 1 and 3 Monday, Lynch Hall.

Cornwall No. 227—Meeting night, 2 and 4 Monday, C O.F. Hall.

Chatham No. 241—Meeting night, 2 and 4 Monday, A.O.U.W. Hall, King street.

Windsor No. 242—Meeting night, every Tuesday, C.M.B.A Hall.

Brockville No. 262—Meeting night, 2 and 4 Thursday, Hall, Comstock Block.

Ingersoll No. 270—Meeting night, 1 and 3 Friday, C.O.F. Hall, King street.

Renfrew No. 282—Meeting night, 2 and 4 Monday.

Ottawa No. 284— Meeting night, 2 and 4 Monday, Hall, 546½ Wellington street.

London No. 298—Meeting night, 2 and 4 Monday, K. of P. Hall.

Ottawa No. 304—Meeting night, 2 and 4 Thursday, Hall, 544 Sussex street.

Prescott No. 306—Meeting night, 2 and 4 Tuesday, Hall, Court Room.

Orleans No. 307—Meeting night, 1 and 3 Saturday.

Hintonburg 324—Meeting night 1 and 2 Monday.

Ottawa No 330—Meeting night, 2 and 4 Wednesday, St. Joseph's L. H. Hall.

Ottawa West No. 344—Meeting night, 1 and 3 Friday, Hall, 132 Rochester.

Ottawa No. 348—Meeting night, 1 and 3 Wednesday, St. Anne's Hall.

Woodstock No. 350—Meeting night, 2 and 4 Tuesday.

Ottawa No. 352—Meeting night, 1 and 3 Wednesday, Hall, Garneau School.

Tweed No. 355—Meeting night, 1 and 3 Friday.

Hastings No. 356—Meeting night, Wednesday, C.O.F. Hall.

Wolfe Island No. 368—Meeting nights, 1 and 3 Tuesday, Masonic Hall

Toronto No. 370—Meeting night, 2 and 4 Thursday, Forester's Hall.

Hawkesbury No. 375—Meeting night, 2 and 4 Monday.

Ottawa No. 376— Meeting night, 1 and 3 Sunday, Broderick's Hall.

Pembroke No. 379—Meeting night, 1 and 3 Monday.

Sault St. Marie No. 386—Meeting night, 1 and 3 Tuesday, School Hall.

Moose Creek No. 390—Meeting night, 1 and 3 Friday, Gagnon's Hall.

Arnprior No. 407— Meeting night, 2 and 4 Wednesday.

Cumming's Bridge No. 429—Meeting night, 2 and 4 Wednesday, Hall, Notre Dame School.

Van Kleek Hill No. 440—Meeting night, 2 and 4 Friday.

London No. 454.

KNIGHTS OF ST. JOHN.

 THE ROMAN CATHOLIC UNIFORMED KNIGHTS OF ST. JOHN are a Catholic, semi-military organization, combining the social with the benevolent element. Its ranks are open to men of all nationalities, provided they are practical Catholics and in sound bodily health. In time of sickness its members are entitled to a sick benefit of $4 a week, and in case of death to a funeral benefit of $50. Where desired, Certificates for $500, or $1,000, or $1,500 are issued to members from what is called the Widows' and Orphans' Fund.

The Order which was established in Rochester, N.Y., about seventeen years ago, and numbers at present about 250 Commanderies, with a membership of about 15,000, 600 in Ontario alone, was introduced into Canada in 1884. In June of that year St. Augustine Commandery No. 62 was organized in Windsor by T. A. Bourke, who has been an officer of the Supreme Council since its organization and was the first Grand President of the Grand Council of Canada, with a charter list of 35 members. Very Rev. Dean Wagner became the Spiritual Director, and still holds the position.

In 1888, with the approbation of his Grace Archbishop Lynch, Leo Commandery No. 2 was organized in Toronto.

COMMANDERIES IN ONTARIO.

Leo No. 2—Organized 1888, meets in St. Vincent's Hall on 1st and 3rd Sundays of every month. Secretary, J. J. Murphy, 25 Montague Place, Toronto.

St. Augustine No. 62—Organized 1884, meets in Mann's Hall, Windsor. 2nd Sunday of every month. Secretary, Thomas Chittle, Windsor.

St. Paul's No. 122—Organized 1863, meets in St. Paul's Hall, Power st., alternate Tuesdays. Secretary, T. K. Haffey, 212 Wilton ave , Toronto.

O'Mahony No. 211—Organized 1892, meets in St. Paul's Hall, Power st., 1st and 3rd Fridays. Secretary, A. Hawkeshawe, 475 Front st., Toronto.

St. Patrick's No. 212—Organized 1892, meets corner McCaul and Queer. sts., alternate Sundays. Secretary, John J. O'Reilly, 120 Chestnut st., Toronto.

St. Mary's No. 216—Organized 1892, meets in Occident Hall 2nd and 4th Sundays. Secretary, Chas. J. O'Brien, 121 Denison ave., Toronto.

Columbus No. 219—Organized 1892, meets in basement of St. Basil's Church, 2nd and 4th Thursdays. Secretary, J. J. Dalton, 9 Ann st., Toronto.

McBride No. 228—Organized 1893, meets in Schoolhouse, Weston, 3rd Monday of every month. Secretary, John Duggan, Weston.

Our Lady of Lourdes No. 253—Organized 1894, meets in Knights of St. John Hall, 68 Adelaide st. W., alternate Sundays Secretary, W. A. Hodgson.

On December 1st, 1893, a meeting of representatives of the different Commanderies was held for the purpose of establishing a Grand Commandery. This resulted in the formation of the Provincial Commandery of Ontario, which was incorporated under the Insurance Corporations Act of 1892. The following are the officers :

Grand Spiritual Advisor and Director—Most Rev. J. Walsh, D.D. Archbishop of Toronto.

President—William H. Cahill, Toronto.

Vice-President—Joseph McEvoy, Toronto.

Secretary—William M. Moylan, 74 Czar st., Toronto.

Treasurer—Charles C. Custance, Jr., Toronto.

Board of Trustees—William Guttenberg, Windsor; John J. Doyle, Toronto.

Committee on Laws and Constitutional Amendment—John Duggan, Weston ; William Ray, Toronto ; T. K. Haffey, Toronto.

Auditors—John H. Kennedy, Toronto ; F. Holiman, Toronto.

CATHOLIC YOUNG LADIES' LITERARY SOCIETY.

" Who shall find a valiant woman ? Far and from the uttermost coasts is the price of her."—Prov. xxxi., 10.

THIS Society was established by Father Henning C.SS.R., as a means for the physical, social, mental and moral improvement of members.

Saint Catharine of Alexandria, whose feast falls on Nov. 25th, is specially invoked by the Society, who have placed themselves under her patronage.

Much of the prosperity of the Society is proclaimed by its members to be due to the enterprise and energy of their first President, Miss O'Reilly, now Mrs. Kavanagh, and, as honorary President of the Society, still most active in promoting its interests.

One ambition that the Society hope soon to see realized is an affiliation with the Catholic Ladies' Mutual Society, whose headquarters are in San Francisco, from which they would reap the benefit of a system of insurance at reasonable rates.

Any Catholic young lady of good character who has reached her seventeenth year may become a member of the Association.

The annual meeting is held on Monday of the second week in November of each year, when also officers for the year are elected.

Regular meetings are held in the McCaul St. Hall every Monday evening at 8 o'clock. An open meeting, to which friends of the Society are cordially invited, and for which the services of an able lecturer are secured, as well as a miscellaneous programme rendered, takes place the last Monday of each month.

Classes for instruction in different branches are formed under the auspices of the Society and good work done.

The officers for 1894-5 are: Honorary President; Mrs. Kavanagh ; President, Miss Lane ; Vice-President, Miss Hart ; Rec. Secretary, Miss M. O'Donoghue ; Fin. Secretary, Miss Moran.

ST. ALPHONSUS CATHOLIC ASSOCIATION.

THE St. Alphonsus Catholic Association of Toronto, founded in 1888 by Father Henning. C.SS.R., as a young men's literary society for St. Patrick's parish, has developed into a city Catholic club, the membership of which is open to all men between the ages of 20 and 35 who are practical Catholics. In 1892 the Club moved into its present club house at No. 184 William street. The club house contains pool and billiard tables, music, reading. card and reception rooms, with a small gymnasium and the nucleus of a library. The building of a larger gymnasium is in contemplation. The house is open every evening, and meetings for business and for debates are held on the first and third Tuesdays of the month. Affiliated with the Club are bicycle and football clubs. During the winter of 1893 a series of public lectures was given, which, it is understood, will be continued during the winter of 1894-5. The election of officers takes place in November. Below we give a list of the officers for 1893-94 :

Spiritual Director—Rev. P. H. Barrett.
President—L. V. McBrady.
Vice-President—M. P. Forbes.
Financial Secretary—E. T. Noland.
Recording Secretary—W. Moylan.
Treasurer—James W. McCabe.
Librarian—P. F. Dolan.
Seargeant-at-Arms—A. McDonagh.
House Committee—J. J. Dalton, C. O'Toole, J. E. Lynes.

LEAGUE OF THE CROSS.

THE Fathers of the Society of Jesus of the Church of Our Lady, Guelph, Ont., organized this Society among their parishioners in June, 1883. The Sodality was erected an Arch-Sodality in 1885, with power to affiliate other similar sodalities.

Those for whom intoxicating drinks is a proximate occasion of sin take on admission the Total Abstinence pledge ; those for whom it is not such a danger and who can safely use it in moderation, pledge themselves not to exceed a stated quantity in twenty-four hours.

The Society has spread throughout Ontario, and will soon be found in every parish. There are two branches in Toronto : St. Paul's—Rev. J. L. Hand, Spiritual Adviser ; William H. Cahill, President; John J. Moran, Secretary. Meets in St. Anne's Hall, Power street, every Sunday : members, 275. St. Joseph's Branch, Secretary, John Howorth, 30 Brooklyn avenue.

THE MOST REV. ARCHBISHOP TACHE.

Written for the Catholic Almanac of Ontario.

THE severest loss which the Church of Canada suffered during the past year was the death of the apostolic and saintly Archbishop of St. Boniface, the Most Rev. Alexander Antonin Taché, who died at his residence on the 22nd of June, 1894.

He belonged to one of the oldest families in Canada, some of whose ancestors were amongst the great historic pioneers of America, e. g. Louis Joliet, the famous discoverer of the Mississippi, and Sieur Varennes de la Verandrye, the hardy ex-plorer of the Red River and the Saskatchewan country. Other members of the Taché family rendered eminent ser-vices to their country, in the government of which they occupied at various periods very distinguished positions. The Archbishop's uncle, Sir Etienne Pascal Taché, died Premier of Canada in 1865. On the side of his mother, who was Miss Bouchor de la Broquerie, he was no less distinguished, she being the great-granddaughter of the founder of Boucherville, and grand - niece of Madame, d'Youville, foundress of the Grey nunnery of Montreal. His father was Charles Taché, who had served in the war with the United States.

Archbishop Taché was born at Riviere-du-Loup in the Province of Quebec July 23, 1824. Whilst very young he lost his father, but had the blessing of a careful training at the hands of an excellent mother, whose only care was to have her sons tread the path of honor and duty in which their forefathers had walked. The future prelate was sent to the College of St. Hyacinthe, where he prosecuted his classical studies, he afterwards proceeded for theology to the Grand Seminary at Montreal. He subsequently returned to St. Hyacinthe, where he was appointed pro-fessor of mathematics.

About this time the arrival in Canada of a few of the Oblate Fathers gave an entirely different turn to the young man's future, and developed his deep religious zeal and natural inclination for a life of adventure and hardship. He applied to be admitted into the Order, and was received into the novitiate in October, 1841. The services of the good Fathers were sought for by Bishop

ARCHBISHOP TACHE.

Provencher for the vast North-West, then a lonely wild whose scattered inhabitants were hunters with no settled abode, or the more nomadic Indians. When the venerable Bishop's proposal was accepted and announced to the community the young novice, Taché, heard a new call : he hastened to consummate the sacrifice he had already made by offering his services. And the very force which in general might have been expected to deter him from it was the very thing which attracted him towards it, the love of his mother. She was at the time suffer-ing from a dangerous illness ; and, in order to obtain her recovery, her son with true filial piety offered to God the sacrifice of home and com-fort to devote himself to the apostolate of that unknown territory which offered only hardship to its missionaries. The offering was accepted : the mother recovered, and had the happiness of being spared for twenty-six years, and the son started on the 4th of June, 1845, for the field of his labors. He thus vividly describes his feelings upon this occasion :

" You will allow me to tell you what I felt when I re-ceded from the sources of the St. Lawrence, on whose banks Providence had fixed my birthplace and by whose waters I first conceived the thought of the Red River. I drank of those waters for the last time, and mingled with them some parting tears, and confided to them some of the secret thoughts and affectionate sentiments of my inmost heart. I could imagine how some of the bright waves of this river, rolling down from lake to lake, would at last strike on the beach nigh to which a beloved mother was praying for her son that he might become a perfect Oblate and holy missionary. I knew that being intensely preoccupied with that son's happiness, she would listen to the faintest murmuring sound, to the very beating of the waves coming from the North-West, as if to discover in them the echoes of her son's voice asking a prayer or promising a re-membrance."

. . . . . " I bade to my native land adieu, which I then believed to be everlasting, and I vowed to my adopted land a love and attachment which I then, as now, wished to be as lasting as my life."

The journey to St. Boniface occupied sixty-two days, and St. Boniface was a thousand miles East of the first scene of the young missionary's labors. After his ordination to the holy priesthood, which took place on the 12th of October, 1845, Father Taché was appointed to accompany Father La-fleche, afterwards Bishop of Three Rivers, to Islo a la Crosse. They started for their station the next summer on the 8th of July, and reached it after two months. Here nothing seemed to daunt his zeal. At one time he is away a hundred miles in one direction baptizing a dying chief. No sooner does he return home, if the mission house could be so called, than he is away in another direction carrying the glad tidings of God's word to Lake Caribou, 350 miles east of Isle a la Crosse. His next mission was to Athabasca, still farther away, where he spent three weeks, baptizing that time 194 Indians. Few could stand the rigors of the winters, the fatigue of the long journeys, the unpalatable food, for they had only pemmican, and, what was severest on the constitution, the want of shelter. Such difficulties try but do not overcome apostolic men. Father Taché counted these years as amongst the happiest of his life, and left a very interesting account how his heart thrilled with joy when at the end of his journey he was welcomed by the untutored savage. Sometimes the picture was reversed. After travelling for hundreds of miles under the most trying difficulties, on arriving at the expected place of meeting he would find the tribe had left a few days before, and had gone further on. Thereupon his own guides would abandon him, seeing that his stock of provisions was low. In order to save his team of dogs he must starve himself, for his safety depends upon them. He starts upon his return and goes days at a time without food. What was the spirit of self-denial and courage which animated this apostolic man may be clearly seen from the following letter written in 1849. Having been informed that owing to lack of funds the missions would have to be abandoned, he writes:

"The news which your letter brings us afflicts us profoundly. We cannot reconcile ourselves to the thought of abandoning our dear neophytes and our numerous catechumens. We will confine our demands upon your assistance to the narrowest limits. We hope that you will always be able to provide us at least with altar breads and wine for the holy sacrifice. We ask only one further favor, which is that we be allowed to continue our present labors. The fishes of the lakes shall supply us with the food we shall require and the wild beasts of the forests with clothing. Again we beg of you, Reverend Father, not to call us away from a work to which our hearts are so much attached."

But God had His providence over both the missions and the zealous missionary whose talents and character had not escaped the notice of the venerable Bishop Provencher. This saintly prelate was now in failing health, and looking about for a coadjutor and future successor his eye rested upon Father Taché, then only 26 years of age. His Lordship called him to St. Boniface, where a letter from his religious superiors instruct-

ed him to sail for France for his consecration. Bishop Tache received his episcopal consecration at Viviers, November 23rd, 1851, from the hands of the Bishop of Marseilles, Mgr. de Mazenod, assisted by Mgr., afterwards Cardinal, Guibert and Mgr. Prince, Bishop of St. Hyacinthe. A brief visit to Rome, and, on his return to America, a few weeks in Lower Canada, occupied the winter, so that it was June before the young Bishop reached St. Boniface. Here Bishop Provencher thought to keep him, but in vain. Bishop Taché again took up his residence at Isle a la Crosse to devote himself with all the greater zeal and success which the unction of his dignity imparted.

Nearly two years after he was raised to the episcopate, Bishop Taché returned to St. Boniface to take possession of his see, rendered vacant by Bishop Provencher's death on June 7, 1853. He entered upon his extended field of labors with his accustomed zeal, and opened convents, colleges, schools and homes of charity. He shared his very table with the orphans, and denied himself of everything that they might want for nothing. As years went on religion advanced; missionary posts were established, the diocese was divided and afterwards sub-divided. It was while on a visit to one of these outlying bishoprics that Bishop Taché suffered the loss by fire of his episcopal residence and cathedral, December 14t 1860. Following closely upon this trial a terrible inundation flooded the district leaving the poor desolate. A few years afterwards the crop the Red River settlement were destroyed grasshoppers, the buffalo chase failed, and famine ensued. Bishop Taché bowed with loving submission to these severe trials, but displayed at the same time the greatest energy in affording relief. His subsequent difficulties were of a severer form and came from other than material loss.

During the political troubles arising of the transfer of the Red River Territory from the Hudson Bay Company to the Dominion of Canada, Archbishop Taché took a very prominent part in restoring peace. He was at the time (1869) attending the Vatican Council at Rome, and on receiving a communication from the Canadian Government hastened home. Upon reaching Ottawa he had a conference with the Ministry, when he received instructions to proceed at once to the North-West and grant a general amnesty for past offences. As the murder of Scott had occurred in the meantime between His Grace's conference and his arrival at St. Boniface, he was severely criticised for having unconsciously exceeded his instructions. He ably justified himself, and showed that his offices for peace were successful, and that he had acted throughout with the utmost good faith for the general welfare of his people.

But the introduction of Manitoba into the Dominion was to cost the zealous prelate further trials, of which he did not live to see the end. It is the Manitoba School Question. Before the public as a political question, before the courts as a judicial one, it is still too burning a subject to be touched upon in a brief biographical sketch. Archbishop Taché was the standard bearer of Christian education in Manitoba. He strove to have provision that the schools in practice at the time should be recognized and maintained by law. For a time all went well, until the Province received a large increase of immigrants. These were mostly English speaking and Protestant; so that two forces were at work, difference of religion and difference of language, tearing down the existing schools. For years the intrepid Archbishop appealed and protested—but to no purpose. He was more of a missionary than politician. He saw the fruits of his sowing, the work of his hands, the dearest object of his zealous love, his schools taken from him and his people, and in the name of law transferred to strangers. It was a hard trial, and served to embitter the last few years of a life which ought to have won from the Province he served so long and well a quiet rest. But the evening was as the day, and the sun went down amidst the storm. A disease contracted many years before told on his constitution, worn out as it was already by the hardships of his missionary labors.

Last spring the state of Archbishop Taché's health caused great anxiety to his friends and flock. An operation was performed, but it was unavailing. He grew worse and finally succumbed. The death-bed scene was of those which close only holy lives, and the farewell words were those of a great soul. Bishop Graudin and a few priests were gathered around him. The dying prelate by a motion of his hands called them closer and blessed them. Then after a few moments he faintly said: " C'est la volonté de Dieu. Je vous dis adieu. Priez Dieu pour moi." (" It is the will of God—Farewell—Pray for me ") and again "Adieu—au ciel " (Farewell, we meet in heaven). With these words and one more fatherly look upon his friends, he breathed away his soul in peace. Thus died at the age of seventy-one the zealous Alexander Antonin Taché, Archbishop of St. Boniface. He was respected by his opponents, beloved by his people, and esteemed by all. He is an honor to the country that gave him birth, the Church he served so well, and the religious community to which he belonged. His memory will be in benediction.

THE CHURCH IN ONTARIO.

CANADA is divided into seven ecclesiastical Provinces : Quebec, Montreal, Ottawa, Kingston, Toronto, Halifax and St. Boniface. Of these three are in Ontario : Toronto, erected March 18th, 1870, comprising the dioceses of Toronto (Metropolitan See), Hamilton and Loudon; Ottawa, erected May 10th, 1887, comprising Ottawa (Metropolitan See) and Vicaria. Apostolic of Pontiac ; Kingston, erected July 28t, 1889, comprising Kingston (Metropolitan See) Peterborough and Alexandria.

I. PROVINCE OF TORONTO.

1. Toronto. 2. Hamilton. 3. London.

1. Diocese of Toronto (Metropolitan See)— This Diocese embraces the Counties of Cardwell, Lincoln, Ontario, Peel, Simcoe, Welland, York—erected Dec. 17th, 1841. Created an Archbishopric March 18th, 1870.

Archbishop (4th) Most Rev. John Walsh, D.D., born 24th May, 1830, at Moncoin, Ireland, ordained priest Nov. 1st, 1854, consecrated Bishop of Sandwich Nov. 10th, 1867, seat transferred to London Oct. 3rd, 1869, appointed Archbishop of Toronto July 24th, 1889, installed Nov. 27th, the same year.

Secretary to Archbishop—Rev. J. Walsh, St. John's Grove, Sherbourne and Earl Sts., Toronto.

Vicar-Generals—Very Rev. Mgr. Rooney, Very Rev. J. J. McCann.

Archdeacon—Rev. K. A. Campbell.

Deans—Very Rev. W. R. Harris, St. Catharines ; Very Rev. E. J. Cassidy, Toronto; Very Rev. J. J. Egan, Barrie.

Archbishop's Council—The Very Rev. Vicar-Generals and Deans.

Catholic population, 57,000 ; Clergy, secular 56, regular 23 ; College, 1 ; Convents, 18 ; Churches or Chapels, 84; Hospitals and Orphanages, 7 ; Parishes, 43.

PARISHES.

There are nine parishes in the City of Toronto. Handsome Separate Schools well equipped, taught by the Sisters of St. Joseph, Loretto Nuns, and Christian Brothers, are in every parish. In the De La Salle High School, Duke street, the more advanced pupils are taught.

The Loretto Nuns have boarding school and select day school at Loretto Abbey, Wellington Place (Mother House) Sup., Rev. M. Ignatia, and select schools at Convent of St. Ignatius, Bond street, Sup., Mother Joachim, and Convent of St. John, Wellesley Place, Sup., Mother Loyola. Sisters of St. Joseph have boarding school and select school at the Mother house, St. Albans street, Sup., Rev. M. De Pazzi, and select school at St. Mary's, Bathurst street, Sup., Mother De Chantal. The House of Providence, Power street,

Sup., Mother Louise, for the aged poor and foundlings; St. Nicholas' Institute, for young boys, Mother Stanislaus, Sup.; Sunnyside Orphanage of the S. Heart, Mother Bernard, Sup., and St. Michael's Hospital, Bond street, Mother Assumption, Sup., are in charge of the Sisters of St. Joseph. Other institutions are: Monastery of Our Lady of Charity (Good Shepherd) Parkdale, Sup., Very Rev. Mother Mary of St. Aloysius Schottmuller, Convent of the Precious Blood, St. Joseph street, Rev. Mother St. Joseph, Sup.

ST. MICHAEL'S COLLEGE, St. Joseph st. — Taught by the Basilian Fathers. Provincial, Very Rev. V. Marijon; Superior, Rev. J. R. Teefy, B.A.; Rev. J. Mulcahy, Director of Studies; Rev. F.X. Frachon, Prof. of Theology; Econome, Rev. J. Guinane, Prof. of Mathematics; Mr. W. D. Heenan, Prof. Rhetoric; Rev. A. P. Dumouchelle, Prof. Belles Lettres; Rev. F. Walsh, First Latin; Mr. King, Second Latin; Rev. A. Martin, Elementary Latin; Mr. Quinlan, First Commercial; Mr. Phelan, Second Commercial; Mr. Ryan, Third and Mr. Collins Fourth Commercial; Rev. E. Murray, Prof. of Music; Rev. A. Martin, Plain Chant; Mr. Cote, Master of Studies; Mr. J. Costello, Master of Recreation, Rev. L. E. Cherrier, chaplain to Sacred Heart Orphanage.

ST. MICHAEL'S SCHOLASTICATE. — Sup., Rev. R. Mc-Brady, with seven scholastics.

MOST REV. JOHN WALSH, D.D.

ST. BASIL'S NOVITIATE, St. Clair Ave.—Superior, Rev. A. Aboulin; assistant, Rev. T. Haydon.

CHRISTIAN BROTHERS, Bathurst St.—Director, Bro. Urbanus.

BLANTYRE PARK, situate east of Toronto is an Industrial School for Catholic children—a work in which his Grace Archbishop Walsh is greatly interested.

ST. MICHAEL'S CATHEDRAL, Bond street—Very Rev. J. J. McCann, V.G., Rev. F. Rohleder, Rev. F.

Ryan, S.J. Under the present Archbishop the whole interior of the Cathedral has been renewed and frescoed, and a chapel built connected by a cloister with the palace. The Conference of St. Vincent de Paul meets after last Mass in St. John's chapel. Altar Society, first Sunday of the month at 4 p.m. in St. John's chapel. Young Ladies' Sodality meets Sundays, 3.30 p.m., in Loretto Academy, Bond street.

Mass—Sundays, 7, 9 and 10.30 a.m. Vespers, 7 p.m. Daily Mass, 6 a.m.

ST. BASIL'S, St. Joseph street, in charge of the Basilians — Parish priest, Rev. L. Brennan, C.S.B., assisted by Rev. F. X. Frachon, C.S.B. Societies — Sodality of B. V. M. for Young Men meets Sundays at 7 p.m.; for young women Sundays at 3.30 p.m. League of the Sacred Heart and Apostleship of Prayer meets Sunday before the first Friday at 4 p.m. with Benediction. St. Vincent de Paul meets Sundays after High Mass. C. M.B.A., Tuesdays. Sewing Society, Thursday afternoons, and Altar Society. Catholic Truth Society has headquarters at St. Michael's College, President, Rev. J. J. Murphy; Sec., W. Kernahan.

Masses — Sundays, 7, 8, 9 and 10.30 a.m. Vespers, 7.30 p.m. Daily Mass, October to June, 8 a.m.; July to September, 7 a.m. inclusive. Devotions in Lent, Advent, June, October and November, Wednesday and Friday evenings at 7.30; every evening at 7.30 in May, First Friday of the month, Benediction of B.S. after 8 o'clock Mass. The chapel in the Novitiate of the Basilian Fathers is open for the accommodation of Catholics in the vicinity.

ST HELEN'S, Brockton—Very Rev. E. Cassidy and Rev. J. C. Carberry.

ST. JOSEPH'S, Leslie St.—Rev. Wm. Bergin.

ST. JOHN THE EVANGELIST, East Toronto Village—Attended every Sunday.

St. Mary's, Bathurst St.—Mgr. F. P. Rooney, V.G., Revs. G. M. Cruise, P. Coyle. Societies— Sodality of B. V. M., Sacred Heart League, St. Vincent de Paul and Confraternity of Expiation.

Masses—Sundays, 7.30, 8.30, 10 and 11 a. m. Benediction for Children of the Sunday Schools, 3.p.m. Vespers, 7.30 p.m. Daily Mass, 7.30 a.m.

St. Peter's, attended from St. Mary's every Sunday—Mass 8.30 and 10.30 a.m.

Notre Dame de Lourdes, corner Sherbourne and Earl Sts.—Rev. Jas. Walsh.

St. Patrick's, William street, in charge of the Redemptorist Fathers since Jan., 1881—Rev. P. H. Barrett, Rector; Revs. S. J. Krein, Cyril Dodsworth, S. Grogan and John Hayden.

Order of Services in St. Patrick's Church : Sundays, a.m.. Low Masses at 7, 8 and 9 o'clock, High Mass and Sermon at 10.30 ; p.m., Catechetical Instruction in Church at 3 o'clock, Vespers, Sermon and Benediction at 7.30. Holidays of Obligation, a.m., Low Masses at 5.30, 6.30, 8 o'clock, High Mass and Sermon at 9 o'clock. Week Days—Masses at 6, 6.30 and 8.15 a.m.

Special Meetings of Societies—Sodality of Children of Mary—Every Sunday at 3.30 p.m. in the School ; Altar Society—Every 3d Thursday of the month at 8 p. m. in the Church ; Confraternity of the Holy Family: 1st, for Married Men : Every 1st Monday of the month at 8 p.m. in the Church ; 2d, for Married Women : Every 2d Tuesday of the month at 8 p.m. in the Church ; 3d, for Unmarried Women : Every 3d Tuesday of the month at 8 p.m. in the Church.

Special Devotions—Every evening in May and October at 7.30 ; every Wednesday and Friday evening in Lent at 7.30 ; every Saturday evening during the year at 7.30 : every 1st Friday of the month as follows : High Mass of Exposition at 8 a.m.; Exposition of the Blessed Sacrament during the day ; Special Services at 7.30 p.m.

Sacred Heart, 428 King street East—Rev. P. Lamarche—for the French citizens of Toronto.

Achill—St. Mary's, attended every Sunday from Adjala.

Adjala (Colgan P. O.)—Rev. J. Kilcullen. Stage from Tottenham on the H. & N. W. Railway.

Albion—See Caledon.

Alliston—Rev. H. J. Gibney. On the H. &. N. W. Railway.

Barrie—On the N. & N. W. Branch of G. T. R., erected a parish in 1855, Father Jamot first pastor, succeeded in 1863 by Father Northgraves, first Dean of Barrie ; Dean O'Connor 1870. Dean Cassidy 1890, Dean Bergin 1891, and in 1893 Dean Egan, present pastor, with Rev. L. Gibra assistant. The church, dedicated to the S. H. of Mary, is Gothic, with a graceful spire nearly 200 feet high. Seats 500. Brentwood, Assumption of B. V. M , and Bell Ewart, Holy Name of Jesus, are attended from Barrie alternate Sundays. The Separate School, established in 1856, is taught by the Sisters of St. Joseph and one lay teacher. A fine four-roomed brick schoolhouse was built in 1893, pupils number 400. The Sisters of St. Joseph have a beautiful and commodious Convent, built in 1885 at a cost of $9,000. Sodality of B. V. M. was established in 1873, League of the S. H. in 1880 and St. Vincent de Paul in 1883. There are over 300 Catholic families in the parish. Mass every Sunday 8.30 and 10 30 a.m. Vespers 7 p.m. Daily Mass, Summer 7.30, Winter 8 a.m.

Bell Ewart—See Barrie.

Beaverton—St. Joseph's, attended from Brock every three weeks.

Black Creek—St. Joseph's, attended from Niagara Falls every Sunday.

Bradford—Japanese Martyrs, attended from Newmarket every two weeks.

Brampton—Angels Guardian, attended from Orangeville every two weeks.

Brentwood—See Barrie.

Brechin—On the Midland Div. of the G.T.R., was erected a parish March 19th, 1884, with Father Davis first pastor. He was succeeded by Father McMahon, and he, in Feb 1893, by Father McRae, the present incumbent. The church is under the invocation of St. Andrew. C M.B.A.—Pres., R.L. Gaughan ; Rec. Sec., John Malone ; League of the Sacred Heart—Sec. Miss M. McRae, and the Altar Society—Pres., Mrs. M. McGrath are established in the parish. A Separate School is taught by one lay teacher ; 93 pupils on the roll Mass—Sundays 10.30 a.m ; Vespers, 7 p.m.; Daily Mass, 8 a.m.

Brock (Vroomanton, P.O.)—Rev. C. Cantillon. Reached by stage from Sunderland on the Midland Div. of the G. T. Ry.

Caledon (Caldwell P O.)—Situate four miles from the Station of the T.G. & B.Ry. was erected a parish in 1867, Father McSpirritt, first pastor, succeeded by Fathers Laboureau, Ray, Egan, Gallagher and Whitney, present pastor. There are 115 Catholic families. The church, Gothic, is dedicated to St. Cornelius and seats 250. Albion—St. John the Evangelist, is attended once in two weeks.

Masses—Sundays, 11 a.m. ; week days, 7.30 a.m.

Christian Island—St. Francis Xavier, attended occasionally by a Jesuit Father.

Church's Falls—Our Lady and St. Patrick, attended from Caledon once a month.

Clareville—St. Clare.

Clifton—Attended from Niagara Falls daily.

Collingwood—St. Mary's, Rev. E. J. Kiernan, on the Ham. & N.W. Ry.

Dixie—St. Patrick, Rev. Jas. Trayling, on the Credit Valley Railway. Fifth Line of Etobicoke—Sacred Heart of Jesus, attended from Dixie every two weeks.

Duffin's Creek—See Pickering.

Flos (Apto P.O.)—St. Patrick, on the Northern Railway.

Fort Erie—St. Joseph, Rev. P. J. McColl, on the Buffalo & Lake Huron Ry.

Georgina—St. Anthony, attended from Brock every two weeks.

Gore of Toronto (Gribbin P.O.)—St. Patrick, Rev. F. McSpirritt.

Grimsby—Patronage of St. Joseph, attended from Smithville every three weeks.

Highland Creek—St. Joseph, attended from Pickering every Sunday.

King—St. Patrick's and St. Mary's attended from Schomberg every two weeks.

Lafontaine—See Ste. Croix.

Lambton—St. Joseph, attended from Dixie every two weeks.

Mara (Uptergrove P.O.)—St. Columbkill, Rev. Jas. Hogan. On the Midland Division of the Grand Trunk Railway.

Markham—St. Patrick's, attended from Uxbridge every two weeks.

Medonte—St. Louis, attended from Flos every two weeks.

Merritton—St. Matthew, Rev. J. F. Smith Electric car from St. Catharines.

Midland—St. Margaret, Rev. J. H. Colin On the Midland Division of the Grand Trunk Railway.

Mono West — St. Cyprian, attended from Orangeville once a month.

Newmarket—St. John Chrysostom, Rev. D. Morris. On the Northern Railway.

Niagara — St. Vincent de Paul, Rev. J. J. Lynett. By boat in Summer from Toronto. In Winter electric car from Niagara Falls.

Niagara Falls—Our Lady of Peace, in charge of the Carmelite Fathers. Very Rev. A. J. Kreidt, Prior ; Revs. A. Brandstaetter, D. F. O'Mallny, D. F. Best, Ambrose Bruder, Paul W. Ryan. This old church was erected a pilgrimage by Pope Pius IX. The Ladies of Loretto have a Boarding School in their magnificent Convent overlooking the Falls. The Carmelite Fathers are building a handsome new Monastery. A home will be extended there to priests who have worn themselves out in the service of the Church.

North Adjala — Immaculate Conception, attended from Alliston every Sunday.

Orangeville—St. Peter, Rev. H. J. McPhillips. On the T. G. & B. Railway.

Orillia—Very Rev. K. A. Campbell and Rev. F. W. Duffy. On the Northern Railway and on the Midland Division of the G. T. R.

Oshawa—Situate about 1½ miles from the G.T.R. station ; was erected a parish in 1842, first resident priest, Rev. Henry Fitzpatrick, 1843, succeeded by Rev. Fathers Nightingale, Smith, Proulx, O'Keefe, Shea, McCann, McEntee, Hand, Jeffcott, the present pastor. The first church, dedicated to St. Gregory the Great, built by Father Kirwan, of Cobourg, in 1842, has been replaced by a fine new structure. The corner stone was laid by His Grace Archbishop Walsh Aug. 19th ; seats 600. Whitby—St. John the Evangelist is attended every Sunday. Separate school, Oshawa, established 1859, is taught by three Sisters of St. Joseph and numbers 100 pupils. C.M.B.A., Altar Society, Sodality of the B.V.M. and League of the Sacred Heart are established. There are about 120 families.

· Mass—Sundays at 9 and 10 o'clock alternately. Daily Mass at 7.30 a.m.

Penetanguishene—On the Northern railway ; erected a parish about 1833 ; the first resident priest was Father Proulx in 1835, followed by Fathers Charest, Ternot, Labaudy, Kennedy and the present pastor, Rev. Th. F. Laboureau. There is a handsome memorial church under the invocation of St. Ann and St. Joseph, erected to the memory of Brebœuf, Lallemant and their companions ; style, Romanesque, seating 800. There is a branch of the C.M.B.A., President, P. J. McDonald. The Public school is Catholic ; four teachers are employed ; pupils number 200. There are about 225 Catholic families. Port Severn i· attended once a month, and stations are held at Wyvale and Muskoka Mills.

Mass—Sundays, 8.30 and 10.30 a.m.; Vespers, 7.15 and 3.30 p.m., according to season ; daily Mass, 7.30 a.m.

Phelpston—Rev. M. J. Gearin, on the Northern railway.

Pickering—St. Francis de Sales, Rev. E. F. Gallagher, on the Grand Trunk railway.

Port Colborne—On the Welland railway, and on the Buffalo and Lake Huron railway, was erected a

parish in 1859. As early as 1844 it was attended from St. Catharines by Father McDonagh, and afterwards by Dean Grattan and Father Conway. Father Voisard was the first resident priest, his parish including Fort Erie. He was succeeded in 1865 by Father Keane, who remained two years. It was attended then from Thorold till 1868, when Father Voisard returned, remaining till 1871. Fort Erie was then made a distinct mission, while Welland was added to Port Colborne, and the parish assumed its pr sent form. Father Kilcullen was then appointed and remained in charge for eighteen years, when the present pastor, Rev. J. J. McEntee was appointed January, 1890. Father Kilcullen had as assistants Fathers P. Kiernan, Hayden, Morris, McCabe and Whitney. The Church, Gothic in style with stained glass windows, is under the invocation of St. Patrick ; will seat, including gallery, 450.

The Altar Society, 1890, and the League of the Sacred Heart—President, Miss Mary Dietrich ; secretary, Miss Ella Reddin ; treasurer, Miss Mary Twohey, are established. There are about 100 Catholic families in the parish of Port Colborne and Welland. The Separate school, founded in 1864, is taught by one lay teacher ; attendance, 70.

Mass—Sundays at 8 and 10 a.m.; alternate Sundays, Vespers at 7 p.m.; daily Mass, 8 a.m. Advent devotions and Lenten devotions, Fridays at 7.30 p.m ; May and October devotions, Wednesday and Friday at 7.30 p.m.

Welland is attended every Sunday. Mass at 8 and 10 a.m. Lenten devotions are held Wednesdays at 7.30, wi·h Mass the following morning at 8 a.m. The officers of the Altar Society in Welland are : President, Mrs Wm. M. German ; vice-president, Mrs. Smith ; treasurer, Miss A. Hobin.

Port Credit—"Star of the Sea," attended from Dixie every two weeks.

Port Dalhousie—"Star of the Sea," attended from St. Catharines every Sunday.

Port Perry—Immaculate Conception, attended from Uxbridge every two weeks.

Port Robinson—See Thorold.

Port Severn—St. Francis, attended from Penetanguishene once a month.

Queenstown—St. Patrick, attended from Niagara every two weeks.

Rama—St. Joseph, attended from Mara every month.

Richmond Hill—St. Mary's new church building, attended from Thornhill every Sunday.

St. Catharines—Was attended as a mission from Niagara as early as 1822. In 1835 the first church, frame, was built by Father Gordon, and in 1841 Father Kilcullen became the resident priest. Fathers Crowley, Cassidy and Rev. Dr. Lee, were connected with this parish—the last nam d is buried under the main wing of the church. Father McDonagh, who was in charge till 1850, began the erec ion of the present church, dedicated to St. Catharine of Alexandria. Fathers Masert and Wardy succeeded him, and in 1852 Father Grattan was made first Dean of the Niagara peninsula. Dean Mulligan succeeded in 1867, and in 1884 Dean Harris, the present pastor, was appointed. The church has been enlarged and beautified during his incumbency at a cost of $22,000, and the main altar ranks as one of the finest in Ontario. The Church, including galleries, will seat about 1,200. In St. Joseph's Mass is celebrated every Sunday at 10 a.m. accommodating the Catholics in the north and north-western part of the city. There are about four hundred Catholic families in St. Catharines. The two Separate Schools are taught by the Christian Brothers and the Sisters of St Joseph. The latter have a select school in their fine convent. The pupils of the schools number 400, teachers, 11. The Societies established are : League of the Sacred Heart, C M.B. A. and the La Salle Literary and Athletic Association. Mass—Sundays, 8 and 11 a.m.; Vespers, 7 p.m.; Daily Mass, chapel of St. Catharine, 8 a.m. : Convent chapel, 6.30 a.m

Ste. Croix (Lafontaine P.O.)—Ex ltation of the Holy Cross, Rev. J. E. Beaudoin ; by stage from Penetanguishene on the Midland. Sisters of the Holy Cross and Seven Dolors from Montreal ; established 1885.

Schomberg—Rev. L. Minehan ; by stage from Aurora on the Northern Railway.

Smithville—St. Martin, Rev. A. Lafontaine ; on the Great Western division of the G. T. railway.

Stayner—On the Northern railway ; erected a parish 1871, Revs. M. McC. O'Reilly, Francis Heydon, P. Kiernan and E. Kiernan in charge of parish in order named ; present pastor, Rev. M Moyna. The church, under the invocation of St. Patrick, is of pure Gothic style and seats 600. There are 70 Catholic families

Mass—Sundays, Winter 11 a.m.; Summer, 10 30 a.m.; Vespers, 4 p.m.; daily Mass, Winter, 8 a.m.; Summer 7 30 a.m.

Tecumseh—St. Margaret, attended from Schomberg every two weeks.

Thornhill—St. Luke, Rev. P. McMahon ; on the Northern railway.

Thorold—Was erected a parish 1853 under Rev. M. Laughlin, succeeded by Rev. Fathers E O'Keefe, Christie, Wardy, Gribbin, O'Reilly, Laboreau and the present pastor, Rev. T. J. Sullivan. A handsome new church was consecrated in 1892 under the invocation of Our Lady of the Holy Rosary and seats 700 people. *Port Robinson* is attended twice a month. The Separate schools, established in 1853, are taught by four sisters of St. Joseph and number 120 pupils. The societies are : League of the Sacred Heart, Pres., Miss C. Freel ; Sec.-Treas., Miss A. Hart; Sodality of B.V.M.; Angels' Society, Pres., Miss Maud O'Neill ; sec., Miss A. Dusian ; Treas., Miss A. McMahon ; and the C.M.B.A , Pres , J. Battle ; Rec. Sec., A. M. Keagan. There are 100 Catholic families.

Mass—Sundays, 8 and 10 a.m.; Vespers, 7.30 p.m.; daily Mass, 8 a m

Tottenham—St. Francis Xavier, attended from Adjala every Sunday.

Uxbridge—Situate on Midland Branch of G.T.R some thirty-five years ago, was attended from Oshawa by Rev. Father Proulx, later by Fathers Braire, Kiernan, Finan, O'Reilly, McEntee, McColl, Egan, Allain, and Keane. The church is dedicated to the Sacred Heart of Jesus, is of brick and holds about 200. *Port Perry* and *Markham* are attended from Uxbridge.

Mass—Sundays, 8 and 10.30 a.m. alternate ; Vespers, 7 p.m.

Victoria Harbor—St. Mary, attended from Midland every three weeks.

Vigo—Our Lady of Purity, attended from Flos every two weeks.

Wabaushene—St. John, attended from Midland once a month.

Warminster—Sacred Heart of Jesus, attended from Orillia once a month.

Welland—See Port Colborne.

Weston—St. John Evangelist, attended from Brockton every Sunday.

Whitby—See Oshawa.

2. DIOCESE OF HAMILTON.

This Diocese embraces the Counties of Brant, Bruce, Grey, Haldimand, Halton, Waterloo, Wellington and Wentworth. Erected Feb. 17th, 1856.

Bishop—Right Rev. T. J. Dowling, born at Limerick, Ireland, in 1840 ; ordained priest at Hamilton, Aug. 7th, 1864 ; consecrated Bishop of Peterborough at Hamilton, May 1st, 1887 ; translated to Hamilton, Jan. 11th, 1889.

Vicar-Generals — Right Rev. Mgr. Heenan, Very Rev. J. Keough, Very Rev. L. Elena.

Bishop's Council—Right Rev. E. J. Heenan, Right Rev. F. P. McEvay, Very Rev. Jno. Keough, Revs. G. Kenny, S.J., L. Elena, Dr. Wm. Kloepfer.

Superintendent of Schools—Rev. J. H. Coty.

Catholic population, 50,000 ; priests, secular, 88, regular, 15 ; College, 1 ; Convents, 15 ; Hospitals, Orphanages, &c., 6.

PARISHES.

CITY OF HAMILTON contains the parishes of St Mary, St. Patrick, St. Lawrence and St. Joseph. The Loretto Nuns have a fine Convent, to which a handsome addition has been recently built, with both boarding and day Schools, Mother Patricia, Superior. Sisters of St. Joseph, Mother house on Park street, Superior Mother Celestine, have greatly enlarged and beautified their Orphanage (inmates, 120), and manage a handsome, splendidly equipped hospital, to which a large addition has been built, most advantageously situated near the mountain—Superior, Sr. M. Antoinette. The Christian Brothers, the Sisters of St. Joseph and the Ladies of Loretto have charge of the Separate schools. The school houses are particularly fine, commodious and well-equipped. Hamilton has a fine cemetery picturesquely situated on Burlington Bav.

ST. MARY'S CATHEDRAL.—Under the patronage of the Immaculate Conception, was erected a parish in 1838 ; first priest, V. Rev. W. P. McDonald, V.G., succeeded by V. Rev. Father Gordon, V.G. The diocese of Hamilton was established in 1856. Rt. Rev. John Farrell, D.D, first Bishop, died Sept. 26, 1873, was succeeded by Rt. Rev. P. F. Crinnon April 19, 1874, who died November, 1882 ; succeeded by Rt. Rev. Jas. Jos. Carberry, O.P., S.T.M., Nov. 11, 1883, died Dec 19, 1887 ; succeeded by the present Bishop, Rt. Rev. T. J. Dowling, D.D, Jan. 11, 1889. St. Mary's Cathedral is built in Gothic style and seats 1,000. The high altar is richly decorated and of handsome design The bell is exceptionally fine. The League of the Sacred Heart, Confraternity of the Holy Rosary, Third Order of St. Francis, Young Ladies' and Children's Sodalities are established. Priests attending St. Mary's Cathedral : Rt. Rev. Mgr. McEvay, Revs. Lehman, J. M. Mahony.

Mass—Sundays, 7, 8.30 and 10.30 a m.; Vespers and Benediction, 7 p.m.; daily Mass, 6.30 and 7.30 a.m.; Rosary every evening at 7 30.

ST. PATRICK, corner King and Victoria ave.—Rev. J. J. Craven, Rev. R. Brady. League of the Sacred Heart, meets 1st Sunday at 4 p. m., n the church. Sodality of the B. V. M., meets every Sunday at 4 p m. Sodality of Holy Angels (girls) meets alternate Sundays at 3.30 p.m. Sodality of Sacred Heart (boys), meets alternate Sundays at 3.30 p. m. Altar Society, meets 1st Sunday at 4.30 p.m. in the chapel.

Mass—Sunday, 7 30, 9 and 10.30. a.m. Vespers, 7 p.m. Daily Mass, 8 a,m.

ST. LAWRENCE—Erected a parish in 1890, with Rev. Geo. O'Sullivan pastor, succeeded by Rev. R Brady, who was succeeded by Rev. J. H. Coty, the present pastor. The church, dedicated to St Lawrence, is of Romanesque order and seats 700. League of the Sacred Heart, Young Ladies' and Children's Sodalities are established.

Mass—Sundays, 8 and 9.30 a.m. Vespers, 7 p.m. Daily Mass, 7 a. m.

ST. JOSEPH—Erected a parish in 1894, pastor, Rev. J. V. Hinchey. A handsome church, Gothic design, seats 500.

Mass—Sundays, 9 30 a.m.; Vespers, 7 p m.; Daily Mass, 8 a.m.

Acton — Holy Rosary, Rev. P. Haley.

Arthur — St. John the Evangelist, Revs. J. Doherty and J. Rube.

Ayton—On the Georgian Bay Division of G. T. Railway dates from 1882, with Rev. P. S. Owens, parish priest. The church, Gothic in style, is dedicated to St. Peter, and seats 400. A large addition is being built. Two Separate schools, with 70 pupils, are taught by lay teachers. C M. B. A. was established in 1889. There are 90 Catholic families.

Mass — Sundays, 10 30 a.m.; Vespers, 3 p.m.; Daily Mass, 7 30 a.m.

Berlin—The first Holy Sacrifice of the Mass known to have been celebrated in this neighborhood was offered up by Rev. Peter Schneider, about three miles from Berlin. For many years the Jesuit Fathers from Guelph had charge of the mission, but the first resident priest was Father Laufhuler, who built the present church, Our Lady of Seven Dolors, in 1854. The parish was placed in charge of the Congregation of the Resurrection in 1858 under Very Rev Eugene Funcken, C.R. In 1890 the present pastor, Very Rev. William Kloepfer, C.R., D.D., took charge. He is assisted by the Rev. Fathers of St. Jerome's College. The societies established are: Sodalities of Our Lady of Mount Carmel and the Immaculate Conception, Ladies' Benefit Society, Mary and Martha Society, organized 1886, Pres., Miss Emma Bauer, meets first Sunday of each month at 3 p.m.; Third Order of St. Francis, 1889; St. Joseph's Mutual Aid Society for the Poles, Pres., A. Duszynski; St. Boniface Benefit Society, 1892, licensed and chartered 1894, Pres., J. Motz, Rec.-Sec., Rev. J. Schweitzer, meets first Monday of the month; and League of the Sacred Heart. There are about 225 Catholic families; a Separate school, established 1858, taught by the School Sisters of Notre Dame, teachers 7, pupils 320.

St. Jerome's College, founded 1865 by the Very Rev. Dr. L Funcken, C R., Rev. Dr. Theo Spetz, Pres., Revs. Dr. Kloepfer, J. Halter, J. Schweitzer, D,D., F. X. Beila, J. Waechter, J. Kosinski, A. Weiler, D.D., Hubert Aymans.

Mass—Sundays, 8 30, with catechetical instruction, and 10.30 a.m.; Vespers, 7 p.m.; daily Mass 8 a m : evening service, 7.30 p.m.

Beverly—Attended from Dundas.

Block—St. Michael's, attended from Owen Sound.

Brant—St. Michael's, attended from Walkerton.

Brantford—St. Basil, Revs. P. Lennon, J. Feeney and F. Kehoo. Sisters of St. Joseph established 1859.

Burlington—St. John the Baptist, attended from Oakville.

Caledonia—St. Patrick, Revs. F. O'Reilly and L. M. Lynch.

Cape Croker—St. Joseph, attended from Owen Sound.

Carlsruhe — On the Georgian Bay Division of G. T. Ry., was erected a parish in 1860, occupied successively by Rev. Fathers Matoga, Laufhuler, Schmitz, Rassaerts, Laussie and Halm, the present pastor. The Church, Roman, dedicated to St. Francis Xavier, seats 500. There are 95 Catholic families. Neustadt is attended from this parish. St. Anne's Altar Society and the C. M. B. A., President, P. Flesch, are established. The cemetery has been improved during the past year.

Mass—Sundays, 10 a.m. Daily, 8 a.m.

Cayuga — St. Stephen, Venerable Archdeacon Laussier.

Chatsworth—St. Stanislaus, attended from Owen Sound.

BISHOP DOWLING.

Chepstow—St. John Baptist, Rev. S. Wadel.

Deemerton—St. Ignatius, attended from Mildmay

Drayton—St. Peter's attended from Macton.

Dundalk—Rev. P. Cassin.

Dundas—As a mission began in 1828 under Rev. F. Campion, succeeded by Revs. John Cullen, 1830 ; J. Cassidy, 1832 ; J. B. Fox, 1838 ; M. R. Mills in 1840 ; James O'Flynn in 1842 ; P. Conolly, 1843 ; P. O'Dwyer, 1845 ; J. O'Reilly, 1847 ; J. Keough, 1885 ; Very Rev. E. J. Heenan, V G., 1889, present incumbent ; Rev. T. J. Maddigan, assistant. The old frame church which had served for about thirty years, having been burned by accident, the corner stone of the present church, under the invocation of St. Augustine, was laid in 1862. It is built in the Gothic style of red brick with free stone facings—the ceiling, groined —seats 600. From Dundas stations are held Christmas and Eastertide at *Ancaster* and *Copetown.* A Conference of St. Vincent de Paul, 1885 ; Sodality of the B. V. M., for girls, 1880 (affiliated 1892 to the Roman Prima Primaria) Prefect, Miss M. Galligan; Secretary, Miss M. Duncan; the Third Order of St. Francis of Assisi, 1889, Sister Superior, Miss M. Shyne; League of rhe Sacred Heart, 1889, President, Mrs. M. Hourigan; Secretary, Miss Kate Shea; St. Augustine Altar Society, and the Confraternity of the Holy Rosary, 1889, President, Mrs. McDonough, are established. There are about 225 Catholic families. The Separate school founded about thirty-five years ago is taught by three Sisters of St. Joseph and numbers 120 pupils. The Sisters of St. Joseph conduct the House of Providence; Sister M. Philip, Superior, sheltering 90 orphan boys and 100 old men and women. The Institution receives a grant from the Government and one from the county. Some inmates pay for their board, voluntary contributions supply the balance of the funds.

Mass—Sundays, 8 and 10.30 a.m.; Vespers and Benediction, 7 p.m.; Holy Days of Obligation, Mass, 5.30 and 10.30 a.m.; Vespers and Benediction, 7.30 p. m.; Daily Mass, 7.30 a.m.

Dunnville—Situate on the Buffalo and Goderich branch of G.T.R., was part of the parish of Caledonia to September, 1880, when it was erected a separate parish, Rev. James Eugene Crinnon first and present resident priest. Since then a new church, St. Michael's (classic Roman), seating 500, and a parochial residence have been built. Two acres of land for cemetery, as well as sites for the church and residence have been purchased. A small debt on the church remains unpaid. C.M.B.A. Society, Pres., Rev. J. E. Crinnon, Rec.-Sec., J. Flanagan, and Altar Society are established.

Mass—Sundays, 10.30 a.m.; week days, 7 a.m.; Vespers and Benediction, 7 p.m; Sunday schools, 10 a.m. and 2.30 p.m.

Durham—Rev. R. Maloney.

Elora—Immaculate Conception, Rev. F Cosgrove.

Elmira—Attended from St. Clements.

Eramosa—Attended from Acton.

Fergus—Church of the Holy Family, attended from Elora.

Formosa—Immaculate Conception, Rev. G. Brohman. Sisters of Notre Dame established.

Freelton—Our Lady of Mount Carmel, Rev. G. Murphy.

Galt—On both the C.P.R. and G.T.R. lines, was erected a parish in 1876, with Rev. J. Ryan first resident priest. Subsequent priests were: Very Rev. T. J. Dowling, V.G., Rev. Fathers O'Reilly, M. J. Maguire, P. McCann, B. J. O'Connell, J. Lennon, R. T. Burke. The present pastor, Rev. E. P. Slaven, has just completed a fine three-roomed school of white brick. The school was established in 1876, and is taught by lay teachers with attendance of 95 pupils. The church, St. Patrick, will seat 500; number of Catholic families, 150. Societies established are: League of the Sacred Heart, 1891, Mrs. J. McTague, president; Sodality of the Blessed Virgin Mary, 1886, president, Miss M. Mullen; C.M.B.A., president, Jas. T. Kelly, secretary, P. Radigan; I.C.B.U., presid., T. Barrett. Hespeler is attended twice every month. There is a League of the Sacred Heart, president, Mrs. Lang; secretary, Miss A. Lang. Also Branch of C.M.B.A., president, J. McMaster; rec. sec., John Murphy; fin. sec., Geo. Collins.

Mass—Every Sunday at 10.30, except the second Sunday of every month, when Mass is at 8.45 a.m.; Vespers, 7 p.m.

Georgetown—Holy Cross, attended from Acton.

Glenelg—St. Peters, attended from Durham.

Griffin's Corners—St. Paul, attended from Owen Sound.

Guelph—Immaculate Conception in charge of the Jesuit Fathers, who conduct a College. Superior, Rev. G. Kenny, with Revs. F. Dumortier, S J., J. O'Loan, S.J. and F. X. Kavanagh, S.J. The Sisters of St. Joseph, 1861, and the Loretto Nuns, are established.

Hamburg—Holy Family, attended from St. Agatha.

Harrisburg—Attended from Paris.

Macton—St. Joseph, Rev. J. S. O'Leary.

Meaford—St. Vincents, attended from Owen Sound.

Melancthon—St. Lawrence, attended from Dundalk.

Mildmay—Sacred Heart of Jesus, Rev. J. Way. Sisters of Notre Dame established.

Milton—Holy Rosary, attended from Oakville.

Morriston—Attended from Freelton.

Mount Forest—Was first attended by the Jesuit Fathers from Guelph. The first resident priest, Rev. P. S. Maheut, was appointed in 1863, succeeded by Revs. R. R. Maurice, 1870; B. J. O'Connell, 1876; P. J. Cassin, 1886; Very Rev. B. J. O'Connell, 1892. On November 3d, 1892. Mount Forest was made a Deanery with Very Rev. B. J. O'Connell, its first Dean. The church dedicated to St. Mary of the Purification, Gothic, seats 600. A set of beautiful stained glass windows have been placed in the church this year. Taere are 160 Catholic families. A Separate school was established in 1863, a second one in 1889. There are 78 pupils taught by two lay teachers. The Altar and Rosary Societies were established in 1876.

Mass—Sundays at 10.30 a.m.; Catechism, 3 p.m.; Nespers, 7 p.m.; Daily Mass, 8 a.m.

Neustadt—Attended from Carlsruhe.

New Germany—St. Boniface, Revs. S. Forster and L. Elena. School Sisters of Notre Dame established.

Nichol—Attended from Elora.

Oakville—St. Andrew, Rev. R. T. Burke. Sisters of St. Joseph established.

Osprey—Attended from Dundalk.

Owen Sound—Assumption, in charge of Basilian Fathers, Revs. F. X. Granottier, P. L. Buckley, P. Shaughnessy. Sisters of St. Joseph established 1886.

Paris—Sacred Heart of Jesus, Very Rev. M. J. Keough, V.G. Sisters of St. Joseph established 1858.

Peel—Attended from Arthur.

Preston—St. Boniface, Rev. F. Weller.

Priceville—Attended from Durham.

Proton—St. Patrick's, attended from Dundalk.

Riverdale—Attended from Teeswater.

Rockwood—Attended from Guelph.

Shelburne—Attended from Owen Sound.

Thornburg—Attended from Owen Sound.

Southampton — St. Agnes, attended from Chepstow.

St. Agatha—St. Agatha, under Resurrectionist Fathers, Revs. Hubert, Aymans. School Sisters of Notre Dame established 1871.

St. Clements—St Clement, Rev. John Gehl. School Sisters of Notre Dame established.

Teeswater—Sacred Heart, Rev. J. Corcoran.

Walkerton—Sacred Heart, Rev. J. T. Kelly. School Sisters of Notre Dame established.

Walpole—St. Anne's, attended from Cayuga.

Waterdown—St. Thomas, attended from Freelton.

Waterloo—E·ected a parish Jan 6, 1891, under Rev. Theobald Spetz, C.R., residing in Berlin. The church (Gothic) dedicated to St. Louis, is well provided for and furnished. The fine basement under the church is used for a school. There are 1½ acres of ground beautified with trees, shrubs, hedges, etc., the whole costing $11,000. There are about 40 Catholic families. Two Separate schools, established in 1891, are taught by two School Sisters of Notre Dame, who reside in the Berlin convent. About 60 pupils attend. Sodality of the B.V.M., 1892; Altar Society, 1891, Pres., Mrs. David Kurz; and C.M.B.A. Societies, 1890, are established.

Mass—Sundays, 10 a.m.; Saturdays, 7.30 a.m.; Vespers, 7 p.m.; Sunday school, 2 p.m.

Wiarton—Attended from Owen Sound.

3. DIOCESE OF LONDON.

This diocese comprises the counties of Bothwell, Elgin, Essex, Huron, Kent, Lambton, Middlesex, Norfolk, Oxford, Perth—erected Feb. 21, 1855 seat transferred to Sandwich, Feb. 2. 1859, transferred back to London, 1869. Patron of the Diocese—Our Blessed Lady in the Mystery of her Immaculate Conception.

Bishop—Rt. Rev. D. O'Connor. D.D., born at Pickering, Ont., March 28, 1841, ordained priest, Dec. 8, 1863, consecrated Bishop of London, Oct. 19, 1890.

Bishop's Council—Dean Murphy, Dean Wagner, Revs. Jos. Bayard, E. B. Kilroy, D.D., D. Cushing, C.S.B.

Catholic population, 60,000; Clergy, secular 56, regular 15; College, 1; Convents, 12; Hospitals, asylums, 4; Parishes, 41; Separate schools in nearly every parish.

PARISHES.

City of London—ST. PETER'S CATHEDRAL—Revs. M. J. Tiernan, M. McCormack, T. Noonan, N. Gahan, J. Tobin.

ST. MARY'S Church, Hill street, attended from Cathedral.

Convent and Academy of the Ladi-s of the Sacred Heart, established 1852, Madame Foley, Superior. Orphan Asylum and Hospital are conducted by the Sisters of St. Joseph, Mother Ignatia, Superior.

Aldboro—Attended from St. Thomas.

Alvinston—Attended from St. Thomas.

Amherstburg—In charge of the Basilian Fathers : Rev. P. Ryan, C.S.B., Rev. L. Renaud, C.S.B.

Ashfield (Kingsbridge P.O.)—Rev. N. Dixon.

Belle River—Rev. J. B. E. Meunier.

Biddulph (Lucan P.O.)—Rev. John Connolly.

Big Point—Rev. C. Parent.

Blenheim—Attended from Chatham.

Blythe—Attended from Wawanosh.

Bothwell—Rev. M. Cummins, new church recently opened.

Brussels—Attended from Seaforth.

Canard River—Situate six miles from Amherstburg Station and ten miles from Windsor, reached by stage, was erected a parish Jan. 20, 1864, under the present pastor, Rev. F. Maiseille. The church, a large substantial frame building with three altars richly decorated, and handsome Stations of the Cross, is dedicated to St. Joseph. There are five common Schools, in which Cathechism is taught every day. By the end of 1894 a Convent and School will be built. There are 210 Catholic families, all French Canadians. The Societies instituted are Bona Mors, 1864 ; Young Men's Temperance Society, 1878 ; League of the Sacred Heart, for men, 1893 ; officers, J. Fayeau, L. Bondy, O. Reaume, and Apostleship of Prayer, P. Bezaire, Laframboise, Rose Drouillard.

Mass—Sundays, 10 a.m. Daily Mass, Winter, 8 ; Summer, 6.30 a.m.

Chatham—St. Joseph, in charge of the Franciscan Fathers, Rev. Paul Alf, O.S.F., Superior, Rev. Theodore Stephen, O.S.F., Rev. Leopold Osterman, O.S.F., and two lay brothers. Ursuline Nuns have a boarding school and select day school, established 1860, Mother Mary Berchmans, Superior. St. Joseph's Hospital, under the Sisters of St. Joseph, established 1890.

Clinton—See Goderich.

Corunna—Situate on the Erie and Huron R. R., six miles from Sarnia, was erected a parish in 1848, with Rev. D. Duranquet, S.J., first parish priest. The present pastor, Rev. J. G. Mugan, appointed Dec., 1889, is the twenty first incumbent. Of these Rev. Michael Moncoq was drowned Dec. 24, 1855, when crossing the St. Clair River to attend a sick call. The present church, St. Joseph's, capacity 1,200, was erected in 1862, by Rev. B. Boubat, renewed and finished in 1882 by Father Ronan. Bell, 1112 lbs., placed in tower in 1891 by Father Mugan. The Separate school, established in 1865, pupils 39, taught by lay teacher. *Courtright*, church erected by Father McGee in 1888, is attended three times a month.

Mass—Sundays, 10 a.m. Daily Mass, 7.30 a.m.

Courtright—See Corunna.

Dover South—Rev. P. Andrieux.

Dresden—Attended from Wallaceburg.

Dublin—Rev. J. Murphy, Dean; Rev. J. A. Kealy.

Dunwich—Attended from St. Thomas.

Essex—Attended from Maidstone.

Fletcher—St. Patrick, Rev. P. McCabe.

Forest—Attended from Parkhill.

French Settlement (Drysdale P.O.)—Rev. J. C. Courtois.

Goderich—Terminus of the Buffalo and Goderich division of G.T.R., was attended in 1843 by Father Schneider, who ministered also to Stratford, Irishtown and the French Settlement. In 1868 Rev. B. Bombat, followed by Revs. Fathers O'Shea, Walters and West, the present pastor. The church, which the congregation hope soon to replace with a new one, is dedicated to St. Peter, and seats 400. *Clinton* is attended from this parish. The Sisters of St. Joseph are established in Goderich, Superior, Mother Angela, and teach the Separate school, which numbers 75 pupils. The C.M.B.A., the Literary and Total Abstinence Society, League of the Sacred Heart and Sodality of the B.V.M. are the societies.

Ingersoll—Rev. J. P. Molphy. Convent and Select school, Sisters of St. Joseph.

Irishtown—Dublin P.O., which see.

Kinkora—Rev. John O'Neill.

Komoka—Attended from London.

La Salette—Rev. P. Corcoran.

Leamington—Attended from Woodslee.

Listowel—Attended from Stratford.

Logan—Attended from Kinkora.

Lucan—Rev. J. Connolly.

Maidstone—Rev. C. E. McGee.
McGilvray—Attended from Mount Carmel.
McGregor—Rev. A. Bechard.
Metcalf—Attended from Strathroy.
Mount Carmel—Rev. H. Traher.
Mount Brydges—Attended from Strathroy.
Norwich—Attended from Woodstock.
Oil Springs—See Wyoming.
Otterville—Attended from Windham.
Oxford East—Attended from Woodstock.
Paincourt (Dover South P.O.)—Rev. P. Andrieux.
Parkhill—Rev. D. A. McRae, Rev. D. Foster.
Petrolia—See Wyoming.
Port Burwell—Attended from Simcoe.
Port Dover—Attended from Simcoe.
Port Lambton—Rev. J. Aylward.
Port Ryerse—Attended from La Salette.
Port Stanley—Attended from St. Thomas.
Princeton—Attended from Woodstock.
Raleigh—Attended from Fletcher.
Ridgetown—Attended from Fletcher (St. Patrick's).
Ruscom River—Rev. A. Lorion.
Sandwich—In charge of Basilian Fathers, Very Rev. D. Cushing, Superior. Basilian Fathers conduct Assumption College, founded 1870.
Sarnia—Was erected a parish in July, 1856, when Father Kirwan was appointed pastor and took up his residence here. Previous to this it had been attended by Father Fluet of Sandwich, Father Fernet of Raleigh and Father Moncoq who was mentioned in the sketch of Corunna as having been drowned on his return from a sick call that had taken him to Algomac, Mich. Father Kirwan was succeeded in 1864 by the Rev. E. B. Kilroy who established the Separate school which is now taught by three Sisters of the Holy Names of Jesus and Mary and one lay teacher. The pupils number 220 In 1860 Rev. R. Beausang took charge, followed in 1874 by Rev. B. Boubat. In 1877 the present pastor, Rev. Joseph Bayard took charge. A handsome Gothic church, seating 1,000, a fine school house and the parochial residence have been built by him. The Sisters of the Holy Names of Jesus and Mary, established 1866, have boarding and select day school, Superior, Rev. Sr. M. Annunciation. There are 230 Catholic families. The Apostleship of Prayer, 1877, and the Sodality of the B. V. Mary are established.
Mass—Sundays, 8.30 and 10.30. a.m.; Vespers, 7 p.m. in Summer and 4 p.m. in Winter.
Seaforth—Rev. J. Kennedy.
Simcoe—Rev. D. P. McMenamin.
Sombra—Attended from Lambton.
St. Augustine—Rev. T. Quigley.
St. Joseph—See Canard River.
St. Mary's—Rev. P. Brennan.
St. Peter—Attended from Big Point.
St. Thomas—Rev. W. Flannery, D.D., P. Quinlan. Sisters of St. Joseph have free and select Schools.
Stony Point—Rev. N. D. St. Cyr.
Stratford—Rev. E. B. Kilroy, D.D., Rev. D. Downey. Ladies of Loretto have boarding and select school in their fine Convent.
Strathroy—Rev. A. J. McKeon.
Tecumseh—St. Anne, Rev. A. P. Villeneuve.
Thamesville—Attended from Chatham.
Tilsonburg—Attended from La Salette.
Tilbury Centre—Rev. P. Langlois.
Vienna—Attended from La Salette.
Walkerville—Rev. L. Beaudoin.

Wallaceburg and Dresden—Rev. J. Ronan.
Wardsville—Attended from Chatham.
Warwick—Attended from Strathroy.
Watford—Attended from Strathroy.
Wawanosh (St. Augustine P.O.)—Rev. T. Quigley.
Windsor—Rev. A. J. Loiselle, Rev. J. Scanlan, Dean Wagner, T. Valentine.
Wingham—Attended from Wawanosh.
West Lorne—Rev. P. Quinlan.
Woodslee—Rev. E. Hodgkinson.
Woodstock—Rev. M. J. Brady.
Wyoming—On the G. T. R. and M. C. R.; was erected a parish in 1867 ; Rev. P. J. Gnam is the present parish priest. Former parish priests are : Fathers Japes, Darragh, Murphy, Ansbro, McCauley.
From Wyoming Petrolia is attended every second Sunday, Oil Springs every fifth Sunday. Magnificent brick churches have been recently built in Wyoming and Petrolia under the present pastor, and the Oil Springs church tastefully remodelled. There are about 35 Catholic families in Wyoming, 75 in Petrolia and 15 in Oil Springs. There is a branch of the C.M.B.A. in Petrolia, also Ladies of Honor Society, 1893, and Sodality of the B.V.M., 1893. Miss Ella Nash is president of the Sodality of the B.V.M., Miss McConnell vice-president, Miss M. Gleason secretary and Miss M. Kelly treasurer.
Mass—Sundays, at 10.30 and 8 a.m. alternately ; Vespers, 7.30 p.m.; daily Mass, 7.30.
Zurich—Attended from French Settlement.

II. PROVINCE OF OTTAWA.

1. Ottawa. 2. Pontiac (Vicariate Apostolic).

1. DIOCESE OF OTTAWA (*Metropolitan See*).

This Diocese, erected 1847, was made the Metropolitan of the Province of Ottawa May 10th, 1887, embraces the Counties of Carleton, Lanark, Prescott and Russell in Ontario, with Agenteuil, Ottawa, Terrebonne and Montcalm in Quebec.

Archbishop—Most Rev. Joseph Thomas Duhamel, D.D., born at Contrecœur Nov. 6th, 1841 ; ordained priest Dec. 19th, 1863 ; consecrated Bishop of Ottawa 28th October, 1874 ; appointed Archbishop of Ottawa June 3, 1886.

Vicar-General—Very Rev. Mgr. J. O. Routhier.
Chancellor—Very Rev. P. McCarthy ; Vice-Chancellor, Dr. J. C. W. Deguire.
Basilica Chapter — Very Rev, Mgr. J. O. Routhier, Archpriest; Very Rev. L. N. Campeau, Archdeacon ; Very Rev. G. Bouillon, Primicerius.
Canons—Very Rev. J. Michel, Very Rev. S. Philip, Very Rev. P. Belanger, Very Rev. D. F. Foley, Very Rev. J. A. Plantin, Very Rev. P. McCarthy.

Catholic population, 117,000 ; Clergy, secular 88, regular 67 ; University, 1 ; Colleges, Convents, 19 : Churches and Chapels, 104 ; Hospitals, Orphanages, etc., 9,

PARISHES IN OTTAWA.

City of Ottawa — In the City of Ottawa, besides the Basilica, there are the parishes of St. Joseph, St. Patrick, St. Anne, St. Jean Baptiste, St. Francois d'Assise, Sacred Heart, St. Bridget and Our Lady of Good Counsel, also many chapels attached to the different religious houses in the city.

The University of Ottawa—Established in 1848, by the Right Rev. J. E. Guigues, O.M.I., D.D., under the care of Rev. Father Tabaret, O.M.I., D.D. Originally incorporated under the title of "College of Bytown," received in 1866 the title of "College of Ottawa," together with power of conferring University degrees—in 1889 by a brief of the Sovereign Pontiff Leo XIII., was raised to the rank of a Catholic University, with all the privileges conferred on such Universities. Apostolic Chancellor, Most Rev. J. T. Duhamel; Rector, Very Rev. J. M. McGuckin, O.M.I.. D.D.; Vice Rector and Professor of Discipline, Rev. A. Antoine, O.M.I., Ph.D.; Director of Theologians, Rev. J. Mangin, O.M.L. D.D.; Secretary, Rev. B. A. Constantineau, O.M.I., M.A.; Prefect of Studies, Rev. N. Nelles, O.M.I.. D.D.; Treasurer, Rev. A. Martin, O.M.I.; Rev. Z. Vaillancourt, O.M.I., Rev. A. Duhaut, O.M.I., Rev. G. Gauvreau, O.M.I., Rev. J. McRory, O.M.I., Rev. E. Jeannotte, O.M.I., Rev. W. Howe, O.M.I., Rev. L. Laganiere, O.M.I., Rev. O. Lambert, O.M.I.. Rev. A. Lajeunnesse, O.M.I., L. Ph., Rev. M. F. Fitzpatrick, B.A., Rev. E. David, O. M.I., Rev. P. Chaborel, O.M.I., Rev. J. Duffy, O.M.I., Rev. A. Newman, B.A., H. Glassmacher, M.A., LL.D., W. A. Herckeurath, M.A., C.E., J. A. Gillis, B.A., Rev. C. Gohist, O.M.I., D.D., Ph.D.. Rev. O. Valeuce, O.M.I., Ph.L., Rev. W. Murphy, O.M.I., M.A., Rev. Wm. Patton, O.M.I..L.Th., Rev. J. Peruisset, O.M.I., Rev. H. Gervais, O.M.I.. M.A., Rev. J. M. Duvic, O.M.I., D.D., Rev. M. Froc, O.M.I., D.D., Rev. J. A. Poli, O.M.I., D.D., Rev. H. Lacoste, O.M.I., D.D., Ph.D., Rev. W. Charlebois, O.M.I., Rev. J. M. Contlee, O.M.I.

Other houses of the Oblate Fathers in Ottawa are, Juniorate of the Sacred Heart, 195 Wilbrod street, Rev. M. E. Harnois, O.M.I., Director, and the Scholasticate, East Ottawa, Rev. J. Duvic, D.D., O.M.I., Superior.

Schools are established in every parish; the boys are taught by the Christian Brothers and the girls, by the Grey Nuns. There are High schools for advanced pupils. The Mother house of the Grey Nuns of the Cross, cor. of Sussex and Water sts., was founded Feb. 20, 1845, by Rev. Mother E. Bruyere, in Ottawa, Superior General, Mother Demers. Branch convents are in nearly every parish. Bethlehem Asylum, Superior, Rev. Sr. St. Olivier, for foundlings; General Hospital, Rev. Sr. M. Phelan; St. Joseph's Orphanage, Superior, Rev. Sr. St. Cecile; St. Patrick's Orphanage, Superior, Rev. Sr. Howley, and St. Charles Asylums, for the poor and infirm. Boarding and select school of Notre Dame du Sacre Cœur are in charge of these Nuns. The Sisters of Our Lady of Charity of the Refuge (Good Shepherd) Prioress Very Honored Mother Mary of St. Bernard Kehoe have two houses. The Sisters of Mercy, engaged in the same work, have also a house. Sisters of the Congregation of Notre Dame have boarding and select schools. The Sisters of the Precious Blood have a monastery in Ottawa. The Capuchin Fathers have charge of the parish of St. Francis of Assissi.

CATHEDRAL NOTRE DAME—Under the patronage of the Immaculate Conception—Basilica—By a special favor of Leo XIII. the Basilica of Ottawa is affiliated to that of St. Mary Major of Rome, with communication of indulgences, spiritual favors and privileges granted by the Sovereign Pontiffs to the Very Holy Patriarchal Liberian Basilica.

The mission of Bytown was formed in 1827, and was attended by Father Angus Macdonell. A small wooden chapel was erected on the site of the present Basilica. In 1831 succeeded Father Cullen; 1835, Very Rev. W. P. Macdonald; 1839, Father Cannon, who built the Basilica. In 1848 the first Bishop of the Diocese of Ottawa, Right Rev. Joseph Eugene Bruno Guigues, D.D., took up his residence in Ottawa and was succeeded in 1874 by the Right Rev. J. T. Duhamel, D.D., who in 1886 became the first Archbishop of Ottawa. Mgr. J. O. Routhier, V.G., the parish priest since 1883, succeeded Rev. D. Dandurand, who had filled the position for 30 years. The magnificent Basilica is in Gothic style, 200 feet by 75 feet. The sanctuary is one of the richest in Canada. There is a fine electric organ. The schools of this parish are taught, the boys numbering 550, by 12 Christian Brothers in the large school La Salle; the girls, 475, of Notre Dame school, by nine Grey Nuns. There is a high school for girls, with 120 pupils, taught by five teachers in the mother house. The number of Catholic families in the parish, 1,290. Of societies there are the Immaculate Conception for Men, Pres., Jos. Vincent: St. Ann, for married women, Pres., Mrs. Laverdure; Sodality of the Immaculate Conception, for young ladies, Pres., Miss Josephine Asselin; and League of the Sacred Heart of Jesus.

Mass—Sundays, 6.30, 8 and 10 a.m.; Vespers, 3 p.m. from October to April, and 7 p.m. from May to September inclusive; daily Mass, 6.30 and 7.30 a.m.

ST. JOSEPH'S—Erected a parish in 1857, under Rev. A. Trudeau succeeded by Revs. J. Corbett, O.M.I., M. Guillard, O.M.I. and A. Paillier, O.M.I., the present parish priest. The church is built in Greek style and seats 1,200 persons. The Societies of St. Vincent de Paul, 1857, President, M. M. Clancy; Living Rosary, 1859, President, Mrs. M. Kehoe, and League of the Sacred Heart, 1892, President Mrs. P. Harty, are established; number of Catholic families, 320. Two Separate schools are taught by three lay teachers and three Grey Nuns; pupils, 200.

Mass—Sundays, 6.15, 8 and 10.30 a.m.; Vespers, 7 p.m.; Daily Masses, 6, 6 30 and 7.30 a.m.

SACRED HEART—In 1888 the construction of this church was begun by the French members of St. Joseph's church. The basement served the purposes of a church up to 1893, when the upper portion was used for the first time. Though not yet finished—the front wall and tower are yet to be done—it has an imposing appearance. It is of Romano Byzantine style of architecture, is 188 feet by 64, with a transept 124 feet, in each end of which is a large circular window 15 feet in diameter. The pinnacle on the back wall is 102 feet high, and the tower, when completed, will be 220 feet in height. It is in charge of the Oblate Fathers. The church was begun by Father Gendreau, O.M.I., continued by Father Harnois, O.M.I., and is nearing completion under Father Valiquette, O.M.I., the present pastor of the Sacred Heart parish. In the parish are societies of St. Vincent de Paul, the Catholic Order of Foresters, a society for married women and one for young girls under the patronage of Our Lady Mary Immaculate. There are 270 Catholic families. Separate school, 1890, taught by two Christian Brothers; pupils, 60.

Alfred—Situate 6 miles from the nearest C.P. Ry. Station, was erected a parish in October, 1871. The first resident priest, Rev. L. A. La Voie, was succeeded in 1890 by Rev. F. Lombard, the present pastor. The church built in Roman style, is dedicated to St. Victor and seats 800. In the Separate Schools are about 300 pupils, taught by 8 lay teachers. The Catholic families number 323.

Mass—Sundays, Summer, 9.30 a.m. ; Winter, 10 a.m. Vespers, 2 p.m.

Almonte—Situate 35 miles from Ottawa, on the main line of C P.R., was erected a parish in July, 1872, with Rev. R., Faure first parish priest, succeeded by Revs. E. J. J. Stinson, 1875 ; J. F. Coffey, 1878 ; B. Casey, 1881, and D. F. Foley, the present pastor, 1882. As a mission Almonte existed from 1823. The first church, St. Mary's, built in 1842, was burned in 1868, re-built larger in Gothic style in the following year. It was enlarged and a sanctuary added in 1875. A peal of three bells chimes from the church tower. The small mission of *Darling* is attended from this parish. There are about 200 Catholic families in the parish and mission. A Separate School was opened in 1873, which now employs 3 lay teachers. The St. Vincent de Paul Society, 1876, the Father Matthew Temperance Association, 1873, the Catholic Truth Society, 1 92, the C. M. B. A., 1884, Rosary Society, Sodality of the B. V. M. and Society of St. Francis of Sales, all flourish in Almonte.

Mass—Sundays, 10.30 a.m.; Vespers, 7 p.m.; daily Mass, 7.30 a.m.

Billiug's Bridge—See Gateville.

Casselman—St. Euphemie, Revs. A. Brausoleil, S. Desjardins.

Clarence Creek—St. Felicite, Revs. Thos. Caron, B. Ducharme.

Curran—Reached by stage, being nine miles from the railway station ; was erected a parish January 4, 1839. Rev. P. Lefaivre was the first missionary priest, assisted in his missions by Rev. C. Cassidy. In March, 1841, succeeded Rev. Wm. Dolan, assisted, from May 31st, 1842 to Oct. 6th, by Rev. C. Cassidy. Rev. P. Lefaivre returned in Dec., 1843 and in July, 1844, P. McEvoy succeeded. On the 21st Jan., 1845, Rev. M. Monaghan became the fi.st resident priest, then followed, in 1846, Revs. John Farrell, in 1848, A. Macdonell, in 1849, P. McGoery, in 1853, T. O'Boyle, in 1855, L. Almiras who was helped by Rev. J. Sterkendries and Rev. F. Hund. In 1859 succeeded P. Bertrand, in 1873 Rev. A. Chaine, in 1875 Rev.C. Gay, in 1880 Rev. F. Lombard, in 1890 the present pastor, Rev. Jas. Pilon. The church, Byzantine in style, is under the invocation of St. Luke. A fine church is in course of construction. There are 263 Catholic families. The Separate schools, established in 1875, are taught by lay teachers.

Mass—Sundays, 7 and 10 a.m.; Vespers, 3 p.m.; Daily Mass, 7 a.m.; prayer, 7 p.m.

Cyrville—Our Lady of Lourdes, Revs. J. B. Bridonneau, H. Richard, P. Audrand, Scholastic of the Rev. Fathers of the Congregation of Mary. Convent of Soeurs de la Sagesse.

Dawson—St. John Evangelist, Rev. A. Contantineau.

Embrun—Six miles from South Indian, Can. A. Ry., reached by stage, was erected a parish Nov. 14, 1858, first priest, Rev. P. Bertrand, subsequent priests, R. R, G. O. Ebrard, O. J. Boucher, J. P. Maurel, F. Lombard, P. Aguel, L. J. Francoeur, J. J. Guay, C. Guillaume and present pastor, Rev. A. Pollion. The church is styled St. Jacques d'Embrun, Gothic, seats 200. There are 8 R. C. Separate Schools, founded since 1886, taught by 2 Grey Nuns and 7 lay teachers. About 425 Catholic families are in the parish. The Societies are : League of the Sacred Heart, established 1886, President, J. Lalonde ; So-

dality of St. Francis of Sales, President, Rev. A. Philion, established Jan., 1886, Sodality of St. Ann, Pres., Mrs. O. Emard, established 1885, Children of Mary, Pres., Miss Z. Morion, established 1885. A new church, which will be one of the finest in the diocese, is about to be built.

Mass—Sundays, 6 and 10 a.m. Vespers, 4 p.m, Daily Mass, 6 and 7 a.m.

Fallowfield—Six miles from the nearest Railway Station, Stittaville, on the C. P. Ry., was a mission from about 1837. For forty years was attended from Richmond by Father O'Connel. In November of 1884 it was erected a parish under Rev. E. J. J. Stenson, who in January, 1887, was succeeded by Rev. J. A. Sloan, the present parish priest. The Church of St. Patrick, Fallowfield, was renovated two years ago, the woodwork painted inside and outside, but it is too small for the congregation, who hope in the near future to put up a substantial stone structure. The grounds about the church and presbytery have been beautifully laid out and embellished with trees, shrubs and flowers. There are 180 Catholic families. *March* (St. Isidore), is attended on the last Sunday of every month. The Separate School, established about 30 years, has 60 pupils, with 1 lay teacher. The Society of St. Francis de Sales was established in Nov., 1885.

Mass—Sundays, 10.30 a. m. Vespers, 4 p. m. Daily Mass, 7.30 a.m.

Fitzroy—St. Michael, attended from Pakenham.

Fourniervillc—St Bernard, 1889, Rev. E. Dacier.

Gateville—St. Thomas Aquinas, Rev. M. Boisseau.

Gloucester (South)—Visitation of B.V.M., Rev. J. McGuire.

Goulbourne—See Richmond.

Hawkesbury Mills—St. Alphonsus Liguori, Rev. S. Philip ; Grey Nuns of Ottawa.

Lefaivre—St. Thomas. Rev. P. Bedard.

L'Original—St. Jean Baptiste, Rev. O. Berube.

Manotic—St. Bridget, attended from Dawson.

March—See Fallowfield.

Metcalf—St. Catharine, attended from Gloucester South.

Notre Dame de Lourdes—Revs. T. Joubert, S.M., J. Pineau, S.M.

Orleans—St. Joseph, Very Rev. L. A. Lavoie ; Grey Nuns, 1869.

Pakenham—St. Peter Celestine, Rev. D. Lavin.

Plantagenet—St. Paul, Rev. E. C. Croteau.

Richmond—Erected a parish about the year 1830, with the Rev. Father Haran the first priest. He was succeeded by Rev. Terence Smith, 1833 ; Rev. P. O'Connell in 1846 ; Rev. J. C. Dunn, 1890, present incumbent. The church is under the invocation of St. Philip, and capable of seating 510. There are 160 Catholic families. A fine presbytery has recently been erected. A mission at *Goulbourne* (St. Sylvester church) is attended from Richmond every second Sunday. The church at Richmond is seven miles from the station.

Mass—Sundays, 10.30 a.m.; daily mass, 7.30 a.m.

Rockland—Is reached at present by small boat ; a branch of Ca. At. will be completed by February, 1895 ; erected a parish June 5th, 1887. Rev. Thomas Caron, of Clarence Creek parish, founded this mission, Rev. E. Barry, curate, ministering to its needs. Rev. P. Grondin succeeded in October, 1887—September, 1888. In December, 1888, Rev. H. M. Clement, O.M.I., assisted Father Caron. On 31st May, 1889, Rev. P. S. Hudon succeeded as resident parish priest. The church, style Roman, is dedicated to the Holy Trinity.

Including galleries, there are 203 pews. There are 312 Catholic families. Separate school, established 1890, is taught by four lay teachers, with an attendance of 260 pupils. Congregation of St. Ann, Sodality of B.V.M., League of the Sacred Heart, Holy Rosary and Holy Family Societies are established, also St. Jean Baptiste, Pres. Joseph Martel, 1st Vice-Pres. Felix Godin, 2nd Vice-Pres. Andre Patrice, Sec. Geo. Bechard. Treas., Nap. Detraitre, Commissary-Orderer, Jules Marie.

Mass—Sundays, from Easter to All Saints' day, 9.30 a.m., rest of the year at 10 a.m.; Vespers at 2.30 p.m.

St. Albert of Cambridge—Rev. A. Gauthier.

St. Eugene—Ten miles from Vankleek Hill, Ont. (Can. At. railway), and 10 miles from Rigaud, P.Q. (C.P.R.), was erected a parish in 1854. First parish priest, Rev. J. J. Collins, succeeded by the present Archbishop of Ottawa, Most Rev. J. T. Duhamel, D.D., who was followed by Rev. F. Towner, present incumbent, with Rev. Eugene Groulx, O.M.I., assistant. The church, St. Eugene, is Gothic, and can seat 600 persons. St. Joachim (Chute a Blondeau P.O.), seven miles distant, is attended every Sunday. There is a fine large new church, dedicated in 1892, Corinthian style, prettily situated on the high bank of the Ottawa river; the steeple can be seen from a long distance. A parish priest has been promised this congregation by next fall. Four Separate schools, established in 1874, with lay teachers, number 240 children. Societies instituted are: St. Francis of Sales, 1880; Sacred Heart of Jesus, 1888; Most Holy Rosary, 1890; Holy Family, 1892. There are 284 Catholic families.

Mass—Sundays, 10 a.m.; Vespers, 3 p.m.; daily Mass, 6.30 and 7.30 a.m.

Ste. Anne de Prescott—Rev. J. E. Coderre.

Ste. Isidore de Prescott—Rev. O. Boulet.

St. Joachim—See St. Eugene.

Sarsfield—St. Hugues, Rev. O. Cousineau.

South Indian—St. Viator, attended from Casselman.

The Brook—Sacred Heart of Jesus, Rev.C. Larose.

Vankleek Hill—On the Can. At. railway, erected a parish August, 1878, with Rev. F. Foley first parish priest, succeeded by Revs. Ph. Brady and P. Dusserre Telmon, present parish priest. The church, dedicated to St. Gregory Naz., is built of stone, with transept and galleries. The Separate school, established in 1886, is taught by eight teachers. Sisters of St. Mary; pupils, 200. The societies are: The S. H. Temperance Society, 1891, and the Catholic Order of Foresters, 1894, officers, Z. Labrosse, J. McMaster, P. Paquette, H. Hurley.

Mass—Sundays, 10 a.m.; Vespers, 4 p.m.; daily Mass, 7 a.m.

Wendover—St. Benoit Joseph, Rev. O. Ferron.

West Huntley—St. Michael, Rev. P. Corkery.

2. VICARIATE APOSTOLIC OF PONTIAC.

This Vicariate, erected by His Holiness Pope Leo XIII. July 11th, 1882, includes the Counties of North and South Renfrew and Pontiac, the territory between 88° and 72°; the height of land at the South, the Hudson Bay, James Bay and the great Whale River at the north.

Vicar Apostolic—Right Rev Narcisse Zephirin Lorrain, born June 13th, 1842 at. St. Martin; ordained priest Aug. 4th, 1867; Vicar-General of Montreal Diocese Aug. 3rd, 1880; consecrated titular Bishop of Cythera, Sept. 21st, 1882, in Notre Dame church, Montreal; residence, Pembroke. Secretary, Rev. John P. Donovan.

Catholic population, 33,000; Priests, 33; Churches, 29; Chapels, 28; Hospitals, 3; Parishes, 21.

PARISHES IN ONTARIO.

Pembroke—Erected a parish in 1856, under Rev. Jno. Gillie, succeeded in 1868 by Rev. O. Boucher, in 1873, S. Jouvent; 1874, Reine Faure. In 1882 was chosen as residence of the Vicar Apostolic of Pontiac, Right Rev. N. Z. Lorrain. Rev. J. P. Donovan and Rev. P. D. Filion are attached to the church, which is entitled St. Columba's Church, style Gothic, seating capacity 1,000. Chalk River and Point Alexander are attended from Pembroke once a month. Two Separate Schools, established in 1864, are taught, the one for girls, by 4 Grey Nuns of the Cross, the other for boys by 5 lay teachers. Pupils number 425. There is also the Grey Nuns Academy with 75 pupils, Sister Nativity, Superior. A general hospital is conducted by the Grey Nuns, Sister Saint Ann, Superior, with 5 Sisters and 5 servants, average number of patients, 18; receives a grant from Government and is supported by voluntary contributions. There are 625 Catholic families. Societies established are: St. Vincent de Paul, 1864, Pres., M. Howe; Vice-Pres., A. J. Fortier; Treas., Jas. Thibeaudeau; Sec., Angus Meehan; St. Zita's, 1884; Holy Rosary, 1888.

Mass—Sundays, 8 and 10 a. m. Vespers, 7 p. m. Daily Mass, 6.15 and 7 a.m.

Arnprior—St Chrysostom, Rev. A. M. Chaine.

Brudenell (Opeongo Road)—St. Mary, Rev. J. McCormac.

Chalk River—See Pembroke.

Cobden—Sacred Heart of Jesus, attended from Osceola.

Deux Rivieres—Attended from Mattawan.

Douglas—St. Michael, Rev. H. S. Marion.

Eganville—St. James, Revs. P. S Dowdall, H. Martel; Grey Nuns of the Cross from Ottawa, Superior, Rev. Sr. St. Thomas.

Golden Lake—Attended from Mattawan and Eganville.

Gower Point—On Ottawa River, vulgarly called La Passe, three miles from Pop. Pac. Junction R. R. (Quebec) and eighteen miles from Cobden on C. P. R. with missions at Fort Coulonge (Q.) and Bristanca (Q.) erected a parish in 1858 under Rev. P. DeSaunhac, succeeded by Revs. J. Ginguet, O. Berube, E. Rochon, G. Motte and 1. Napoleon LeMoyne, present pastor. Church, dedicated to Our Lady of Mount Carmel, Gothic, seats 225 people.

Mass—Sundays, 10 a.m.; Vespers, 7 p.m.; Daily Mass, 7 a.m.

Griffith—Our Lady of the Holy Rosary, attended from Mount S. Patrick.

Hagarty (Emmet)—St. Stanislaus.

Mattawan—House of the Oblate Fathers, St. Ann, Rev. P. E. Gendreau, Superior, P Simonet, O. M.I.; Rev. A. Berneche, O.M.I.; Grey Nuns of the Cross from Ottawa, Superior, Rev. Sr. St. Basil, conduct hospital and parish school.

Mackay Station—Attended from Mattawan.

Maynooth—St. Ignatius, Rev. Jos. Barrette.

Mount St. Patrick—Rev. R. J. McEachen.

Nosbonsing Lake—On the C. P. Railway, erected a parish April 4th, 1886, under present pastor Rev.

Thos. E. Gagnon, comprising four townships, with population of 324 Catholic families. The church. St. Philomena, is three-quarters of a mile from the station, seats 350 people. The three missions, *St. Thomas, Sacred Heart* and *St. Lewis*, are attended once a month. The five Roman Catholic Separate schools are taught by five lay teachers and number 170 pupils. Another school, 35x50, will soon be added. The Societies established are, League of the Sacred Heart, Holy Rosary and Ladies of St. Ann, Pres., of the last-named, Mrs. Luc Lemieux.

Mass—Sundays, 10.15 a.m.; Vespers, 3 p.m.; Daily Mass, 8 a.m.

Osceola—St. Pius, Rev. F. M. Devine.

Point Alexander—See Pembroke.

Renfrew — St. Francis Xavier, Rev. P. T. Ryan. Sisters of the Holy Cross and Seven Dolours, also Christian Brothers.

Renton—Attended from Mattawan.

Rockliffe—Attended from Mattawan.

Round Lake—Attended from Eganville.

Sand Point—St. Alexander, attended from Arnprior.

Springtown — St. Raphael, attended from Renfrew.

Sebastopol — Attended from Brudenell.

III. PROVINCE OF KINGSTON.

1. Kingston ; 2. Peterborough ; 3. Alexandria.

1. Diocese of Kingston (Metropolitan See).

This Diocese, established Jan. 27, 1826, constituted a Metropolitan See Dec. 28, 1880, comprises the territory from the western boundary of Hastings county. This includes the counties of Addington, Dundas, Frontenac, Grenville, Hastings, Lanark, Leeds, Lennox and Prince Edward.

Archbishop—Most Rev. James Vincent Cleary, D.D., born Sept. 18, 1828, at Dungarvon, Waterford county, Ireland; ordained priest Sept. 20, 1851 ; consecrated at Rome Nov. 21, 1880 ; promoted to Archiepiscopal dignity, Dec. 28, 1889. Secretary, Ven. Archdeacon Kelly ; Vicar-Generals, Rt. Rev. Mgr. Jas. Farrelly and Very Rev. C. H. Gauthier ; Archdeacon, Ven. Thos. Kelly ; Vicars Forane, Very Rev. J. S. O'Connor, Very Rev. John Masterson, Very Rev. C. B. Murray.

Catholic population, 65,500 ; Priests, 40 ; Convents, 18 ; Hospitals and Orphanages, 4 ; Churches or chapels, 66 ; Parishes, 80.

City of Kingston—CATHEDRAL—St. Mary Immaculate, Most Rev. J. V. Cleary, D.D., Ven. Archdeacon Thos. Kelly, Revs. J.V. Neville, J. P. Kehoe, J. Collins and A. Carson. Church of the Good Thief, in suburbs, attended by Rev. J. V. Neville. Chapel of St. James (contiguous to Cathedral), Chapels at Hotel Dieu and House of Providence, Chapels for Catholic worship exclusively in the Penitentiary, attended by Rev. J. V. Neville ; and in Rockwood Asylum, attended by Rev. J. P. Kehoe. The Sisters of Notre Dame (Congregation), Superior, Rev. Sister St. Wilfrid, established 1841, teach Boarding and Select schools ; Hospital Sisters of St. Joseph, established 1845, have charge of Hospital and Female Orphanage, Superior, Rev. Sister Hopkins ; Sisters of Charity (Providence), founded by Bishop Horan in 1860, conduct the House of Providence for the sick and infirm, also a male orphanage.

RT. REV. N. Z. LORRAIN, D.D.

Amherst Island — St. Bartholomew's, attended from Loborough.

Ardoch—St. Kilian's, attended from Bedford.

Athens—St. Denis, attended from Yonge.

Bathurst—St. Vincent's, attended from Burgess.

Bath—St. Linus', attended from Loborough.

Bedford—Sacred Heart of Jesus, attended from Sharbot Lake.

Belleville—St. Michael's, Rt. Rev. Mgr. James Farrelly, Rev. J. O'Brien. Ladies of Loretto conduct boarding and day school.

Blessington (Read P.O.) St. Charles Borromeo, Rev. Thos. McCarthy.

Brewer's Mills — St. Barnaby's, Rev. Thos Carey.

Brockville—St. Francis Xavier, Very Rev. C. H. Gauthier, V.G., Sisters of Notre Dame (Congregation) 1878, Superior, Sr. St. Eugenie ; Hospital of St. Vincent de Paul conducted by Sisters of Charity (Providence).

Burgess (Stanleyville P.O.)—St. Bridget's, Rev. T. P. O'Connor.

Camden — St. Anthony of Padua, Rev. P. J. Hartigan.

Cardinal—Sacred Heart of Jesus, attended from Prescott.

Carleton Place—St. Mary de Mercedes, Rev. M. O'Rourke.

Chesterville—St. Mary's, Very Rev. Dean O'Connor.

Chippewa—Annunciation, attended from Camden. **Cushendall**—Holy Name, attended from Kingston.

Deseronto—St. Vincent de Paul, attended from Napanee.

Erinsville—Assumption of Blessed Virgin Mary, Rev. G. Cicolari.

Ferguson's Falls—St. Patrick's, attended from Carleton.

Flinton—St. John the Evangelist, attended from Erinsville.

Frankford—St. Francis Assisi, Rev. Jas. Connolly.

Gananoque—St. John Evangelist, Rev. John D. O'Gorman.

Howe Island — St. Philomena, attended from Gananoque.

Hungerford—St. Edmund, attended from Tweed.

Iroquois—St. Pius, attended from Morrisburg.

Kemptville—Exaltation of the Cross, Rev. M. Macdonald.

Kitley—St. Philip Neri, Rev. M. J. Spratt.

Lansdown—St. Patrick, attended from Gananoque.

Lob·rough—St. Patrick, Rev. C. A. McWilliams.

Macdonald's Corners—St. Columbanus, attended from Sharbot Lake.

Madoc—Sacred Heart of Mary, Rev. Thos. Davis, Rev. Thos. Murtagh.

Marmora—Sacred Heart of Jesus, attended from Madoc.

Matilda—St. Anne, attended from Morrisburg.

Merrickville—St. Anne, revs. M. C. O'Brien, J. McCarthy.

Morrisburg—St. Mary Immaculate, Rev. D. A. Twomey.

Mountain—St. Daniel, attended from Kemptville.

Napanee—St. Patrick, Rev. John T. Hogan.

Odessa—St Bridget, attended from Loborough.

Palmerston—St. Leo the Great, attended from Sharbot Lake.

Perth—St. John Baptist, R·v. C. J. Duffus. Sisters of Charity (Providence).

Phillipsville—St. Malachy, attended from Kitley.

Picton—St. Gregory the Great, R·v. J. H. McDonagh.

Prescott—St. Mark Evangelist, Very Rev. Dean Masterson.

Queensboro—St. Henry, attended from Madoc.

Read—See Blessington.

Richmond—St. John Baptist, attended from Blessington.

Rockport—St. Brendan, attended from Yonge.

Sharbot Lake—St. James Major, Rev. C. J. Killeen.

Sheffield—Attended from Erinsville.

Smith's talls—St. Francis de Sales, Rev. M. J. Stanton.

Spencerville—St. Lawrence O'Toole's, Rev. W. E. Walsh.

Sterling—St. James the Less, attended from Frankford.

Toledo—St. Columbkille's, attended from Kitley.

Trenton—St. Peter 'in Chains, Very Rev. Dean Murray.

Trevelyan—See Yonge.

Throoptown—St. Michael, attended from Spencerville.

Tweed—St. Carthagh's, Rev. John Fleming.

Tyendinaga—Holy Name of Mary, Rev. J. S. Quinn.

Wellington—St. Frances of Rome, attended from Picton.

Westport—St. Edward, Rev. P. A. Twohey.
Mass—Sundays, 10.30 a.m.; daily Mass, 7 a.m.

Winchester—St. Columban, attended from Chesterville.

Wolfe Island—Sacred Heart of Mary, Rev. T. J. Spratt.

Yonge (Trevelyan P.O.)—St. James Major, Rev. J. J. Kelly.

2. DIOCESE OF PETERBORO'.

This Diocese comprises the Counties of Durham, Northumberland, Peterboro', Victoria and the Districts of Algoma, Muskoka, Parry Sound and western portion of Nipissing; erected a diocese July 11th, 1882.

Bishop—(3) Right Rev. R. A. O'Connor, born at Listowel, Ireland, in 1838; ordained priest Aug. 2nd, 1861; consecrated Bishop of Peterboro' May 1st, 1889. Vicar-Generals: Very Rev. P. D. Laurent, Very Rev. J. Brown; Sec., Rev. D. J. Scollard.

Catholic population, 36,500; Priests, secular 26, regular 20; Churches, 60; Hospitals, 2; Parishes, 25.

PARISHES.

City of Peterboro'—CATHEDRAL ST. PETER IN CHAINS—Ven. Archdeacon Casey, Rev. D. J. Scollard, Revs. T. Collins, D. O'Connell. Sisters of Congregation of Notre Dame, established 1867, teach girls' Separate schools; two other fine Separate schools in city, lay teachers: Sisters of St. Joseph, Sup. Mother Vincent, have a fine hospital.

Algoma Mills—Attended from Massey.

Alnace—St. John Evangelist, attended from North Bay.

Blind River—Attended from Wickwemikong.

Bobcaygeon—St. Joseph, attended from Fenelon Falls.

Bowmanville—St. Joseph, attended from Peterborough.

Bracebridge—St. Joseph, Revs. P. McGuire and T. Fleming.

Brighton—Holy Angels, Rev. Wm. J. McCloskey.

Bruce Mines—Attended from Garden River.

Burnley—St. Peter, Rev. J. Nolan.

Byng Inlet—In Muskoka district, two boats a week, was erected a parish in 1871, Rev. Paul Nadeau, S.J., first priest, succeeded by Rev. P. Hamel, S.J., Rev. S. Dufresne, S.J., present pastor. The church, dedicated to the Holy Family, and the presbytery were burned down in April, 1893, in a conflagration that consumed Burton's Mill, the industry of the village. The population has diminished since, but another mill is building this summer (1894) and by October, it is expected, the new church and presbytery will be completed. The priest or missionary resides in Byng Inlet at different intervals averaging one third of the year. The Catholics are mostly French Canadians; about forty-six families. *French River*, twice a month, *Collins Inlet, Grumbling Point, Kiviti Kitigaming, Kabekona, Shawanga, Parry Island* (opp. Parry Sound) *Beau Soleil Island, Christian Island* (Toronto diocese) *Cape Croker and Tangeur* (Hamilton diocese) are visited three times a year. All are Indian reserves except French River and Collins Inlet. In another year one or more schools will be established. Handsome chapels are at French River and Cape Croker.

Callender—Attended from North Bay.

Campbellford—Visitation of B. V· M., Rev. M. Connelly.

Cartier—Attended from Sudbury.

Chandos—Purification of B. V.M., attended from Peterboro'.

Chapleau—Attended from Sudbury.

Chelmsford—Attended from Sudbury.

Cobourg—Situate on main line of G.T.R., erected a parish in 1837 under Rev. A. F. Kerwan, succeeded by Revs. W. Dolan, M. Timlin and E. H. Murray, present pastor, The church, dedicated to St. Michael, seats 500. There are 200 Catholic families. A Separate school was established in 1883. Four Sisters of St. Joseph teach 150 pupils. The I.C.B.U., the C.M.B.A. and the Sodality of B.V.M. are established.

Mass—Sundays at 8 and 10 a.m.; Vespers, at 7 p.m.; Daily Mass, 7 a.m.; Benediction at Convent chapel Fridays at 5 p.m.

Cockburn Island—Attended from Wickwemikong.

Cook's Mills—Attended from Massey.

Codrington—Church of Most Holy Rosary, attended from Brighton.

Downeyville—See Emily.

Douro—St. Joseph, Rev. Wm. J. Keilty, Very Rev. J. Browne.

Emily—St. Luke, Rev. C. E. Bretherton (Downeyville P.O.)

Ennismore—St. Martin, Rev. W. J. McColl.

Fenelon Falls—St. Aloysius, Rev. T. B. O'Connell.

Fort William, *Indian Mission*—In 1849 Rev.Father Choue, S.J., came from Pigeon River, U.S.A., where he had been stationed with Father Fremiot, S.J., and Brother Depooter, S.J., and founded the present mission of Fort William. His successors were Revs. F. Fremiot, Blebuer, Duranquet, Ferard, J. Hanipaux, Gagnon, Hebert, Specht, Baudin, all Jesuit Fathers. Rev. F. Gagnieur, S.J., with Rev. Joseph Specht, S. J., and three Brothers are now in charge of the mission.

Fort William, on the C.P.R., is situate on the Kaministiquia river, which is 300 feet wide at this point. Street cars pass within seven minutes' walk of the mission. The church, which is under the invocation of the Immaculate Conception, is built of logs, clapboarded ; the exterior is neat and clean ; inside some little repairing is needed. There are seats for 300. The societies established are: Sodality of the B.V.M., Arch-Confraternity of the Sacred Heart of Jesus, Temperance Society of the S. H., 1893, and the Apostleship of Prayer, 1894. In 1869 the Daughters of Mary opened an orphan asylum and school, with Miss Martin superior, which they conducted for 18 years. The Sisters of St. Joseph are now in charge, Superior Mother Incarnation ; there are about 70 children, white and Indian. The institutio is supported but meagrely by the Government ; collections and private contributions enable the work to be carried on. A school for girls is taught by the Sisters in the Convent, some of the girls boarding in

RT. REV. R. A. O'CONNOR, D.D.

the Convent ; the few boys in the village are taught by a lay teacher.

We give the missions in Ontario attended from Fort William, with the number of Catholic families : Nepigon, 30 ; Pays Plat, 16 ; Pic, 22 ; Montizambert, 15 ; White River, 8 ; Chapleau, Michipicoten, 22 ; Aycwang, 10 ; Savanne, Nepigon Lake, 32 ; Long Lake, 51.

Beaver Bay, 5 ; Grand Marais, 22 ; Grand Portage, 27, attended from Fort William, are in the United States.

There are Separate schools at Nepigon Lake (pupils 22), Pays Plat (pupils 18), Pic (pupils 14), Nepigon, 2 schools, pupils 14. The school at Michipicoten has been closed since 1882, but will be open this year (1894) ; lay teachers are employed. In the village of Fort William there are but two unbaptized Indians, and they dare not practise their superstition openly, but around Nepigon Lake and Long Lake there are hundreds of pagans yet. Rev. Father Spetz visits all these missions once, twice, three, four times a year, and oftener when possible. Nepigon Lake, 100 miles from a railway station, is reached by water.

Fort William East—In charge of Rev. Father Arpin, S.J.

Fort William West—In charge of Rev. F. Devine, whose P.O. address is Schreiber, on C. P. Ry. (Algoma District), where he resides the greater part of the year.

French River—See Byng Inlet.

Garden River—Immaculate Heart of Mary, Revs. J. A. MacDonald, E. Caron, S.J., and V. Artus, S.J.

Goulais Bay—St. Peter, Apostle, attended from Sault Ste. Marie.

Galway—Immaculate Conception, attended from Fenelon Falls.

Grafton—St. Mary, Rev. M. Larkin.

Hastings—Our Lady of Mount Carmel, Rev. John Quirk.

Kearney—St. Patrick, attended from Bracebridge.

Keane — St. John, Evangelist, attended from Douro.

Killarney—St. Joseph, attended from Wickwemikong.

Lakefield—St. Paul, attended from Peterboro'.

Lindsay—Purification of B. V. M.. Rev. P. D. Laurent, V.G., Rev. T. F. Scanlan. Mother House and Novitiate of the Sisters of St. Joseph of Peterboro' diocese, Superior, Mother Austin, boarding and select School. The Separate Schools are taught by the Sisters and lay teachers.

Little Current—St. Vincent de Paul, attended from Wickwemikong.

Massey Station—Revs. P. Nadeau, S.J., R. A. Cote, S.J.

Michipicoten—See Fort William.

Mississigna—Attended from Wickwemikong.

Nepigon—See Fort William.

North Bay—St. Mary of the Lake, Rev. Eugene Bloem.

Norwood—St. Paul, Rev. P. Conway.

Old Fort—Attended from Port Arthur.

Parry Sound—St. Peter, attended from Bracebridge.

Percy—St. Jerome, attended from Campbellford.

Pic River—St. Francis Xavier, see Fort William.

Port Arthur—Was erected a parish in 1873, under Rev. R. Baxter, S.J., succeeded by Revs. C. Vary, S.J., J. Blethier, S.J., F. Arhaud, S.J., J. Chandon, S.J., P. Hamel, S.J., H. Hudon, S.J., R. Chartier, S. J. and J. Connolly. S.J. The church is dedicated to St. Andrew and will hold 300 people. There is one Separate School, established in 1881, taught by three Sisters of St. Joseph and attended by 140 pupils. The Hospital, which receives a grant from the Government and municipality, is conducted by the Sisters of St. Joseph, Rev. Mother Clotilda, Superior. The Sodality of B. V. M., 1887, President, Miss Mary Gehl; Treasurer, Miss S. McFadden, and the C. M. B. A., 1894, are established.

Mass—Sundays, 7.30 and 10.30 a.m. Vespers—7 p m. Daily Mass—7 a.m.

Port Hope—Our Lady of Mercy, Rev. M. Lynch.

Sault Ste. Marie—Sacred Heart of Jesus, Rev. O. Neault.

Schreiber—Rev. F. Devine.

Sheshegueuning — Attended from Wickwemikong.

Silver Islet—St. Rose of Lima. See Fort William.

RT REV ALEX. MACDONELL, D.D.

South Bay—Attended from Wickwemikong.

St. Joseph's Island—St. Joseph, attended from Garden River.

Sturgeon Falls—Revs. Thos. Ferron, A. L. Desaulniers.

Sudbury—St. Anne, Revs. T. Lussier, S.J., E. Lefebvre, S.J., P. Hamel, S.J., A. Primeau, S.J.

Thessulon River—St. Ann, attended from Garden River.

Trout Creek—Rev. A. F. Kelly.

Verner—Attended from Sturgeon Falls.

Victoria Road—Our Lady Help of Christians, Rev. Jas. Sweeney.

Walford—Attended from Massey Station.

Warren—Attended from Sturgeon Falls.

Webbwood—Attended from Massey Station.

West Bay—Immaculate Conception, attended from Wickwemikong.

White Fish Lake—Attended from Wickwemikong.

White River—Attended from Port Arthur.

Wickwemikong, Manitoulin Island — Invention of the Holy Cross, Very Rev. D. Duranquet, S.J., Revs. J. Paquin, S.J., J. Richard, S.J., S. Dufresne, S.J. Daughters of the Immaculate Heart of Mary, founded 1870, Superior, Mme. Lucy Haessley, School and Orphanage. Free school and Industrial School for boys conducted by Jesuit lay Brothers.

Wickwemikonsing—Attended from Wickwemikong.

Wooler—St. Alphonsus, attended from Brighton.

Young's Point—Our Lady of Good Counsel, attended from Douro.

3. DIOCESE OF ALEXANDRIA.

This diocese, erected Jan. 23rd, 1890, embraces the counties of Stormont and Glengarry.

Bishop – Right Rev. Alexander Macdonell, D.D. born at Lochiel, Glengarry county, Nov. 1st, 1833; ordained priest Dec. 20th, 1862; consecrated in Alexandria, Oct. 28th, 1890.

Catholic population, 22,-000; Priests, 14; Churches, with resident priests, 10; without, 8; Academy, 1; Convents, 3.

PARISHES.

Alexandria— CATHEDRAL ST. FINNAN — Right Rev. Alexander Macdonell, Revs. D. R. Macdonald, R. A. Macdonald. St. Margaret's Convent, conducted by Sisters of the Holy Cross, Superior, Sister M. de St. Antonin ; pupils, 200. Separate school for boys, 200 pupils.

Cornwall — St. Columban, Rev. George Corbett, pastor; Rev. D. A. Campbell, assistant.

Cornwall East—Nativity of B. V. M., Revs. Paul A. De Saunhac, pastor ; Rev. A. Xouale, assistant.

Crysler—Reached by stage from Wales, on G.T.R. Erected a parish May 10th, 1870. First priest, Rev. Thomas Davis ; succeeding priests, Revs. T. J. Spratt, C. J. Duffus, Wm. Fox, John Twomey and Wm. McKinnon, present pastor. The church is dedicated to the Immaculate Conception, seats 800. There are 170 Catholic families, two Separate Schools, established 1874, with two lay teachers and 120 pupils. League of Sacred Heart, established Aug., 1894, Pres., Mrs. J. B. Lafrance ; Sec., Mrs. Dr. Boileau ; Treas., Mrs. Toussaint Hebert. South Finch is attended every Sunday from Crysler.

Mass—Sundays, 10.30 a.m. Daily Mass, 7 a.m.

Dickinson's Landing—St. Patrick, attended from Cornwall W.

Glennevis—St. Margaret, Rev. D. C. McRae.

Glen Robertson—St. Martin of Tours, attended from Glennevis.

Greenfield—St. Catharine, attended from Lochiel.

Lochgarry—St. Stephen, attended from Alexandria.

Lancaster—St. Joseph, attended from Williamstown.

Lochiel—St. Alexander, Rev. Wm. M. Fox.

Martintown—St. Ita, attended from Williamstown.

Moose Creek—Situate on the Can. Atlantic railway, was erected a parish Dec. 28th, 1882, under the present pastor, Rev. M. J. Leahy. The church, dedicated to Our Lady of Angels, is a plain wooden building painted white, with tower, bell and small spire, accommodating 300 people. Two separate schools, one established 1885, the other in 1891, are taught by two lay teachers and attended by 121 pupils. There are 265 Catholic families. The Catholic Order of Foresters opened a court Jan. 18th, 1894.

Mass—Sundays, 10 a.m.; Catechism, 9 a.m.; Vespers, 3.30 p.m.; daily Mass, 7 a.m.

Munroe's Mills—St. Columbkille, attended from St. Raphael.

Monkland—Our Lady of Angels, attended from St. Andrew's.

South Finch—St. Bernard, attended from Crysler.

St. Andrew's—Rev. Wm. A. Macdonell, pastor.

St. Raphael's—Rev. Terence Fitzpatrick, pastor.

Williamstown—Situate four miles from Lancaster on G.T.R.; erected a parish in 1848 under Rev. Francis McDonagh, succeeded by Rev. J.J. McCarthy and Rev. C. H. Gauthier, and by present pastor, Rev. John Twomey. The church, St. Mary's, is Gothic, built of stone and seats 800. There are 300 Catholic families. Lancaster every second Sunday, and Martintown once a month, are attended from Williamstown.

CATHOLIC POPULATION OF ONTARIO.

A census taken in 1783 under the direction of the Bishop of Quebec showed that the number of Canadian Catholics was 113,000, with 135 priests and 234 nuns. Four of the priests were stationed in Western Canada (now Ontario), but the number of Catholics under their care is not given. The total population of Western Canada at this date is estimated to have been about 10,000, and the Catholics probably numbered between three and four thousand.

Dr. Thomas Rolph, in his "Statistical Account of Upper Canada," published in 1836, gives the Catholic population in 1834 as 52,428, out of a total population of 321,145. The clergy consisted of a Bishop, his coadjutor and 20 priests; and there were 35 churches and three in course of erection.

In 1842 the first official census by religions was taken, and the Catholic population of Upper Canada is reported to be 65,203 out of a total population of 487,053.

The subsequent reports are as follows:

1848—	Catholic Population	.118,810	Total Population..	725,879
1851—	"	..167,695	"	..952,004
1861—	"	..258,151	"	..1,396,091
1871—	"	..274,166	"	..1,620,851
1881—	"	..320,839	"	..1,923,228
1891—	"	..358,300	"	..2,114,321

SEPARATE SCHOOL STATISTICS.

	No. of Schools.	No. of Pupils.	Average Attendance.	No. of Teachers.
1871	160	21,206	10,371	249
1881	195	24,819	13,012	374
1892	312	37,466	21 560	662

ABBREVIATIONS OF THE NAMES OF RELIGIOUS ESTABLISHED IN CANADA.

C., Cistercian, Trappist.

C.M. Congregation of the Mission, Lazarist.

C.P. Congregation of the Passion, Passionist.

C.PP.S. Congregation of the Most Precious Blood.

C.R., Congregation of the Resurrection, Resurrectionist.

C.R.I.C., Canon Regular of the Immaculate Conception.

C.S.R. Congregation of St. Basil, Basilians.

C.S.C., Congregation of the Holy Cross.

C.S.P., Congregation of St. Paul, Paulist.

C.S.Sp., Congregation of the Holy Ghost.

C.SS.R., Congregation of the Most Holy Redeemer, Redemptorist Father.

C.S.V., Congregation of St. Viatur.

Eud., Eudist.

O.C.C., Order of Calced Carmelites, Carmelite.

O.M.Cap., Order of Minor Capuchins, Capuchin.

O.M.C., Order of Mi or Conventuals, Black Franciscan.

O.M.I., Oblates of Mary Immaculate, Oblate.

O.P., Order of Preachers, Dominican.

O.S., Order of Servites, Servite.

O.S.A., Order of St. Augustine, Augustinian.

O.S.B., Order of St. Benedict, Benedictine.

O.S.D., Order of St. Dominic, Dominican.

O.S.F., Order of St. Francis, Franciscan.

P.P., Parish Priest.

S.J., Society of Jesus, Jesuit.

S.M., Society of Mary, Marist.

S.P.M., Society of the Fathers of Mercy.

S.S., Saint Sulpice, Sulpitian.

ALPHABETICAL LIST OF THE ARCHBISHOPS, BISHOPS AND PRIESTS IN ONTARIO.

ARCHBISHOPS.

Cleary, Most Rev. Jas. Vincent; residence, Kingston.
Duhamel, Most Rev. Jos. Thomas ; residence, Ottawa.
Walsh, Most Rev. John; residence,Toronto.

BISHOPS.

Dowling, Right. Rev. T. J.; residence, Hamilton.
Lorrain, Right Rev. N. Z.; residence, Pembroke.
Macdonell, Right Rev. Alex.; residence, Alexandria.
O'Connor, Right Rev. D.; residence, London.
O'Connor, Right Rev. R. A.; residence, Peterboro'.

PRIESTS.

Alexis, O. M. (Ott.)*, St. Francois d'Assisse, Ottawa.
Alf, Paul, O.S.F. (Lon.), Chatham.
Allain, L. A. H. (Tor.), St. Catharines.
Allard, J. (Ott.), Bouchette, P.Q.†
Allard, T. (Ott.), Monte Bello, P.Q.
Andrieux, P. (Lon.), Dover South.
Antoine (Ott.), University, Ottawa.
Arnauld, A. (Ott.), Lac Ste. Marie, P.Q.
Arpin, L., S.J. (Pet.), Fort William East.
Artus, V., S.J. (Pet.), Garden River.
Audrand, P., S.M. (Ott.), Cyrville.
Aylward, T. (Lon.), Port Lambton.
Aymans, Hubert, C.R. (Ham.), St. Agatha.
Barrett, P.H., C.SS.R. (Tor.), St. Patrick's, Toronto.
Barrette, Jo . (Pon.), Maynooth.
Beaudoin, A. (Pet.), Byng Inlet.
Bayard, Jos. (Lon.), Sarnia.
Beauchamp, P. (Ott.), St. Ann's, Ottawa.
Beaudoin, J. C. (T. r.), St. Cerix.
Beaudoin, L. (Lon.), Walkerville.
Beausoleil, A. (Ott.), Creuelman.
Bechard. A. (Lon.), McGregor's.
Bedard, P. (Ott.), Lefaivre.
Bella, F. X., C.R. (Ham.), Berlin.
Belanger, J. P. (Ott.), St. Andre Avellin, P.Q.
Belanger, D. (Ott.), St. Phillipe d'Argenteuil, P.Q.
Bellemarie, C. (Ott.), St. J. Bap., Ottawa.
Benoit, (Ott.), St. Jean Baptiste, Ottawa.
Bergin, V. Rev. Wm. (Tor.), St. Joseph's, Lesliville.
Bernecha, A., O.M.I. (Pon.), Mattawan.
Bertrand, P. (Ott.), Masham Mills.
Bernhe, O. (Ott.), L'Original.
Best, D., O.C.C. (Tor.), Niagara Falls.
Best, Philip, O.C.C. (Tor.), Niagara Falls.
Bloem, Eugene (Pet.), North Bay.
Bloudin, L. (Ott.), Lowe, P.Q.
Boisseau, M. (Ott.), St. Malachy, P.Q.
Boisrance, P. (Ott.), University, Ottawa.
Bonaventure, O. M. C. (Ott.), St. Francois d'Assisse, Ottawa.
Boubat, B., London invalided.
Bouchet, A. (Ott.), Notre Dame de Montfort, P.Q.
Boulet, O. (Ott.), St. Isidore de Prescott.
Bouillon, O. (Ott.), Archiepiscopal Residence, Ottawa.
Bourget, P. (Ott.), Notre Dame de Montfort, P.Q.

* The name of the diocese is bracketed and abbreviated—Ott., Ottawa ; Al., Alexandria ; Ham., Hamilton ; K., Kingston ; Lon., London ; Pet., Peterboro' ; Tor., Toronto ; Pon., Vicariate Apostolic of Pontiac.
† All post-offices in this list are in the Province of Ontario, exce pt those marked P.Q., Province of Quebec.

Brady, R. (Ham.), Hamilton.
Brady, M. J. (Ham.), Woodstock.
Brennan, P. (Lon.), St. Marys.
Brennan, J., asst. (K.), Prescott.
Brennan, L., C.S.B. (Tor.), St. Basil's, Toronto.
Bretherton, C. F. (Pet.), Downeyville.
Bridonnetu, J. B. (Ott.), Cyrville.
Brohman, Geo. (Ham.), Formosa.
Brunette, F. (Ott.), Archiepiscopal Res., Ottawa.
Browne, V. Rev. Jos. (Pet.), Douro.
Burkley. P., C.S.B. (Ham.), Owen Sound.
Burke, R. T. (Ham.), Oakville.
Campeau, L. X. (Ott.), Archiepiscopal residence, Ottawa.
Campbell, D. A. (Al.), Cornwall.
Campbell, K. A. (Tor.), Orillia.
Cantillon, C. (Tor.), Vroomanton.
Carberry, J. C. (Tor.), Toronto.
Carey, Thos. (K.), Brewer's Mills.
Caran, E. (Pet.) Garden River.
Caron, Thos. (Ott.), Clarence Creek.
Carson, A. (K.), Cathedral, Kingston.
Casey, Very Rev. D. J. (Pet.), Peterboro'.
Cassien, O.M. (Ott.), St. Francois d'Assisse, Ottawa.
Cassidy, Very Rev. E. (Tor.), Brockton.
Cassin, P. (Ham.), Dundalk.
Cashron, A., S.M. (Ott.) Arundel, P.Q.
Chalorel, T. O.M.I., (Ott.), University, Ottawa.
Chaine, A. M. (Pon.), Arnprior.
Chamberland, M. (Ott.), Suffolk, P.Q.
Champagne, T. (Ott.), Templeton, P.Q.
Charland, P. (Ott.), St. Jean Baptiste, Ottawa.
Charlebois, G. (Ott.), Oblate Scholasticate, Ottawa.
Chatelain, J. (Ott.), Thurso, P.Q.
Cherrier, C.S.B. (Tor.), St. Michael's College, Toronto.
Chevaller, J. A. (Ott.), Mani aaki,P.Q.
Cicolari, G. (K.), Erinsville.
Coderre, E. (Ott.), St. Anne de Prescott.
Cohn, J. (Tor.), Midland.
Cole, T. (Ott.), Dawson.
Collins, J. C.S.B., (Lon.), Sandwich.
Collins, Jas. (K.), Cathedral, Kingston.
Collins, T. (Pet.), Peterborough.
Connelly, M. (Pet.), Campbellford.
Connolly, Jas. (K.), Frankford.
Connolly, J., S.J. (Pet.) Port Arthur.
Connolly, J. (Ham.), Lucan.
Constantineau, H., O. M. I. (Ott.), St. Joseph's, Ottawa.
Conway, P. (Pet.), Norwood.
Corbeil, A. (Ott.), St. Faustin, P.Q.
Corbeil, O. (Ott.), Templeton, P.Q.
Corbett, G. (Al.), Cornwall.
Corcoran, J. (Ham.) Teeswater.
Corcoran, P. (Lon.), La Salette.
Corkery, P. (Lon.), West Huntley.
Cosgrove, P. (Ham.), Elora.
Coty, J. H. (Ham.), Hamilton.
Cote, J., C.S.B. (Lon.) Sandwich.
Cote. R. A. S.J. (Pet.), Massey Station.
Courtois, J. C. (Lon.), Orvada e.
Cousineau, O. (Ott.), Rockland.
Coutbee, A., O. M. I. (Ott.) University, Ottawa.
Coyle, P. (Tor.), St. Mary's, Toronto.
Craven, J. J. (Ham.), St. Patrick's, Hamilton.
Crinnon, J. F. (Ham.), Innisville.
Cruise, J. M. (Tor.), Toronto.
Crespin, A., C.S.B. (Tor.), Toronto.
Cummins, M. (Lon.), Bothwell.
Cushing, C. C.S.B. (Lon.), Sandwich.
Dacier, E. (Ott.), Fournierville.
David, C., O.M.I. (Ott.), University, Ottawa.

Davis, Thos. (K.), Madoc.
Dawson, Very Rev. Æ. McD. (Ott.), Ottawa.
Deguire, J. C. W. (Ott.), Basilica, Ottawa.
DeSaunhac, Paul (Al.), Cornwall, East.
Desjardins, A. (Ott.) Papineauville, Ont.
Desmond, A. P. (Tor.), Uxbridge.
Desaulniers, A. L. (Pet.), Sturgeon Falls.
Deslauriers, C. (Ott.), Chute aux Iroquois, P.Q.
Devine, E., S.J. (Pet.), Port Arthur.
Devine, F. M. (K.), Osceola.
Devine, F., S.J., S brieber.
Dixon, N. (Lon.), Ashfield.
Dodsworth, Cyril, C.SS.R. (Tor.), Toronto.
Doherty, J. (Ham.), Arthur.
Donovan, J. (Al.), Pembroke.
Dowdall, P. S. (K.), Eganville.
Downey, D. (Lou.), Stratford.
Dube, J. (Ham.), Arthur.
Ducharme, L. (Ott.), Clarence Creek.
Duffy, F. W. (Tor.), Orillia.
Duffus, C. J. (K.), Perth.
Dufresne, S. (Pet.), Wickwemikong.
Duhaut, A. E. (Ott.), University, Ottawa.
Dumortier, F., S.J. (Ham.), Guelph.
Dumouchelle, A. B., C.S.B. (Tor.), St. Michael's College, Toronto.
Dunn, J. (Ott.), Rich + ond.
Dupret, invalided, (Lon.), London.
Dunoyer, L., O.M.I.C. (Ott.), Lac Nominingue, P.Q.
Duranquet, D. (Pet.), Wickwemikong.
Duserre—Telmon (Ott.), Vankleek Hill.
Duvic, J. M., O.M.I. (Ott.), Oblate Scholasticate, Ottawa.
Egan, V. Rev. J. J. (Tor.), Barrie.
Falar, F. X., O.M.I. (Pon.), Albany, Hudson Bay, P.Q.
Farrelly, Rt. Rev. Mgr. J. (K.), Belleville.
Fautcux, (Lon.), invalided, London.
Feeney, J. J. (Ham.), Brantford.
Ferguson, M., C.S.B., (Lon.), Sandwich.
Ferreri, V. (Pon.), Vinton, P.Q.
Ferron, O. (Ott.), Wendover.
Ferron, Thos. (Pet.), Sturgeon Falls.
Filion, F. D. (Pon.), Pembroke.
Fitzpatrick, T. (Al.), St. Raphael.
Flannery, W., D.D. (Lon.), St. Thomas.
Fleming, T. (Pet.), Bracebridge.
Fleming, John (K.), Tweed.
Foerster, Stephen (Ham.), New Germany.
Foley, J. (Ott.), Almonte.
Foley, D. P. (Ott.), Almonte.
Forget, A. (Ott.), St. Andre Avellin, P.Q.
Forget, J. W. (O t.), Perkin's Mills, P. Q.
Forster, D. (Lon.), Parkhill.
Fox, Wm. (Al.), Lochiel.
Frachon, F. X., C.S B. (Tor.), St. Michael's College, Toronto.
Francœur, J. L. (Ott.), retired, Casselman.
Froy, M., O. M. I. (Ott.), University, Ottawa.
Gagnieur, W., S.J. (Pet.), Fort William Indian Mission.
Gagnon, T. G. (Pon.), Nosbonsing Lake.
Gahan, N. (Lon.), Cathedral, London.
Gallagher, E. F. (Tor.), Pickering.
Gapihan, J. (Ott.), Notre Dame de Mont fort, P.Q.
Garon, P. (Ott.), Donat, P.Q.
Gascon, Jos. (Ott.), Greenville, P.Q.
Gauthier, A. (Al.), St. Albert.
Gauthier, Very Rev., V.G. (K.), Brockville.
Gauvreau, E, (Ott.), St. Jean Baptiste, Ottawa.
Gauvreau, G. (Ott.), University, Ottawa.
Gauvreau, T. (Ott.), St. Jean Baptiste, Ottawa.
Gay, C (Ott.), Gracefield, P.Q.
Gear'n, M. J. (Tor.), Phelpston.
Gek, J. (Ham.), St. Clement .

Gendreau, P. E., O.M.L (Pon.), Mattawan.
Georges, F., O.M.I. (Ott.), Hull, P.Q.
Gorvals, H. (Ott.), University, Ottawa.
Gibbons, J. (Tor.), Penetanguishene.
Gibney, R. J. (Tor.), Alliston.
Gibra, L. (Tor.), Barrie.
Gnani, John (Lon.', Hosson.
Gnam, P. (Lon.), Wyoming.
Gohiet, F., O.M.I. (Ott.), University, Ottawa.
Grandfils, J. B., O.M.I. (Ott.), Hull, P.Q.
Grannotier, B., C.S.D. (Lon.), Sandwich.
Grannotier, F., C.S.B.(Ham.), Owen Sound.
Grogan, S., C.SS.R. (Tor.), St. Patrick's, Toronto.
Groulx, E. (Ott.), Archiepiscopal res., Ottawa.
Guay, J. (Ott.), Ripon, P.Q.
Guogon, M. (Ott.), Maniwaki, P.Q.
Gueynard, J s., O.M.I. (Pon.), Albany, Hudson Bay, P.Q.
Guillaumie, A. (Ott.), St. Felix de V., Ch neville, P.Q.
Guinane, J J., C.S.B. (Tor.), St. Michael's College, Toronto.
Haley, P. (Ham.), Acton.
Halm, M. (Ham.), Carlsruhe.
Halton, Jos., C.R. (Ham.) Berlin.
Hamel, P., S.J. (Pet.), Sudbury.
Hand, J. L. (Tor.), St. Paul's, Toronto.
Harnois, M., O.M.I. (Ott.), 196 Wilbrod st., Ottawa.
Harris, Very Rev. W. R. (Tor.), St. Catharines.
Hartigan, P. J. (K.), Camden East.
Hayden, J., C.SS.R. (Tor.), St. Patrick's, Toronto.
Hayes, T., C.S.B. (Lon.), Sandwich.
Heenan, Rt. Rev. E. J. (Ham.), Dundas.
Hinchey, J. (Ham.), St.Joseph's,Hamilton.
Hodgkinson, E. (Lon.), Woodslee.
Hogan, John (K.), Napanee.
Hogan, J. (Tor.), Brechin.
Howe, W., O. M. I. (Ott.), St. Joseph's, Ottawa.
Hudon, P. S. (Ott.), Rockwood.
Jacques, (Ott.), St. Jean Baptiste, Ottawa.
Jankowski, B. (Pon.), Wilno.
Joannotte, J. E., O.M.I. (Ott.), Church of Sacred Heart, Ottawa.
Jeffcott, M. J. (Tor.), Oshawa.
Joubert, Thos. (Ott.), Notre Dame de Lourdes.
Kavanagh, F. X., S.J. (Ham.), Guelph.
Kealy, J. A. (Lon.), Dublin.
Keane, J. J. (Tor.), Uxbridge.
Kehoe, F. (Ham.), Brantford.
Kehoe, J.P. (K.), Cathedral, Kingston.
Keilty, Wm. J. (Pet.), Douro.
Kelly, A. F. (Pet.), Trout Creek.
Kelly, T. J. (Ham.), Walkerton.
Kelly, Thos., Archdeacon (K.), Kingston.
Kelly, J. J. (K.), Trevelyan.
Kelly, M., C.S.B. (Lon.), Sandwich.
Kennedy, Jos. (Lon.), Seaforth.
Kenny, G., S.J., (Lon.), Guelph.
Keough, John (Lon.), Paris.
Kiernan, B. (Pon.), Quyon, P.Q.
Kiernan, E. J. (Tor.), Collingwood.
Kilcullen, J. (Tor.), Cobau.
Killoen, C. (K.), Sharbot Lake.
Kilroy, Dr. E. B. (Ham.), Stratford.
Klopfer, Dr. Wm., C.R. (Ham.), Berlin.
Kosinski, Jno., C.R., Berlin.
Kroldt, A. J., O.C.C., Prior (Tor.), Niagara Falls.
Krein, S., C.SS.R. (Tor.), St. Patrick's, Toronto.
Labelle, A. A. (Ott.), St. Paul's, Aylmer, P.Q.
Laboureau, Th. F. (Tor.), Penetanguishene.
Lacoste, H., O. M. I. (Ott.), University, Ottawa.
Lafontaine, A. (Tor.), Smithville.
Laganiere, L. (Ott.), University, Ottawa.
Lamarche, P. (Tor.), Church of S. Heart, Toronto.
Lambert, O., O. M. I. (Ott.), University, Ottawa.

Langlois, J. B. (Ott.), Angers, P.Q.
Langlois, P. (Lon.), Tilbury Centre.
Laniel, A., O.M.I. (Ott.), Maniwaki, P.Q.
Laporte, C., O.M.I. (Ott.), Maniwaki, P.Q.
Larkin, M. (Pet.), Grafton.
Larose, C. (Ott.), The Brook.
Laurent, Very Rev. P. D. (Pet.), Lindsay.
Laussier, Dean (Ham.), Cayuga.
La zon, L., O.M.I. (Ott.), Hull, P.Q.
Lavin, D. (Ottawa) Pakenham.
Lavoie, L. A. (Ott.), Orleans.
Leahy, M. J. (Al.), Moose Creek.
Leclerc, J. (Ott.), Chute a Blondeau.
Locl ch, J. (Ott.), Notre Dame de Montfort, P.Q.
Leduc, D. (Pon.), Allumette Island, P.Q.
Lefobvre, E., S.J. (Pet.), Sudbury.
Le Gendre, F. (Ott.), St. Philomene, P.Q.
Legault, H., O.M.I. (Ott.), Hull, P.Q.
Lo Cuyader (Pon.), Renfrew.
Lohman (Ham.), St. Mary's C thedral, Hamilton.
Lemay, O. (Ott.), Amherst, P.Q.
Lemon, P. (Ham.), Brantford.
Lo Moyne, F. N. (Pon.), Gower Point.
Lewis, L. V., O.M.I. (Ott.), Hull, P.Q.
Lombard, F. (Ott.), Alfred.
Loiselle, A. A. (Lon.), Windsor.
Lorlon, A. (Lon.), Kuscom River.
Lórtie, J. (Ott.), B ckingham, P.Q.
Louise Marie, O.M.I. (Ott.), St. Francis d'As-isse.
Lussier, T., S.J., Sudbury.
Lynch, G. M. (Ham.), Caledonia.
Lynch, J. J. (Ham.), Niagara.
Maddigan, P. J. (Ham.), Dundas.
Mahony, J. M. (Ham.), St. Mary's Cathedral, Hamilton.
Major, L. H. (Ott.), Cassel an.
Malmartel, J., O.M.I. (Ott.), Oblate Scholasticate, Ottawa.
Martin, A. (Ott.), University, Ottawa.
Marseille, F. (Lon.), Canard River.
Macdonald, Donald R. (Al.), Alexandria.
Macdonald, R. A. (Al.), Alexandria.
MacDonald, J. A., S. J. (Pet.), Garden River.
MacDonald, Michael (K.), Kemptville.
Macdonell, W. A. (Al.), St. Andrew.
MacRae, Donald C. (Al.), Glennevis.
McBrady, R., C.S.B. (Tor.), St. Michael's College, Toronto.
McCabe, Patrick (Lon.), Fletcher.
McCann, V. Rev. J. J. (Tor.), St. Michael's Cathedral, Toronto.
McCarthy, J. (K.), Merrickville.
McCarthy, P. (Ott.), Ste. Brigitte's, Ottawa.
McCarthy, Thos. (K.), Read.
McCauley, W. (Ott.), St. Patrick's, Ottawa.
McCloskey, Wm. J. (Pet.), Brighton.
McColl, P. J. (Tor.), Fort Erie.
McColl, W. J. (Tor.), Ennismore.
McCormac, Jos. (Pon.), Brudenell.
McCormack, M. (Lon.), Cathedral, London.
McCrory, C', O.M.I. (Ott.), University, Ottawa.
McDonogh, J. H. (K.), Picton.
McEachen, Ronald (Pon.), Mount St. Patrick.
McEntee, J. (Tor.), Port Colborne.
McElvay, Rt. Rev. F. P. (Ham.), St. Mary's Cathedral, Hamilton.
McGee, C. E. (Lon.), Maidstone.
McGovern, F. J. (Ott.), Almonte, (sick retired).
McGrath, M. (Lon.) Sandwich.
McGuire, J. (Ott.), South Gloucester.
McGuire, M. J. (Pet.), Brighton.
McGuire, P. J. (Pet.), Bracebridge.

McGuckin, J., D.D., O.M.I. (Ott.), University, Ottawa.
McKeown, A. (Lon.), Strathroy.
McKinnon, Wm. (Al.), Crysler.
McMahon, P. (Tor.), Thornhill.
McMenamin, D. P. (Lon.) Simcoe.
McPhillips, H. J. (Tor.), Orangeville.
McRae, D. (Lon.), Parkhill.
McRae, K. J. (Tor.), Brechin.
McRory, J., O. M. I. (Ott.), University, Ottawa.
McSpirritt, F. (Tor.), Gribbin.
McWilliams, C. A. (K.), Loborough.
Medolce, J. M., O.M.I. (Pon.), Temiskaming, Hudson Bay, P.Q.
Mounier, J. B. E. (Lon.), Belle River.
Michel, M. J. (Ott.) Buckingham P.Q.
Minehan L. (Tor.), S homhroy.
Moise, O. M. (Ott.), St. Francois d'Assisse, Ottawa.
Molphy, Jos. (Lo n), Ingersoll.
Montour, L. (Ott.), Sr. Philippe d'Argenteuil, P.Q.
Montreuil, A., C.S.B. (Lon.), Sandwich.
Morris, D. (Tor.), Newmarket.
Moreau, S. A. (Ott.), Ste. Agathe, P.Q.
Motard, A. (Ott.), Cantly, P.Q.
Motrior, C. (Pon.), Temiskaming, Hudson Bay, P.Q.
Moyn, M. (Tor.), Stayner.
Mugan, Jas. (Lon.), Corunna.
Mulcahy, J., C.S.B. (Tor.), St. Michael's College, Toronto.
Mungovan, M., C.S.B. (Lon.), Sandwich.
Murphy, G. (Ham.), Freelton.
Murphy, J. J. (Lon.), Dublin.
Murphy, W. (Ott.), University, Ottawa.
Murphy, T., O.M.I. (Ott.), University, Ottawa.
Murray, E., C.S.B. (Tor.), St. Michael's College, Toronto.
Murray, Very Rev. C. B., Dean (K.), Trenton.
Murray, E. H. (Pet.), Cobourg.
Murtagh, Thos. (K.), Madoc, Assistant.
Myraud, J. (Ott.), Billing's Bridge.
Nadeau, P. (Pet.), Massey S ation.
Neault, O. (Pet.), Sault Ste. Marie.
Nolles, N., O.M.I. (Ott.), University, Ottawa.
Neville, J. V. (K.), Kingston.
Nolan, J. (Pet.), Burnley.
Nolin, A. (Pon.) Quyon, P.Q.
Noonan, S. (Lon.), London.
O'Brion, John (K.), B Heville, As-istant.
O'Brien, M. (K.), Merrickville.
O'Connell, B. J., Dean (H m.), Mount Forest.
O'Connell, D. (Pet.), St. Peter's Cathedral, Peterborough.
O'Connell, T. B. (Pet.), Fenelon Fal s.
O'Connor, Very Rev. Dean (K.), Chesterville.
O'Connor, T. P. (K.), Stanleyville.
O'Gorman, John D. (K.), Gananoque.
O'Leary, J. S. (Ham.), Macton.
O'Leane, J., S.J. (Ham.), Guelph.
O'Malloy, A. (Tor.), St. Catharines.
O'Malley, D., O.C.C. (Tor.), Niagara Falls.
O'Neill, J. (Lon.), Kinkora.
O'Reilly, F. (Ham.), Caledonia.
O'Rourke, M. (K.), Carleton Place.
O'Sullivan, L., O.S.F. (Lon.), Chatham.
Ouimet, S. (Ott.), St. Jovite, P.Q.
Pailller, A (Ott.) University, Ottawa.
Paquin, J., S.J., (Pet.) Wickwemikong.
Parent, Charles (Lon.), Big Point.
Patrico, O. M. (Ott.), St. Francois d'Assisse, Ottawa.
Pattren, F (Ott), University, Ottawa.
Pelletier, A. (Ott.), Masson, P.Q.
Phillion, A. (Ott.), Embrun.
Philip, S. (Ott.), Hawkesbury.
Piau, E., O.M.I. (Ott.), Maniwaki, P.Q.
Picotte, G. A. (Pon.), Calumet Island, P.Q.
Pilon, J. (Ott.), Curran.
Pilon, V. (Ott.), Curran.
Pinsault (Ott.), Notre Dame de Lourdes.

Plantin, J. A. [Ott.], Archiepiscopal Residence, Ott·wa.
Poli, J. A., O.M.I. [Ott.], Oblate Scholasticate, Ottawa.
Poulin, C. [Ott.], Chelsea, P.Q.
Prevost, M. [Ott.], Hull, P.Q.
Prim·au, A., S.J. [Pet.], Sudbury.
Proulx, C. [Ott.], St. G·r·rd, P.Q.
Quigley, T. [Lon.], St. Augustine, P.O.
Quinlan, P. [Lon.], West L·rne.
Quinn, J. S. [K.], Marysville.
Quirk, John [Pt.], Hastings.
Reddin, J. [Tor.], St. Paul's, Toronto.
Renauvl, L., C. S. B. [Lon.], Amherstburg.
Richard, J., S J [Pet.], Wickwemikong.
Richard, H [Ott], Cyrville.
Richer, D [Ott.], Nctr· Dame de la Salette, P·Q
Rion, E., C.R.I.C. [Ott.], Lac Nominingue. P·Q.
Rochon, E. [Ott.], Papineauville, P.Q.,
Rohlleder, F. [Tor.], St. Michael's Cathedra, Toronto.
Ronan, J· hn [Lon], Wallaceburg.
Rooney, Rt. Rev. Mgr. [Tor.], St. Mary's, T ronto.
Routhier, Very Rev. J. O. [Ott.] Archiepiscopal Residence, Ottawa.
Ryan, F., S.J [Tor.], St. Michael's Cathedral, Toronto.
Ryan, P. C.S B [Lon], Amherstburg.
Ryan, P. T [Pon.], Ren frew, P.Q.
Sea lan, J [Lon.], Windsor.
Scanlan, Thos. F. [Pet.], Lindsay.

Schneider, London, invalided.
Schweitzer, C. R. [Ham.], Berlin.
Sc·llard, D J [Pet.], Cathedral, Peterboro.
Semande, F., C.S.B [Lon], Sandwich.
Shaloe, M. [Pon.], Sheenboro', P.Q.
Shaughnessy, P., C.S.B. [Ham.], Owen Sound.
Simonet, P., O.M.I. [Pon.], Mattawan.
Slaven, E. [Ham.], Galt.
Sloan, J·· [Ott.], Fal'owfield.
Smyth, F. [Tor.], Merritton.
Specht, Jo·., S.J. [Pet], Victoria R·ad.
Sp·tz, Theo·. C.R [H·m], Berlin.
Spratt, M. K [K], Kitley.
Spr·tt, T. J. [K.], Wolfe Island.
Stanton M. J. [K.], Smith's Falls
St. Cyr, W. D. [Lon.], Stony Point.
Stephen, Theo·., O.S.F. [Lon.], Chatham.
Sullivan, T. [Tor.], Thorold
Sweeney, Jas. [Pet], Victoria Roa·t.
Talbot, G. [Ott.], Case·lman, [retired].
Tangnay, C. [Ott], Church St., Ottawa
Tulfy, J. R., M.A., C.S.B. [Tor.] St. Michael's College, Toronto
Therien, F. X., O.M I [Pon.], Temiskaming, Hudson Bay, P.Q.
Ti· man, M. J. [Lon.], London.
Tobin, J. [Lon], London.
Tonch·tte, H. [Ott], St Eugene.
Towner, F. [Ott], St. Eugene.
Traher, H. [Lon.], Mount C·rmel
Trayling, J. [Tor.], Dixie.
Treacy, J P., D.D. [Tor.], St. Mary's, Toronto.

Trinquier, E. [Ott.], Notre Dame d° Lourdes, P·Q.
Twohey, P. A. [K], Westport.
Twomey, Denni·A [K], Morrisburg.
Twom y, J. [Al], Wi lliamstown.
Vaillancourt, Z., O.M.I. [Ott.], 196 Wilbrod street, Ottawa
Valence, O. [Ott.], Oblate Scholasticate, Ott·wa
Valenti·, T. [Lon.], Windsor.
Vatiquotte, A., O.M I. [Ott.], 196 Wilbrod street, Ottawa.
Va'lule, P. [Ott.], Arundel, P.Q.
Victor, O. M. [Ott.], St. Franc·is d'Assirse Ottawa.
Villeneuve, A. P. [Lon.], Tecumseh.
Vuaillet, I. M., O.M.I.C [Ott.], Lac Nominingue, P.Q.
Wadel, Stephen [Ham.], Cher·stowe.
Waechter, J., C.R. [Ham.], Berlin.
W gn·r, J. T., Dean [Lon], Windsor.
Walsh, F., C.S.B. [Tor], St. Michael's College, Toronto.
Walsh, Jas , [Tor.], N. D. de Lourdes, Toronto
Walsh, W. E. [K.], Spence·ville.
Weiler, F. [Ham], Preston.
West, T. [Lon], Goderi·h.
Wey, Joseph [Ham], Mi'dmay.
Whelan, M. J. [Ott.], St. Patrick's, Ottawa.
Whitney, P. [Tor], Caldwell
Xouale, A. [Al.], Cornwall East, assist.

SOME EVENTS OF 1894.

Archbishop Tache died in St. Boniface June 22nd, 1894. A sketch of the career of this great missionary Archbishop is given elsewhere.

Marie Francois Sadi Carnot, President of France, was assassinated at Lyons by an anarchist named Santo as he was sitting in his carriage about to drive to the Grand Theatre on June 24th, 1894. He has been succeeded by M. Casimir-Perier.

Joan of Arc, by a formal enactment, was made patron saint of the Third Republic and her birth-day proclaimed a national holiday. France has followed ardently the Church in her pronouncement that this noblest of French women is worthy of veneration.

Mgr. Satolli, Apostolic Delegate to the United States, visited Canada in October, and was tendered a grand reception in Montreal and Quebec.

The Comte de Paris, after a lingering illness, died at Stowe House on Sept. 10th, 1894. He was the grandson of King Louis Philippe. Large numbers of French Legitimists journeyed to England to pay a last mark of respect to one whom they regarded as the King of France. The Comte de Paris, with his brother the Duc de Chartres, served on Gen. McLellan's staff during the American War. In 1864 he married the eldest daughter of the Duc de Montpensier.

Hon. C. F. Fraser.—At the right of the main entrance of the Parliament Buildings, if the visitor look closely at the red sandstone capping the six columns, he will see carved the monogram of the Hon. Christopher Finlay Fraser, to whose honest and faithful administration we are indebted for the stately buildings that loom up over the city, the first object that catches the eye from whatever direction the city is approached.

Mr. Fraser was the recognized leader of the Catholics in Ontario, which no doubt contributed somewhat to his rapid advancement, though his brilliant talents would have brought him to the front irrespective of influence. His indomitable spirit and unfailing energy were manifested in his close attention to the exacting duties of his office in spite of bodily infirmity—his health had been failing for some years. His sudden death occurred on the 24th of August, 1894, in Toronto, whither he had returned after a tour of inspection of the Registry offices, and in those very buildings whose construction he had watched as a father watches a child.

Christopher Finlay Fraser was called a man of the people, a man who had risen by his own merits to distinction, and whose career ought to be an inspiration to all young Canadians who cherish the desire to serve their native land—a career eloquent of honesty, fidelity and sturdiness of conviction. He was born in Brockville in 1820. His father was a Highlander, his mother, Sarah Burke, of Irish birth and patronage. After many struggles for his education he was called to the bar in 1865, and in 1867 entered political life. He was twice defeated in his candidature for Brockville, but was elected member for South Grenville in 1871, and in 1879 was elected member for Brockville, which constituency he represented till his retirement from political life. In 1874 he was gazetted Commissioner of Public Works, and superintended the building of the Mercer Reformatory, Mimico Asylum, Orillia and Brockville Asylums.

He was the ablest speaker on the Government side. Of his eloquence and ability as a debater the Toronto *Empire*, politically opposed to him, said : " There are many who will recall memorable nights in the Legislature, when they have listened with delight to the impetuous torrent of his eloquence, for during the twenty-two years which he sat in the House, until weakness, in the atter years, made his abstention compulsory, he was ever in the front in debates. Many a time when the tide of debate was going against his political friends, have they looked to the Minister of Public Works to come to the rescue, and rarely did he fail them. With a genius rarely equalled for grasping the salient points and marshalling the arguments in the most effective way, he would take up the lagging debate and drive home the contention of his side with a force and eloquence which always evoked the enthusiastic applause of his friends, while his opponents, if not convinced, would at least listen with pleasure and admiration of his talents."

Sir Frank Smith has always been identified with the Catholics of Ontario as their representative in public affairs at Ottawa, and the honor of knighthood recently conferred upon him by the Queen has been a gratification to his coreligionists. And not only to them, but to all ambitious youths who see in his success the reward of honesty, uprightness, faithful and conscientious discharge of business obligations.

SIR FRANK SMITH.

Sir Frank Smith was born at Richill, near Armagh, Ireland, in 1822, emigrating to Canada ten years later with his father and settling near Toronto. He went into business as a wholesale grocer at London, Ont., in 1849, which business he continued in Toronto until comparatively recently. His knowledge of affairs, his probity, his shrewd business sense have served well the Conservative Government, of whose Cabinet he is a member.

Father Lawlor.—The heroism of Father Lawlor at Hinckley and Sandstone during the terrible forest fires that ravaged the States of Wisconsin and Minnesota in the drought of 1894 puts to shame the cowardice of the ordinary man's conduct. He stripped himself of his coat, which he tore in two that he might dip it in the water and so shield somewhat the suffering women and children from the scorching heat.

Rev. Walter Elliott, of the Paulists, who has been giving missions to the non-Catholics in the Diocese of Detroit, has begun a mission in Ohio.

Mr. George W. Kiely, whose sudden death occurred July 17th, 1894, left to charitable institutions $17,000. Of this sum $10,000 is in the hands of certain persons with power to bestow on such charities as they may deem most require it. In his lifetime Mr. Kiely was noted for his generosity to the Church.

Hospice of the Carmelites at Niagara Falls.—On the 16th of July, 1894, His Grace Archbishop Walsh laid the corner-stone of the new Hospice of the Carmelite Fathers, to cost $100,000, at Niagara Falls. The sermon on this occasion was preached by a Franciscan friar, Rev. Raphael Fuhr, of St. Francis College, Quincy, Ill. It was a Franciscan, Father Hennepin, who was the first white man to see the Falls.

The ceremony was witnessed by numbers of the clergy from the neighboring dioceses, while hundreds of pilgrims to the shrine of Our Lady of Peace gathered to assist at the interesting ceremony. The building will be of Medina sandstone three stories in height, with circular towers on the front entrance. The roof will be of red tile.

Monsignor Begin, who succeeds Cardinal Taschereau in the Quebec See, was a priest of the archdiocese of which he has now become the head, and during his sacerdotal days he was the principal of the Laval Normal School in Quebec. On the death of the first Bishop of the Diocese of Chicoutimi, Monsignor Racine, he was consecrated his successor in that See Oct. 28, 1888. Three years later he was recalled to Quebec to become the auxiliary of Cardinal Taschereau, and he was then appointed Archbishop of Cyrene *in partibus*, with the rights of succession. The succession has now come to him, and he can be trusted to continue the wise and conservative policy which characterized the administration of his illustrious predecessor.

Catholic Scientific Congress.—All the nations of the civilized world were represented at the Catholic Scientific Congress held in Brussels in September, 1894—France, Holland, Germany, Austria, Hungary, Switzerland, Italy, Spain, England, America. Among the American representatives were the distinguished rector of the Catholic University of Washington, and two of its professors, viz., Drs. Bouquillion and Grennan and the well-known scientist and author, Father Zahm, of Notre Dame, Indiana.

St. James' Cathedral, Montreal.—The magnificent Cathedral of Montreal, St. James', built upon the plan of St. Peter's at Rome, and about one-third the size, was blessed on Easter Sunday, 1894. It was begun 24 years ago by Mgr. Bourget and continued by Mgr. Fabre. The sanctuary is immediately under the large dome, and extends the whole width of the church. There will be 30 marble altars in it when completed.

On Feb. 4th, 1894, His Grace Archbishop Walsh solemnly blessed and dedicated St. Mary's new school at Barrie, a handsome red brick building with four lofty and spacious rooms.

A handsome church 120 feet in length by 54 in width has been recently finished in Oshawa. It is built of red pressed brick and dressed with Ohio sandstone.

The corner-stone of the fine new church of St. Mary, Richmond Hill, was laid by His Grace Archbishop Walsh on the 17th June, 1894.

The new church in Phelpston has been completed at a cost of $12,000.

A Memorial Window was placed in St. Paul's church, Toronto, to the memory of William O'Connor, champion oarsman.

His Grace Archbishop Cleary, of Kingston, presented to Principal Grant, the representative of the Board of Governors of the General Hospital, Kingston, a handsome monument which is placed over the graves of the 1,400 Irish victims of the plague who were buried there in 1847. The monument represents the angel of the Resurrection, "The trumpet shall sound and the dead shall rise again incorruptible."

On May 30th His Grace Archbishop Cleary blessed and laid the corner-stone of the new church in connection with the Hotel Dieu, Kingston, in the presence of the clergy of the diocese and a large number of citizens.

On July 16th His Grace the Archbishop of Kingston laid the corner-stone of the church of St. Denis the Areopagite in the village of Athens. After the ceremony His Grace delivered a sermon explaining the necessity of sacrifice in the worship of God, and what the Church meant to Catholics.

On June 24th, 1894, the church of St. Joseph, Hamilton, was dedicated with impressive ceremonies. Pontifical High Mass was celebrated by His Lordship Bishop Dowling. The church was blessed at the opening of the service by Mgr. Heenan. His Grace the Archbishop of Toronto preached the sermon on the occasion.

Mr. Hugh Ryan, of Toronto, has bestowed a princely gift upon the Church in Toronto in building the handsome new wing of St. Michael's Hospital, Bond street. This new wing possesses a particularly fine operating-room, and is equipped in the most approved modern style. The City Council of Toronto on April 30th refused to send city patients to St. Michael's Hospital. A motion was introduced by Ald. Bailey requiring " The Medical Health Officer to send all city patients to the Toronto General Hospital and Grace Hospital so long as these hospitals are able to furnish accommodation, but in the event of these two hospitals being overcrowded, then the Medical Health Officer shall be empowered to issue orders for city patients to any other hospitals willing to admit them."

The Manitoba School Question. — The decision of the Privy Council was against the Catholics in the Manitoba school question, and the people who colonized the province, and the Church who preserved it to the Crown are denied the privileges of their own schools which were solemnly and repeatedly promised them.

The Catholic Summer School of America held a most successful session at Plattsburg, N.Y., on Lake Champlain. The officers of the Summer School are : President, Rev. Thomas J. Conaty, D.D.; First Vice-President, Rev. P. A. Halpin, S.J.; Second Vice-President, Thomas B. Fitzpatrick ; Treasurer, Rev. Morgan M. Sheedy ;

Secretary, Warren E. Mosher, A.M. Messages expressive of cordial feeling and best wishes were interchanged between the Chautauqua School and the Catholic Summer School.

The Catholic College of Stonyhurst celebrated its 100th anniversary in July, 1894

Cardinal Vaughan is about beginning the building of the Cathedral of Westminster. Bentley, of London, is preparing a design; the style is to be Roman.

Father John C. Drumgoole.—A statue to the memory of the venerable priest and apostle of the poor boys of New York, Father John C. Drumgoole, was unveiled before a crowd of 51,000 persons. Father Drumgoole's successor, Father

Dougherty, introduced Judge O'Brien, who delivered the eulogy on Father Drumgoole and his work.

For being a model reformatory the Monastery of the Good Shepherd, Troy, N.Y., received a gold medal from the Chicago Exhibition Commissioners.

In St. Mary's church, St. Catharines, is a relic of St. Anne, the mother of the Blessed Virgin. A novena of special devotion to St. Anne begun Oct. 8th resulted in the reception of the holy sacraments of Penance and Eucharist by unprecedented numbers, while several cases of relief from physical infirmities were also witnessed.

ERRATUM.

On page viii., line 4, "Nazareth" should read *Bethlehem.*

ADDENDUM.

In the Archdiocese of Kingston, by a Papal Indult, the Feast of St. Patrick is a double of the First Class; hence in the year 1895 it will be kept liturgically on the 17th March as usual in the Diocese of Kingston.

ACKNOWLEDGMENT.

The editor desires to acknowledge the help and encouragement she has received from the Hierarchy and Clergy of the Church in Ontario, and to thank those who have been generous in giving their time and talents towards the production of this book.

The Sisters of the Precious Blood have found friends outside Ontario also who have assisted them: Rev. Father Finn, S.J., of the Faculty of Detroit (Mich.) College has contributed one of his inimitable boy's stories; Rev. Father Hill, S.J., of Kentucky, has written an account of an interesting miracle that he himself witnessed, and Miss Jessie Willis Broadhead, of Detroit, has sung of the Night Watches of the Sisters of the Precious Blood. The Calendar was prepared by Rev. Father Cruise of St. Mary's, Toronto. Every page has been specially written for the

Almanac. The cover is the design of Mr. J. S. O'Higgins, whose original sketches illustrate the short stories.

There is a word of regret that the information concerning parishes is not more complete. Particulars were asked from every parish, but all did not respond.

The hope is expressed that the different Catholic societies will find the Almanac a happy medium of communication—that their interest in the success of the Almanac will be a personal one. Information concerning societies should be sent in for publication not later than September.

Indulgence is craved by the editor for any inaccuracies and omissions in this first issue of A CATHOLIC ALMANAC OF ONTARIO.

24 Elgin avenue.   E. O'S.
Toronto, Oct. 24th, 1894.

TABLE OF CONTENTS.

FIRE INSURANCE

INCORPORATED BY ROYAL CHARTER AND EMPOWERED BY SPECIAL ACT OF PARLIAMENT.

National Assurance Co.
OF IRELAND.

Established 1822. Head Office, 3 College Green, Dublin.

CAPITAL	£1,000,000
INCOME (exceeds)	300,000
INVESTED FUNDS (exceed)	500,000

BOARD OF DIRECTORS.

SAMUEL BEWLEY (Samuel Bewley & Co.)
MAJOR WILLIAM GIBTON.
HENRY PERRY GOODBODY.
JONATHAN HOGG (Wm. Hogg & Co.), Director of the Bank of Ireland.
BRINDLEY HONE, Director of the Royal Bank of Ireland, Commissioner of Irish Lights, Director of the Dublin, Wicklow & Wexford Railway Company.
WILLIAM HONE, Director Dublin & Kingstown Railway Company.
HARRY W. JAMESON.
THOMAS ALIAGA KELLY (T. W. & J. Kelly)
GEORGE KINAHAN, J. P. (Kinahan & Co. Limited), Director of the Bank of Ireland.
LUKE J. M'DONNELL, D.L., Director of the Bank of Ireland, Director of the Great Southern & Western Railway Company, Director of the Great Northern Railway Company (Ireland).

HUGH O'CONNOR.
JOSEPH R. O'REILLY, D.L.
SIR GEORGE E. OWENS, M.D., J.P.
THOMAS PIM (Pim Brothers & Co.)
JAMES TALBOT POWER, D. L., Merchant, (John Power & Son).
EDWARD ROBERT READ, (Joseph Watkins & Co.)
J. HAMILTON REID, M.A.
WILLIAM ROBERTSON, Director of the Bank of Ireland, Director of the Great Southern & Western Railway Company, Director City of Dublin Steam Packet Company.
GEORGE BLACK THOMPSON (Thompson, D'Olier & Co.)
GRAVES SWAN WARREN, Director of the Dublin & Kingstown Railway Company.
HAROLD ENGELBACH, Secretary.

Ontario Branch	*J. H. EWART, General Agent,*	Offices—16 Wellington St. East, Toronto.

Correspondence is invited as to Agencies.

HOME COMFORT

WROUGHT STEEL FRENCH RANGES
STEEL HOTEL AND FAMILY RANGES.

CARVING AND STEAM TABLES,
BROILERS, MALLEABLE WATERBACKS, ETC., ETC.

MADE OF MALLEABLE IRON AND WROUHT STEEL, and will **LAST A LIFBTIME** if properly used.

This Style Family Range is sold only by our Travelling Salesmer from our own wagons at one uniform price throughout Canada and the United States.

Sales to January 1st, 1895,
289,327.

Above Honors Were

THE
Home Savings and Loan Comp'y
LIMITED.

Established under Legislative authority.   CAPITAL   -   - $2,000,000.

OFFICE : No. 78 CHURCH STREET, TORONTO.

DIRECTORS:

HON. SIR FRANK SMITH, Senator, President.   EUGENE O'KEEFE, Vice-President.
WM. T. KIELY, JOHN FOY, EDWARD STOCK.

Solicitor : JAMES J. FOY, Q.C.

Deposits received from 20 cents upwards, and interest at current rates allowed thereon.
Money loaned in small and large sums at reasonable rates of interest, and on easy terms of
repayment on Mortgages on Real Estate, and on the collateral security of Bank and other Stocks
and Government and Municipal Debentures.
Mortgages on Real Estate and Government and Municipal Debentures purchased.   No valuation
fee charged for inspecting property.

Office Hours—9 a.m. to 4 p.m. Saturdays—9 a.m. to 1 p.m and from 7 to 9 p.m.

JAMES MASON, MANAGER.

A. A. POST.   A. W. HOLMES.

POST & HOLMES,

ARCHITECTS.

Manning Arcade, 24 and 26 King St. West,
Toronto.

Ecclesiastical Architecture a Specialty.

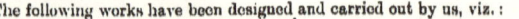

The following works have been designed and carried out by us, viz. :

Monastery of the Precious Blood, Toronto.   St. Mary's Church, St. Mary's, Ont.
St. Bernard's Church, Bradford, Pa.   St. Gregory's Church, Oshawa, Ont.
St. Patrick's Church, Niagara Falls. Ont.   St. Michael's Hospital, Toronto

AND MANY OTHERS THROUGHOUT ONTARIO.

St. Michael's College,

(In Affiliation with Toronto University.)

UNDER THE SPECIAL PATRONAGE OF

HIS GRACE THE ARCHBISHOP OF TORONTO,

AND DIRECTED BY THE BASILIAN FATHERS.

Full Classical, Scientific and Commercial Courses.

Special courses for Students preparing for University Matriculation and Non-Professional Certificates. Terms, when paid in advance—Board and Tuition, $150 per year ; Day Pupils, $28. For further particulars apply to

REV. J. R. TEEFY, PRESIDENT.

Loretto Abbey

WELLINGTON PLACE.

TORONTO, CAN.

THIS Institution for the EDUCATION OF YOUNG LADIES is conveniently situated near the business part of the city. yet sufficiently remote to secure the quiet and seclusion so conducive to study, combines the advantages of the city with those of the country, having the full benefit of the PURE AIR OF THE LAKE, whilst it is both sheltered and ornamented by a beautiful belt of forest trees surrounding the shrubbery.

The Course of Instruction in this Academy embraces
Every Branch suitable to the education of young ladies.

Modern languages are taught by natives. The Studio is affiliated with the Government Art School. MUSIC, in its various branches, is assiduously cultivated and taught by accomplished and experienced teachers, whose system is modelled on that of the European Conservatories.
. Commercial Course, Stenography, Type Writing, etc., taught to all the pupils who may desire it.

Special Course for Pupils Preparing for Matriculation.

FOR FURTHER PARTICULARS ADDRESS :

LADY SUPERIOR.

- - - *"Truth is mighty and must prevail."* - - -

The Toronto Radiator Manufacturing Co., Ltd.

TORONTO, ONT.,

— **ARE THE** —

Largest Manufacturers under the BRITISH FLAG.

Radiator for Hot Water and Steam Heating,

"SAFFORD PATENT."

THE ONLY RADIATOR BUILT WITHOUT BOLTS OR PACKING.

INSTALLED IN THE FOLLOWING:

St. Michael's College, Toronto.
House of Providence, "
St. Joseph's Hospital, "
Loretto Convent School, "
St. Mary's Convent, "

St. B.ail's Novitiate, Toronto.
Sunnyside O phanage, "
Loretto Convent, Niagara Falls.
R. C. Church, Brockville.
". " Belleville.
St. Peter's Cathedral, Montreal.

Immaculate College, Montreal.
Hotel Dieu, Quebec.
Convent School, St. Boniface.
Lor- tto Convent, Hamilton.
Notre Dame de St. Roch, Quebec.

Made only by **The Toronto Radiator Mfg. Co., Toronto, Ont,**

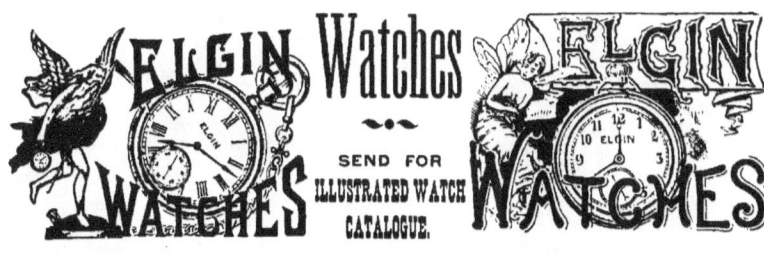

www.ingramcontent.com/pod-product-compliance
Lightning Source LLC
Chambersburg PA
CBHW020030030726
47499CB00007B/2361